Quicks

By Kevin Waltman

Cinco Puntos Press
El Paso ❀ Texas

QUICKS: D-Bow's High School Hoops. Copyright © 2016 by Kevin Waltman. All rights reserved. No part of this book may be used or reproduced in any manner whatsoever without written consent from the publisher, except for brief quotations for reviews. For further information, write Cinco Puntos Press, 701 Texas Avenue, El Paso, TX 79901 or call 1-915-838-1625.

FIRST EDITION
10 9 8 7 6 5 4 3 2 1

Library of Congress Cataloging-in-Publication Data

Names: Waltman, Kevin, author.
Title: Quicks / by Kevin Waltman.
Description: First edition. | El Paso, TX : Cinco Puntos Press, [2016] |
Series: D-Bow's high school hoops ; book 4 | Summary: "Marion High, an inner-city school in Indianapolis, has never had a state championship. It's D-Bow's senior year, his A-Game is ready, big-time colleges are taking notice, and he's dreaming big. What's rattling D-Bow is the cocky white guy, Daryl. He wants D-Bow's job at point. It's time for D-Bow to man up. He needs to be the team leader, and he needs to bring that A-Game. —Provided by publisher.
Identifiers: LCCN 2016014621| ISBN 978-1-941026-62-5 (paperback) |
ISBN 978-1-941026-61-8 (cloth) | ISBN 978-1-941026-63-2 (e-book)
Subjects: | CYAC: Basketball—Fiction. | High schools—Fiction. | Schools—Fiction. | African Americans--Fiction. | BISAC: JUVENILE FICTION / Sports & Recreation / Basketball. | JUVENILE FICTION / Boys & Men. | JUVENILE FICTION / People & Places / United States / African American. | JUVENILE FICTION / Social Issues / General (see also headings under Family).
Classification: LCC PZ7.W1728 Qu 2016 | DDC [Fic]—dc23
LC record available at https://lccn.loc.gov/2016014621

Book and cover design by Anne M. Giangiulio

For Gram and Mah and Dack

PART I

1.

On these blocks, it's different. The numbers in official box scores? Sure, those matter. Those let you leap to college. To the L. But they don't count the same way as skills on the blacktop. That's the real proving ground.

My Uncle Kid for example. Never scored a D-I deuce. Flamed out in Juco. And now he's middle-aged and crashing at our house because he doesn't have the scratch for his own place. But he can still get out there on that Fall Creek court and bring it. So he can strut all summer because he can run off ballers half his age.

It's early August, the threat of school staring us in the face. And it's brutal hot. So after a few games, the crowd thins. Now it's just a three-on-three battle on the other end, while Kid feeds me on this one. My boy Fuller—locked in at the three spot for Marion East this fall—watches us while he unlaces his kicks and takes big swigs from a Gatorade.

I catch baseline, rise in a smooth motion. Bucket. Then to the wing behind the stripe. Wet again.

"I'm telling you, D," Uncle Kid says, "don't sweat this Gibson guy. I've seen him run. Nothing special."

Kevin Waltman

"He's got a little burst," Fuller chimes from the sideline.

I catch the rock at the top of the key, then stop mid-stroke. I stare at Fuller. "What you trying to say?"

He holds his hands up apologetically. "Nothing, man. He's got quicks. But no real J to respect. Too small to finish at the rim. Just quicks."

I nod at Fuller to let him know it's cool. Then I go back to my work. Next shot's back rim, the rebound soaring so high that the rock arcs across the sun in the distance. Kid chases.

Burst. Quicks. That's the last thing I need to hear. I'm still lugging around this brace on my knee. Still feeling that old tightness after my step-up exercises. Still have to wait until the court clears so I can come work on my J—the only hoops I can have until I get clearance. And I've still got the scar from the surgery—a reminder that one wrong step can wipe out a season, a career.

I spent the summer entertaining home visits from coaches and setting up official visits to high majors. I've got the stars next to my name. Got the scholly offers. Got the stats from three seasons of tearing it up at Marion East. But quicks is the one thing I'm still missing.

Fuller polishes off the last of his Gatorade. He arcs the empty at a trash can fifteen feet away. True. He smiles. Doesn't matter if it's trash in the garbage or leather through the nylon—finding bottom is always good. "Later, D-Bow," he tells me, then starts hoofing it toward home. I finish my workout with Uncle Kid in silence, then we hit it, too.

For a while the only sound is the traffic. It's thick on Fall Creek, then dwindles to a couple creeping cars once we're into the neighborhood. A thumping bass here. A squealing tire there.

"You can't seriously be sweating Darryl Gibson," Kid finally says.

I shrug. "Nah. You kidding? Everyone always hypes the new kid just because. No worries."

Kid bobs his head in agreement. We're a block from Patton now. My knee's just the littlest bit tight after the workout. "That's right," Kid says. "Gibson's flavor of the day. But I mean, he had two years to prove himself down in Bloomington, and he barely made a dent in the stat sheet."

We keep talking as we walk. We spill out all the reasons not to worry. I've still got a couple months to get right. No way Coach Bolden would hand over my starting spot now, not after all we've been through.

"And let's face it," Kid says as we open the door. "Ain't no white boy gonna transfer to Marion East and steal minutes from you."

He gives me a playful punch on the shoulder and laughs. But it's short-lived. There's Mom on the couch, sending a severe frown his way. "What kind of mess are you putting in Derrick's head now?" she asks.

"Oh, let it go, Kaylene," Kid says. "I'm just making a little noise at him."

She rises up a few inches from the cushions. "Don't you tell me to let it go. Not in my house. Not about my son." Then her focus snaps to me. "And don't you go listening to some garbage about white-boy-this or white-boy-that. Racist nonsense."

Kid can't take this. "Oh, come *on*. It's not racist. I'm not saying he's evil. Just saying Darryl Gibson can't be much of a baller."

Mom stops him with another look. "You think I've lived a black woman's life in Indianapolis and don't know racism? But I am not letting my son think turning that kind thing around on white people helps him one single bit."

Kevin Waltman

And that's the word in this living room, true as if it's chiseled in stone. One, because it's my mom's living room, and it's best not to mess with Kaylene Bowen. Two, because she's nearing the end of her second trimester. And she's thirty-eight. And it's swamp-ass August outside. She gives a little *humph* then settles back into the couch, wincing with the effort.

Thing is, it makes a difference. Gibson being white, that is. I know my mom's right. I mean, we've talked about this since I was a kid. There are plenty of things to be bitter about—the way the city lets our schools drown and our streets break into a million potholes. Or the way they press on a kid from the neighborhood who steps out of line while teenagers up in Hamilton County run pharmacies out of their bedrooms. Or how they stitched the Monon Trail right over our neighborhood, so rich people could bike or walk their dogs across our patch of land without actually having to see us. But resenting white people won't change a thing. Makes it worse, my dad says, but I still only halfway believe him on that.

Still. It matters. Getting pushed by a new kid would hurt no matter what. But when a white person shows up at Marion East they're either lost or logging community service hours. So I can't lose minutes to a white kid. I just *can't*.

"Dinner's almost ready!" Jayson calls. And for the first time I snap out of my train of thought and take in the chaos behind Mom.

Dad and Jayson are whipping together dinner, but that means a circus of water boiling over and dirty spoons scattered on the counter and strands of spilled spaghetti squashed on the floor. Meanwhile, my girl Lia is setting the table, as serene as my dad and little brother are chaotic. She glances up at me and smiles, quickly blows a little kiss before anyone else can see. Then she goes back to smoothing out napkins and arranging glasses. My head swims at the sight. Mainly because she's as fine as a girl can be, and she's cool to hang with, and she's been there for me every step of the way on my rehab. But it's that last part that has a troubling little undercurrent—*she's been there all the time.* When I met her she made me chase a little, kept me off balance. Now she hovers like we're married. But what am I supposed to tell her? Stop being so nice to me?

Everyone crowds in. Reaching. Grabbing. Slopping pasta on plates. Mom clears her throat, just once, and then everyone settles down while she says a quick prayer. She's never been real religious. She hits up church out of habit but doesn't Jesus you to death. But she's been insisting on prayers before meals lately. Mostly, I think she's hoping for divine intervention so she can feed the extra mouth that's coming in a few months.

"Amen," she says at last. Then there's the briefest pause before everyone dives into their food. It's a flurry. And with six of us squeezed around our little table, I can barely get enough elbow room to grab a fork.

"You okay, Derrick?" It's Lia, her eyebrows pinching down at me like I just spit on the salad.

"Fine."

"You're quiet," she says. "You sure you're okay? Workout go all right?"

"Good," I say.

"*Okay*," she says, clearly not believing me. In terms of couple drama, this isn't even a blip. I just start to dig in, but my right elbow

Kevin Waltman

keeps bumping Dad every time I take a bite. We go through a few rounds of *Sorry* and *No problem*, before I sigh and let my fork clank down on my plate.

"You sure you're okay?" Lia asks again.

"I'm *fine*," I snap. Lia looks away, simmering. Mom stares at me like she's about to climb across the table—belly and all—and smack some manners into me. "I'm sorry," I say, trying to undo as much damage as I can. "I didn't mean to be a jerk." I look back at my plate. "I just can't get any room."

2.

Already you can feel the heat easing up. The cool is coming. And with it, hoops. First practice in three weeks.

I'm in senior study hall, killing time. At Marion East, if you keep your head down and plug away—don't show up high, don't get arrested—you're golden. Sure, I've got to keep cranking in trigonometry and English and on and on, but I've got this game down. Hell, at this point they basically tell you exactly what's going to be on the tests, so I'm not sweating it. So I use this time to get my head right.

Except Darryl Gibson keeps intruding on my thoughts. He's a surly guy. Doesn't say much. But his legend grows daily. He's still wrecking it at the Fall Creek court, to the point that he's earned an obnoxious nickname—D-Train, after the way he barrels to the rim. And at school, he's earned a rep of someone not to be messed with. Word is a couple thugged-out guys tried to jump him the first week and he put them both on their asses in the bathroom. Probably just a story, but people believe it.

Just this morning, he came cruising down the hall while I was

Kevin Waltman

kicking it with my teammates and he barely nodded at us. Like he's too good or something. It makes me think back to when I was a newcomer. I used to walk these halls thinking I had something to swagger about, too. I remember how I resented Nick Starks—he was the senior point I was trying to uproot from the lineup—and maybe that's how Gibson sees me. Whatever. That's his problem, not mine.

"Bowen," a voice calls. I come out of my daydream. There's Mr. Mason, in front of me. He's holding up a hall pass with one hand, his other propping up his head like it weighs a hundred pounds. "Looks like you got a get out of jail card." He's got retirement in his eyes, and he gives no shits at all. Doesn't even look at me while I walk up and pluck the pass from his hand. First couple weeks of study hall, kids would try to get a rise out of him. They'd pull out phones and play games at full volume. They'd drop f-bombs in casual conversation. They'd stretch out on the floor, plop down their bookbag for a pillow, and nap. Mason never blinked.

Now some people actually study. What's the point of acting out if you can't get a teacher to notice?

I check the clock, see there's only twenty minutes left in the period. "Do I need to come back here before next bell?" I ask.

Mason shrugs. He opens his desk and pulls out a bag of chips, opens them with a loud crinkle. "No point, I guess."

Then I'm gone. As I walk down the hall, I check all the slogans.

Belief Efficiency Schoolwork Tenacity = B.E.S.T.
We Are the Hornets. Our Strength is in the Hive.
Always Aiming Upward!

They've been there forever. Same slogans and signs since the first day I set foot in Marion East. Every school has them—constant attempts to keep kids motivated. When you're young, they seem to mean something. Like a little life instruction manual written on the walls. Then you hit junior year. Senior year. Things change. You see kids who had promise spiral down. You see kids who graduated full of hope stuck in their parents' house, no better prospects than minimum wage jobs. Over and over and over.

Then again, what's the choice? To not believe in possibilities? To just give up? No way. And whenever I get that kind of feeling, I've got something to save me—hoops. There the rules make sense. Nobody's going to change them on you mid-game either. Give me the rock. Get me between the lines. Then I'll show you what's *B.E.S.T.*

I hover outside of Coach Bolden's door before I knock. I've been called down here so many times over the years that I don't even worry. Sometimes it's been a pep talk. Sometimes a brutal lecture. Sometimes it's been to take a long look at my mid-term grades.

I knock.

"It's open," a voice says.

Then, when I duck my head in, there's no Bolden. Instead, the other two seniors on the squad—Fuller and Chris Jones, our big who spent all summer bulking up—sit silently in folding chairs. Across from them, behind Bolden's big old desk, sits Lou Murphy, Bolden's long-time assistant. He points at one last chair that leans against the brick wall. "Grab a seat, Derrick," he says.

I do as I'm told, but my senses are on high alert.

Once I sit and face Murphy, he clears his throat. He clasps his

Kevin Waltman

hands in front of him and sits them on the desk, then decides against it and lays them palms-down as he leans forward. Murphy's always been our go-to guy, that players' coach who strokes our egos when Bolden comes down too hard. But now he just looks too young. Instead of his smooth, copper-colored face and that nervous smile behind the desk, there should be Bolden's hawkish scowl—dark, wrinkled, ready to attack.

Finally, Murphy just pops up, like the seat's full of thorns. He claps his hands. "Let's just get to it," he says. "I wanted to let the seniors know first. Coach Bolden isn't coming back this year." As he says it, he motions back to the chair. Maybe he meant it as a sign of respect—like it'll *always* be Bolden's seat—but it makes it feel like the old man's dead.

"What's wrong?" Fuller asks. He's a senior in high school whose forehead wrinkles up like a senior citizen's. He's a bull, always moving straight ahead, on the court and off. "Something happened to him, right?" he says, as much an accusation as a question.

"No, no," Murphy says. "It's nothing like that. He just decided it was time to retire."

I don't say anything, but I'm angry. I'm not sure why, but it seems like a betrayal. Jones must feel the same way, and he doesn't hold back. "Just like that?" he yells. "The old man said forget it right before my senior year? After all the work? After all the damn suicides I've run for him, he just walks?"

Murphy nods, understanding. "I hear you," he says. Then he catches himself and takes a harder tone. "But Jones, it is what it is. Man up about it. Coach was getting up there. If he wants to spend his days doing the crossword and watching cable, he's earned it."

Nobody says anything after that. We just let the news settle over us the way a January snow silences the city as it falls. There's just the wheeze and rattle of the air conditioning unit. I start remembering all my go-rounds with Bolden—the fight over playing time my freshman year, his crazy lineups that put me at the four-spot, the heart-to-hearts during my sophomore slump, his fire-breathing lectures when I let my head get too swole as a junior. And then his patience and counsel through my recruitment and my injuries. It's hard to imagine Marion East hoops without him prowling the sideline, chewing out officials, stomping his foot on the hardwood. *Gone.* Retirement isn't death, I guess, but it kind of feels like it to the people left behind.

"So?" Jones asks at last.

"What?" Murphy says.

"So who's the new coach?"

Murphy widens his eyes. "I am," he says, a little too defensively. Then he softens, remembering that he didn't exactly explain that part to us. And finally, he lets a little smile creep in. He shakes his head. "The old man didn't really give the school much of a choice to do anything else," he says. "He just dropped the news on them yesterday. Probably knew it all summer long, but held out so they'd have to let me have a crack at it."

Then he cuts us loose. We're under orders not to tell anyone until the other players hear in person from him. The three of us walk together down the halls. Right now they're empty, but any second that bell will ring and the whole school will spill out. Noise. Clamor. Chaos.

"Well, what do you guys think?" Fuller asks.

"I think it's some bullshit," Jones says. He's a hulking 6'8", but when he acts this way his face sags into a mope. It makes him look soft, not menacing. "My senior year."

Kevin Waltman

"*Our* senior year," I remind him. But I don't say anything else. Truth is, I'm as sad as I am angry. But ballers aren't gonna sit around and cry for the dearly departed. Next man up.

"Whatever," Jones says. "I spent all summer banging weights and this is what I get." He storms off, leaving Fuller and me standing under that big red sign: *We Are the Hornets. Our Strength is in the Hive.*

Then the bell rings and everyone swarms out around us.

Those slogans are flat-out lies.

There's no time to sulk. After school, it was just a quick *Catch you later* to Lia, and then I hopped in my car to trek here: the doctor's office. One last check-in before the season starts. Lia offered. My parents offered. Hell, even Jayson offered. But I didn't want company on this one. Some things you have to do solo. If I get a bad report now, I don't want to have to face anyone to talk about it.

Hanging in the waiting room about kills me. It's worse than watching another player step to the line with the game in the balance. Nothing you can do but hope. Thing is, I should be more confident. The knee doesn't give me any problems anymore. Not even tightness after workouts. But I don't get to turn it loose without the doctor's say-so.

"Bowen. Derrick." I look up to see a nurse with a clipboard. She looks around, then sees me rising. She motions me to follow.

First things first. She gets me on the scales. "One-ninety-two," she mutters to herself and writes it down. It's a little more than I've weighed in the past, but no surprise. The one thing I could do while injured was add some bulk. If there's any extra fat, it'll burn off with a week or two of practice. Then she has me stand straight to measure my height. I'm not even really paying attention—just hoping to get this over with and get a green light from the doc—but when she reads it off I ask her to repeat herself.

"Six-four," she says, narrowing her eyes at me. It's like she thinks I called her a liar or something. Then she relents. "Okay. Six-four-and-a-half. That better?"

I nod, but she's misreading me. I didn't think she was cheating me of an inch. It's just that I topped out at 6'3" before freshman year and haven't grown a millimeter since. No wonder my kicks have felt tight. But, hey, I'll take it. An extra inch and a half? That's another board per game. Another bucket or two among the bigs. Maybe a dozen more blocks over the course of a year.

Provided I get to wear a uni at all.

After that, she ushers me to a smaller room and tells me the doctor will be right with me. *Right*. That means I sit there in silence for half an hour. I thumb through an *SI* and a *SLAM*, but even they can't distract me. I look at pictures on the wall, some signed photos of semi-famous athletes this doctor's put back between the lines.

Finally, the door swooshes open and in he comes. He's young, thin. His skin is honey-colored, but it's impossible to figure out what ethnicity he is. He speaks in a clipped but cheery tone—the kind of thing that usually bothers me, but he's been a pretty steadying force through this whole journey with my knee.

"How we doing today, Derrick?" he asks. He extends his hand.

I rise, shake his hand. "I guess how I'm doing depends on what you tell me."

No more small talk then. He knows I need him to get down to

Kevin Waltman

business. He measures the circumference of my leg and writes it down. He quizzes me on my workouts. *Any swelling? Soreness? Am I hitting full speed running? Any problems after downhill running?*

It's a little weird. I mean, I know what the right answers are. But I try to be honest with myself and the doctor—the last thing anyone wants is another injury. So I give him the truth. I haven't had any soreness or swelling in over a month. Everything feels good. Except one thing. "I hit top speed," I tell him, "but I don't feel like I get there as fast as I used to."

The doctor nods. Then he frowns a little and scans a chart in front of him. He flips a page. Then another. It's like he's on the beach, browsing some summer read while I'm in deep water in need of saving.

He looks up at me again. He smiles, but I can tell there's something lurking behind it—the way a parent might smile right before they drop the hammer on you, like *I hate to do this to you, but your ass is grounded.*

"What you're experiencing is normal," he says. "I could count on one hand the number of athletes I've had who felt they had the same power. For most of them, it takes at least a full year from their injury. And yours was in"—he double-checks his chart—"late January. So, like I said, totally normal. You'll get that power back as your knee returns to form." Then he taps his temple with his finger a few times. "But some of it's in here, too. Tearing your ACL isn't like stubbing a toe, Derrick. Sometimes our mind holds us back a little longer until we feel safe." I stare at him, still waiting on the verdict. I didn't come to the doctor for some psychology lesson. He must sense it because he waves his hand in the air, as if to say *Forget all that nonsense.* "You're good to go, Derrick."

"For real?" As badly as I want to believe it, the thought almost scares me somehow. Like any second, a camera crew's going to pop out and let me know the doc was punking me.

"You check out," he says. "Every test up and down the line. We're going to want a brace on you for a good while longer, but you can resume full basketball activities."

"Right away?"

"Derrick, as far as I'm concerned, if there's a court on the other side of that door, you can start a pick-up game."

Kevin Waltman

3.

First, the kicks. Fresh out of the box. I went to Ty's Tower to buy them this weekend. My mom forked over the cash, but this time—more than all the times in the past—it seemed to cause her physical pain to hand that stack to me just so I could put something on my feet. But you don't tell a musical phenom to go buy a used instrument, and you don't tell a baller to skimp on kicks.

Now I have to deal with Wes at Ty's Tower. We don't hang too much anymore. Last year, he got himself tangled up with some for real bad people. He's still paying off some debt he owes those guys, scrubbing floors at the same seedy bar where Uncle Kid works. It's not the kind of place that puts him in contact with good influences. Hell, it's illegal for him to even be working there, but they can just give him some cash off the books and he works cheap. So after all that, I keep pretty clear of my boy, even if he does still live right up the street. Still, the guy's the biggest sneakerhead I know. It would just feel like a betrayal if I bought my senior kicks without him as wing man.

First thing I do is point to the LeBron XIIIs. Used to be I'd rock the

D Roses, but after his sexual assault case my mom said she'd cut off my feet if I put his shoes on. But here, I get all told from Wes instead. "Gotta step up your sneaker game for senior year," he says. He practically begs me until I try on some Hyperdunks and some Melos. Even some funky Brandblack Raptors. "That's what I'm talking about," he says. "Some real flavor." As he points to the shoes, I see fresh ink on his arms—namely a dollar sign on the inside of his wrist. Tats don't come cheap, I know, and I shudder to think about where he's getting that extra flow. But I don't press it. Not now.

In the end I come right back to the LeBrons. "Come *on, D*," Wes pleads. But I'm not here for anything new, other than a jump in size for proper fit.

Wes knows it too. The whole time he was pointing out other shoes, he knew it. Him changing my mind isn't the point. The two of us hanging a little is. It'll never be like when we were pups again. Too much has changed. And it'll be a long time before I can trust him again. When it all went down last year, I had to put myself on the line for him—and I damn near got popped doing it.

We head out to the street. Wes immediately digs a pack of smokes from his pocket and starts packing them. Then he sees me watching him and tucks them back away. Not that I care. He's smoked a lot more than a few Marlboros in his day. But anything like that is just this little reminder that we've hit different paths in our lives.

"How's work?" I ask.

He laughs. There's no joy in it—it's the laugh of someone bitter. "I mop puke off the floor three days a week," he says. "And every dime I get goes to JaQuentin Peggs."

JaQuentin. That was the guy. I still seem him around now and

Kevin Waltman

then, and every time he just looks more dangerous. "Well," I say, but I just let it trail off.

"Yeah, I know," Wes says. "Nobody's fault but mine." But the way he says it sounds like he's accusing someone else.

"Wanna grab a Coke somewhere?" I ask. For some reason, I don't want my time with Wes to be over yet. Truth is, I miss the kid, even if I know I'm better off without him dragging me down.

"Nah," he says. "I'm tired. I think I'm gonna hit it."

Around me, the locker room's humming. Every last player in Marion East is full of themselves. Talking trash. Yapping about dropping twenty a game. Going undefeated. It's this way in every locker room in the state right now. Soon enough, the season will come along and knock some woof out of people. But today? Everyone's still perfect.

Across from me, Darryl Gibson sits in his locker, headphones on. He bobs his head in silence, the only guy in the locker room not running game. He feels me checking him and looks up. He lowers the headphones down around his neck. "'Sup, Derrick," he says.

I shrug. "What's up with you?"

He shakes his head. *Nothing.* That's been the sum total of our exchanges in school. But what is there to say? We both want the same thing and only one can have it. I check him now. He keeps a sneer on his face like he's some banger ready to tear it up. Even has a little ink—a "D" on fire on the inside of his right forearm. "I know you're not used to seeing white point guards around here," he says, "but you don't have to eye me like I'm some animal in the zoo."

Around us, a few guys quiet down. Of course, *everybody* has been wondering about it to themselves—how it's going to go down between me and Gibson.

"Ain't about white, black, or green," I tell him. "It's about who's got the orange in their hands and what they do with it. And you're the *back-up* point guard."

That gets a reaction from guys. The underclassmen all laugh—a little too hard maybe, trying to get on my good side. But Jones, my fellow senior, bellows across the room. "Know the truth when you hear it, Gibson." It's the first thing I've heard come out of his mouth since our meeting with Murphy.

Then Josh Reynolds, a wiry junior who's set as our two-guard, bounces over. He sways and struts, then tells us, "Don't matter who's bringing the rock up the court. Just find me when I pop open." Then he goes through an elaborate, slow-motion charade of his jumper. He fades back as he does it, then nods his head as if he's seen the rock find bottom. "Wet," he says. "All day every day." Then he cups his hands by his mouth and mimics a crowd roar, like he's just sunk a game-winner. It's all play. The stuff that kids do from the first time they touch leather. Gibson and I both laugh, then check each other and serious up again.

I've got my eye on Reynolds though. He's always been flaky. He bailed on us halfway through the first practice his freshman year, then had to beg forgiveness to get back on the team. And even last year when he slid into the rotation he was the kind of guy you had to keep calm. Quick to take a shot. Quick to panic. And already this year he seems even jumpier, like there's an itch all over his skin. I'll have to manage that mania, I can tell. I've learned that a point guard's job is more than just driving and dishing—it's also massaging egos and pep-talking and squashing tension.

But enough of that. The locker room door swings open. Murphy stands there, whistle draped over his neck. His eyes gleam with energy—maybe what we'll miss in Bolden's wisdom will be made up for by Murphy's enthusiasm. He pounds his fist on the heavy door—*thump thump thump*—and smiles at us. "What the hell you boys waiting for?" he shouts. "Season starts *now!*"

No joke. Time to hit the hardwood.

Early on, Murphy sticks to Bolden's old practice script. Namely, he runs us till our lungs burn and our legs go wobbly. I don't care. It feels good. The thunder of kicks on the hardwood and a real sweat soaking through my shirt. I didn't know how much a person could come to miss wind sprints.

I don't ease up, either. Not now. And when I get a glimpse of Jones slowing down at the end of one, I don't let it slide. "Come on, big man," I say. It's cool and off to the side. No need to call him out for the freshmen to hear. Still, he squinches up his face like he doesn't want to hear it. "Naw, let's do it, Jones," I say. "Senior year. Make it count." That at least coaxes a fist bump from him before Murphy lines us up and blows his whistle. Off again.

The only thing gnawing at me is Gibson. We finish neck and neck pretty much every time, but I have to make up ground in the second half of the sprint. It's like he's to the free throw line before Murphy's finished blowing his whistle. Just *zip*. Gone. That burst I've heard about is real. And he knows it. There's no talk between us, but every once in a while I'll see him glance over at the end to see if he's outpaced me.

Finally, it happens. The annual ritual. A freshman bows out. This time it's another big—Xavier Green—who can't hack it. He stumbles on one sprint, then on the next he doesn't go. Just stands there on the baseline sucking wind while the rest of us rattle it off. I don't really know Xavier, but his big brother Moose was our beast in the post for my first two years. I was hoping maybe Xavier would bring that same kind of heat to the floor. But one look at him, doubled over gasping, and the only thing I can tell is that he hasn't arrived at the first practice in playing shape any more than Moose used to.

Murphy, hands on his hips, walks over to Xavier. *This is it*, I think. *This is where Murphy lays down the law.* Under Coach Bolden, it was a rite of passage—first one to cave on the sprints got chewed out mercilessly.

Off to the side, I hear Reynolds laugh a little. Two years ago, he was the one who got the earful from Coach so I'm sure he loves watching it happen to some other poor freshman.

Murphy puts his hand on Xavier's back. "You okay there, X-Man?" he asks.

Xavier, still unable to stand up straight, just nods a few times. But then he holds up a hand to say he needs a second.

Murphy nods, understanding. He turns to the rest of us and says we did a good job. "Now let's start drills. Bigs down here with X-Man. Perimeter players on the other end."

We stand there for a second, dazed. "For real?" Reynolds whispers. I know where he's coming from. It's like Murphy just walked on Coach Bolden's grave. I don't care who Xavier's older brother was, kid dies on a sprint he's supposed to get jumped. And this *X-Man*

Kevin Waltman

business? Excuse me if I pass on the nicknames for someone who hasn't scored a single high school bucket yet.

"Come on, let's go!" Murphy shouts. But even then there's no anger. He sounds like the same old Assistant Murphy, encouraging and cajoling. Not like a head coach at all.

Then, there's drills. Two ends of the floor. One coach. I know this one's not Murphy's fault—he probably hasn't had time to scrounge up an assistant yet—but it makes him look unprepared. The guy knows hoops, but if knowing hoops was all it took, then my Uncle Kid would be the next Coach K.

Sure enough, when Murphy strolls down to us and turns his back on the bigs, it's a mess. He starts us in a weave drill, but behind him the big guys are just gaming the system. First it's Xavier acting the fool, chucking up twenty-footers instead of working his post moves. And, after a minute, they're all into it, even Jones who should know better.

Murphy must see me looking past him, because he stops our drill and wheels around. Just as he turns, Xavier is launching a hook shot from the hash mark.

"Hey, come on," Murphy yells. "Let's be grown-ups, aight? Work the way I showed you." But there's no heat, no old-fashioned Bolden bite. So they nod at Murphy and act all sorry, but in another minute it's back to the same-old.

I try to focus on our drills, but when I hear laughing from the other end, that tears it. I stop mid-weave. I let a pass from Reynolds just sail toward the sideline. I take three big steps to mid-court. "Hey, Xavier," I yell. He turns, a big goofy grin on his face. I used to like that grin on his older brother, but at least I knew he would bust ass when the time came. "This is a practice for men who want to play basketball. Not kindergarten. You might think you can come here and just fuck around all day, but don't expect to be getting minutes when the season rolls around."

"Okay," he says. He rolls his eyes a little bit and gives a *whatever* shrug.

"Hey!" I yell and start marching toward him.

That's when Murphy cuts me off. He grabs me by the elbow and gets in my ear. "Easy," he says. "You don't have to be the coach, too. Let me handle this."

I stare at him for a second, but he doesn't blink. He still doesn't seem angry, and that lack of anger *infuriates* me. Hell, I don't know what practice is without somebody screaming. "Fine," I say, and I turn back to our end of the court.

Murphy starts us in another drill—one-on-one at the top of the key, offensive player only gets three dribbles—and then heads back to the bigs. As he goes, he calls to Green—"Hey, now, X-Man, let's get with it"—like they're long lost pals.

A bad start.

And it gets worse. I'm up first against Rider, my back-up from last year. Easy pickings. I give him a shot fake, lean right, and then just duck past him left. I don't even have to explode too hard, just get my shoulders past and scoop to the rim. Then I turn to see who's on deck for me. It's Gibson, straight out of the gate. He's got a little sneer when I bounce him the rock.

He waits for me to come out to check him. Then he tucks the ball into a triple-threat position and I lower into my crouch. He takes

Kevin Waltman

a lazy dribble to his left—death in this drill, where you can't waste any motion. I hop to cut him off.

Then *boom*. He's vapor. Hits me with a simple cross-over, but it's so quick—violent, really—that I don't have time to recover before he's to the rim. He can't dunk it. Just a lay-in. But his point's made. A few of my teammates murmur and whistle.

As I walk past him to the end of the line, Gibson gives me a parting shot. "D-Train's comin' down the tracks, old man. Best step out the way."

4.

We're hanging at Lia's place. Her dad's gone. That ought to mean taking things back to her bedroom. But it's been ten full minutes since either of us said a word. I made some snarky little comment about Gibson, Lia told me to let it go, I told her I wasn't just gonna "let go" of my senior season. And that puts us here. Watching a movie on her couch—but both of us kind of eyeing the other, waiting for an apology that isn't coming.

Then, at a commercial, Lia stretches her leg over and jabs my calf with her toe. I don't react, so she does it again. "Come *on*, Derrick," she says. "We don't have to give each other the silent treatment just because the night got off to a bad start."

That's all it takes for me to thaw. For whatever reason it's like I *want* us to be mad at each other sometimes. But as soon as she gives an inch I cave. "Awww, I'm just being a pain in the ass," I say.

"No," she says, "I know how much ball means to you." She's letting me off the hook easy, I know. But right now I'll take it. "But, D, this kid Gibson can't be all that, right?"

I nod. It's the same stuff I've been telling myself. But then every day at practice it's the same old—we get iso'd on the perimeter and he rips it past me. "I guess," I say, trying to sound more confident than I am.

"I've been to your bedroom, D," she says. I smile. A little too big. "Okay, big man," she goes on, "you just enjoy that one. But I'm not talking about *that*. I mean the stack of recruiting letters in your room. You think Darryl Gibson has that kind of notice? You think anyone's gonna have a press conference for him when he announces where he's going to school?"

It's a nice ego boost. And I know I should be a lot more grateful than I am to have a girlfriend like Lia.

She jabs me with her toe again. Playful. "Come on, boy," she says. "Lighten up."

I glance at her and grin. "How much longer your dad gone?"

She smiles right back, and I know it's on again. But as I follow her to her room, I still can't shake the knowledge—I flat-out can't keep Gibson in front of me. The only other point I've ever had trouble with like that is Dexter Kernantz down at Evansville Harrison, and they've won State twice in a row. I think—I *know*—I'm a better all-around player than Gibson. But every time Gibson goes by me I feel an extra ounce of that thing no baller can stand—doubt.

We're in Lia's room now, lights dimmed. "Look, Derrick. You want to mope out there"—she points to the living room—"fine. But in here you better be with me a hundred percent. Got it?"

"Oh, I got it," I say. And when she kisses me I'm not lying.

"For the love of God, just clean up your room!"

I hear that all the way from the other side of the front door. Makes me want to turn right around and speed back to Lia's. We called it a night after her dad came home, but still—ten o'clock is late to be arguing about cleaning the house.

I turn my key and go on in. Mom—her finger in mid-air while she hollers at Jayson—freezes and then points that finger at me instead. "There he is," she says.

I run a quick inventory of things that could have made her mad. I've steered clear of real trouble since last year with Wes. I bombed a history quiz, but it didn't kill my mid-term. There's what Lia and I just finished up an hour ago, but it's not like that would be some shocker to my mom. "What?" I finally ask.

"The deal was you had the kitchen this week and Jayson had the room," Mom snaps.

A quick glance at the kitchen reveals that all the dishes are cleaned and put away. All the pots scrubbed spotless. I open my mouth to point this out, but Dad leaps in. "Son, you'll want to clean the counters like you promised," he says. He loops his arm around my shoulder and leads me to the kitchen. Behind us, I hear Jayson's footsteps thump toward our room as he finally obeys Mom.

When she turns the television volume up, I lean toward Dad. "How long is she gonna be so crazy?" I ask.

Dad leaps back like I just rolled a grenade at his feet. "Son, how stupid are you? Your mom's pregnant. There are rules to follow." He starts clicking them off on his fingers. "First, whatever she asks, do it. She wants an ice cream sundae at three in the morning, make it. She wants the kitchen cleaned, do it. Second, we *do not* complain. Any man who complains about a pregnant woman isn't a real man. And finally—most importantly—you never *ever* refer to a pregnant woman as crazy. You might think she's crazy, but really she's just been made acutely aware of all of our shortcomings. She's *saner than she's ever been*, okay?"

I nod, then laugh a little, but even that gets the spooky eye from my dad. I mean, he's right. As I scrub down those counters, I think that it can't be an easy draw—pushing forty and pregnant, crowded into a house with Dad and me and Jayson and Kid? I guess Mom can be however she wants to be.

In my room, Jayson hasn't even started on the mess. He's sitting on his bed, thumbing through a script for a school play. He looks up for a second, offers me a *'Sup*, and then goes back to his thing.

Truth is, I can't blame him. Since Uncle Kid had to move in with us, Jayson and I have been crammed into what used to be just my room. And with the baby coming, nothing's going to change—except for Kid getting booted to the couch or, maybe, finding his own place—until I split for college. We've got the beds pushed against two walls, our clothes spilling out of drawers, our school books and papers fighting for room in the corner. That leaves a few feet for Jayson's X-Box, its wires snaking up to a little hand-me-down T.V. on the dresser. We could clean, but first we'd need twice the space. I step over Jayson's book bag and go toward the closet so I can peel off my clothes and get into something clean for night-time. Even there, I've got no room. Jayson's got a lifetime's worth of dirty socks and underwear piled in the center.

And scattered around that is my recruiting mail. When it first started rolling in I kept it in organized boxes, but somewhere along the way it just spilled into an avalanche. You can see the school logos on the envelopes—Purdue, Georgetown, UAB, Dayton. Thing is, there are a few names that aren't adding themselves to that stack anymore. When I tore up my knee last year, the flood of letters—and texts and tweets and calls—diminished to a stream. I still have an offer from Indiana, but the other elites have cooled on me. I'm damaged goods.

I kick at Jayson's pile until there's some free floor space to set down my bag. I scan the room. We've got to at least make a dent, or Mom's going to come in here in the morning and blow the place up. But first, I plop down next to Jayson. He scoots over, annoyed.

"It's not like we've got privacy anymore," I say. "Might as well just tell me what you're checking."

He sneers. "Man, they're making us do *A Raisin in the Sun*. Like there hasn't been a black play written in the last fifty years or something." He acts too tough for it, but here he is memorizing lines. He doesn't want to think of himself as an actor, but he can make you a believer the minute he steps on the boards. "What about you?" he asks. "Hook it up with Lia?"

"Shut up," I say, but he laughs. Like I said, no privacy. I can't keep track of how many times I've caught him snooping through my texts.

He sets his script down. "How's hoops?"

"All good," I say. Only I'm not as good an actor as Jayson.

"For real?" he asks. "You been sighing around this place like you're about to cry."

Kevin Waltman

"Nobody's gonna cry," I say. I scan the room again. "Unless Mom sees this room and whips both our hides."

That spurs him into action. We do what we can—cram clothing into drawers, combine our dirty laundry into one pile, stack our books on the shelves, tuck his X-Box to the side of the dresser. But as we do it, all I can think about is that stream of recruiting letters. And what I wonder is how much of it would dry up—even from my main schools like Indiana and Clemson—if they knew I was getting turned inside-out by some scrub white boy in pre-season practices.

It's 2:00 in the morning when I hear it. The *ka-thunk* of a basketball being dunked—the sound of an incoming text on my phone. I fumble for my phone in the dark.

You up?

I smile at the message, though I probably shouldn't. I yawn, then tuck the phone under the sheet so the light won't wake Jayson. **Am now**, I hit back.

The text comes back quick, and I try to muffle the sound by shoving the phone under my pillow. Too late. "Who the hell is that?" Jayson asks, his voice annoyed and raspy with sleep.

"None of your business," I whisper.

"Good luck with that," he says.

I take a quick peek at my phone: **Just up. Thinking about you. Want to get together soon?** It might be the middle of the night, but that's all it takes to get my pulse racing.

Jayson keeps after me. "It's Lia, isn't it? She sending pics? Man, if she's sending pics you've got to let me see." He's getting louder every second. The last thing I need is for Mom, sleepless again, to come in here and start asking questions.

"It's not Lia," I seethe. While I whisper-shout at Jayson, I knock out another text. A simple **Sure**. Not too eager. No definite date. Just enough to keep the conversation open.

"Oh, come on, D," Jayson says. "It's Lia. Ain't nobody gonna text you in the middle of the night but her." He climbs out of his bed now and stands over me—hand out, expecting the phone.

I slap his hand away. "Get back in your bed," I say. "It's not Lia." He just stands there, hands on his hips, not believing me. "It's not," I insist. "It's Jasmine."

"Jasmine Winters?" he asks.

I don't have to answer that one. Then there's a heavy footstep in the hallway. Probably Mom. Maybe Kid or Dad prowling for late-night eats. Either way, it saves me from more questions. Jayson slips back into his bed soft as a free throw finding nothing but net.

I turn to the wall and check my phone again. On cue, the text comes back—**Cool. Soon then**. It kind of pulls back on her previous urgency. But there it is—texts from Jasmine. The first I've heard from my ex in months. *Ex*. Crazy to think about her in that term because, somehow, it always feels like we're still together, even when we go forever without talking.

I don't text back. I just try to be quiet and get some sleep. But not before I delete the whole conversation so Lia never sees it.

Kevin Waltman

5.

I know better than to pay attention to a list. What matters is what happens between the lines. But I can't help it.

The *Indianapolis Star,* with the season starting tonight, has listed its "Top 20 Indiana Basketball Prospects." When I was a freshman I popped on these very pages, listed as the top underclassman. Now? Well, they've got it in black and white.

Rank	Name	Class	Height	High School	College
1.	Dexter Kernantz	Sr.	6'2"	Evansville Harrison	Ohio State
2.	Alphonse Harrell	Jr.	6'10"	Bloomington South	Undecided
3.	Devin Drew	Sr.	6'2"	Pike	Illinois
4.	Scotty Sims	Sr.	6'8"	Evansville Harrison	Undecided
5.	Kalif Trueblood	So.	6'6"	Hamilton Academy	Undecided
6.	Will Holliday	Sr.	6'3"	Jeffersonville	UAB
7.	Martavis Richardson	Sr.	6'7"	Lawrence North	Dayton
8.	Andrew Bone	Sr.	6'5"	South Bend Central	Butler
9.	Jeff Stanski	Sr	6'2"	Muncie Central	Ball State
10.	Scout Thurmond	So.	6'6"	Pike	Undecided
11.	Derrick Bowen	Sr.	6'3"	Marion East	Undecided

I stand in our kitchen and stare at it. I got up early this morning, even before Mom, because I knew this would be in the paper, and I wanted to see it before anyone else. So now I've got some quiet time. Except all I want to do is scream. Ten guys in front of me? Two from Pike and two from Evansville Harrison? Two *sophomores* in front of me? And *four* guards? Kernantz has at least earned it. He's a two-time champ and Ohio State bound. And Drew's a beast at Pike. But Holliday? *Stanski?* I could have turned those guys inside-out on my crutches.

I don't scream, of course. Waking up the house won't help a thing. I slide open the drawer next to the sink instead. Pull out the scissors. I flatten the paper on the counter and start to snip into it. I might as well make this my hit list. Knock 'em off one at a time. Hell, I'll post it in my school locker so it'll be there first thing every morning.

I hear the creak of a floorboard. I wrap my hand around the scissors, turning them into a dagger in my hand. Pure instinct. Then I wheel around, ready to face the intruder. There's Jayson, yawning. "You scared the shit out of me," I say. "What are you doing up this early?"

He sneers at me. "You're not as quiet as you think," he says. "And my bed's only about five inches from yours."

We stare at each other in the dim light of the house for a few seconds. I hear rustling from the room that used to be Jayson's, the one Kid now takes. Kid's got to get his own place before the baby comes. He says he's on it, but there's no evidence of him looking for apartments as far as anyone else can tell.

"What you doing there?" Jayson asks. He points to the scissors.

"Nothing," I say.

Kevin Waltman

Jayson takes a few steps toward me, squinting as he walks. He sees the paper on the counter behind me. "What you clipping?"

I just point to the paper, let him see for himself. Jayson taps the list of players. "You could ball out over all these guys," he says.

"I know," I say, but I can tell Jayson's just trying to pump me up. "I was gonna tape the list to my locker. Motivation, you know?" But as I explain it, I feel embarrassed. Every player has their motivational tools, but explaining it to a non-player is like trying to convert a non-believer to your religion. You realize you must just sound crazy.

"I'll do you one better," he says. He walks to the stove and slides open a drawer beside it. Out comes a book of matches, and Jayson holds them overhead like they're some kind of trophy. "Make it a burn list."

I see that old mischief in his eyes. We're so on top of each other these days we've forgotten that we used to have fun together. Still, I shake my head no. "I'm not setting fire in our kitchen."

"Oh, come on," he pleads. He points toward the bedrooms. "All Mom does is complain about this paper anyway. How many times a week does she threaten to cancel her subscription because of some racist nonsense this rag puts out?" He's got a point. I'm still not up for burning the thing, but Jayson takes my hesitation as approval. He opens the matches and strikes one. Then he holds it up in the air like a torch. "Come on," he pleads again.

I look at that list. Ten guys in front of me. *Ten.* Some of them not even going to high majors. "Fine," I say, and I grab the paper impulsively. I hold it over the sink while Jayson lowers the match to it. It catches immediately, the edges blackening and curling up. I hold it for a while longer, watching the names surrounding mine get swallowed by the flame. Jayson shakes the match down into the sink. It lands in

· a cup of water with a hiss. Then, once I see every name above mine reduced to ash, I drop the list and the rest of the Sports section into the sink, too. The flame moves faster, engulfing the whole section. Smoke twists up from the sink. I look at Jayson and wink. I have to admit there's something cathartic about this.

"Only one thing to do now," I say.

"What's that?"

"Turn the heat up on Warren Central tonight, too."

We both laugh, trying to keep our voices down. Any minute now people will start getting up for the last day of a workweek, but there's no sense in waking them early. Then the alarm goes off—not from some bedside table, but the smoke alarm above the sink. I'd forgotten about it, but now it screeches insistently. Jayson starts to scramble for a chair, but I just give a quick jump and press the button to stop it. Then we open the kitchen window and the smoke starts escaping to the cold air outside.

The damage is done. I hear Dad hollering for my mom to stay put while he checks it out. He's the first one to the front of the house, with Kid on his heels. They both look around frantically, their eyes on high alert for danger, death and destruction. Soon enough their gaze lands on me and Jayson where we stand by the sink, guilty as hell.

Dad runs his hand across his face angrily. "Please have some kind of explanation for this!" he demands.

I start to sputter out a response, but the more I explain the more ridiculous I sound. I watch my dad's face grow darker and angrier. Behind him, Kid just shakes his head, stifling a laugh. Finally, Jayson steps up. "It was my idea, Dad. I'm sorry."

Kevin Waltman

Somehow that pacifies Dad. An admission of guilt goes a long way with him. Instead, he hollers to the whole house. "No fire here! Just two dumbass teenage boys doing whatever dumbass teenage boys do!" Then he thumps his way to the kitchen, muttering something about at least deserving some coffee before the day goes haywire.

Mom comes in and surveys the scene, hands on her hips. She looks bleary and beaten down. "I live with morons," she says to nobody in particular.

That sends Kid over the edge. He starts laughing in short spurts, then just lets it out. Jayson's not far behind, then finally Dad, and even Mom. Finally I feel safe enough to laugh, too.

Then Mom makes her way to the kitchen and starts making breakfast for everyone. She's clearly exhausted, but she's still smiling to herself at the absurdity of it all. I've known it all along, but it makes me realize it all over again—my mom is a true saint on this earth.

6.

Warren Central. Their gym. So much for kicking off the season with an easy win. Their star from last year—Rory Upchurch—graduated and is getting minutes at Xavier now. But it's not like he was lugging a bunch of scrubs up and down the floor last year. They might not have a star, but they're talented and deep. Their center, Ricky Curry, is going to be a load for Jones. And they've got a senior point guard, J.T. Cox, who's a savvy vet. We better lace 'em up for real.

The clock's dwindling on warmups. I call Fuller over to me, and we take turns with the ball on the perimeter. Shot fake, one dribble, pull up with the other one offering mock D. For me, it's just about testing out that knee one last time. In my head, I know it's good, but it hasn't faced real game action yet. Every time I pull up, I'm thinking more about the knee than my follow-through on my J.

The crowd noise starts to swell as the clock dips under a minute. Season's about on. I bump fists with Fuller, then step out to the three point stripe. I dribble the clock away, then with a few ticks left, fire a step-back three. Splash.

On the bench, Murphy gives us a few last words before they call out the starting lineups. He's still flying solo, no assistant. "Run on misses," he shouts. "We're letting Jones play Curry solo, but sink down and show him some extra hands. On our end, keep your spacing to give room to drive. Got it?" I swear his voice almost cracks on those last words. And something about it seems off anyway. Coach Bolden never would have asked us if we "got it"—it was assumed that what he said was law. Murphy's nervous.

I scour my brain for some way to give Murphy support. Some way to buck him up without sounding condescending. But there's no time. The announcer starts in on the starting lineups, and I'm called first. As soon as *Bowen* resonates in the gym, I sprint to center court—and I'm greeted with a swell of boos and jeers. Truth? I love it. All it means is that I've broken their hearts a bunch over the last few years. Every baller knows that if the opposing fans hate you, you're doing something right.

The only thing that bothers me is that I know Gibson is lurking on the bench. When Murphy wrote my name on the board pre-game, I heard this little *pffft* come from Gibson. He gave just the slightest shake of his head in dismay. I know where he's coming from. When I was a freshman, I felt the same way every time Coach wrote Nick Starks' name on the board instead of mine.

I scan the crowd for my people. They all sit together now. Dad and Jayson flank Mom, like they're protecting her against the press of the crowd. Lia sits in front and gives me a quick wink when she sees me looking. Then, behind them, stands Kid. Arms folded. Sneer on his face. All business. He's packed on too many pounds to play at pace, but the look on his grill says he'd love to shed those street clothes and pop on a uni tonight. When he makes eye contact, he just nods real long and slow.

They finish announcing our starters, and then the whole squad leaves the bench to join us. We huddle near our free throw line while the crowd buzzes in anticipation of the Warren Central starters. Then, as the announcer starts calling their names, the crowd loses their minds—basketball's back at last. I get in the middle of our squad. "Game time," I shout. "Game *time*." I scan them, make eye contact with everyone. Even Gibson. "This is what we sweat for. What we wait all summer for. Game *time*." I point above and around us. "Nobody here thinks we've got the goods this year. But we got news for them. The bodies right here on this patch of hardwood are destined for something special. I feel it. I know it." Then I put my hand in the center and everyone layers theirs on top. "Starts tonight. Right now."

Then we all shout *Team!* and it's game on.

What I said to them? I don't really know. I mean, I *do* feel that way, but so does every player on every squad in every corner of the state. But now I know there are no guarantees. All you can do is ball out while you can. And when the ref lofts that rock into the air and Warren Central controls, I dig into Cox and begin to do just that.

Cox comes into the frontcourt and decides to test me right out of the gate. He gives a little shudder then throws a crossover at me. It's quick enough to get a step and he darts into the lane. It's Xavier Green's job to help, but he's slow to recognize, and Cox has a clean path to the rim.

But I've still got my size. I time him up and rise. Years past I'd try to swat that orange hard enough to pop it. Now I just tap it straight to Green. He corrals, outlets to Reynolds. He crosses the mid-court stripe, pushing, then centers the ball. Fuller runs, widening to the wing. Jones is hustling on the other wing, hoping for an easy run at it, while

Green and I trail. Reynolds knifes into the lane, then kicks to Fuller who's spotted up. The D jumps to him, so he drives past. He looks for a lob to Jones, but by this time Warren Central has everyone back, pinched into the paint. For a second Fuller's stuck. Creases of concern spread across his face. But he's a year wiser. He knows there's no need to panic. He pivots away from the pressure to get a clean look back to the perimeter—just in time to spot me filling out top.

I don't even have to shout for the rock. He just puts it in my mitts and I rise in rhythm. True from the moment it leaves my hands.

From their pocket behind our bench, the Marion East crowd explodes. Always good to see the first bucket go down. But it's more than that, I know. There's a little extra throat to that roar, and it's because I was the one to bury the shot. First touch, post-surgery. I point to our crowd in recognition. Then I point to my knee, as if to say it's all good.

It's not like Warren Central is going to stop the action to hand me the game ball though. Cox is right back on top of me, challenging again. He drives all the way down into the paint, but this time I stay pinned to him and he has to push it back out. I can see it in his body language though—it might not have ended in a bucket that last trip, but he got past me. I'm going to be dealing with his drives all night long.

As soon as I finish that thought, Xavier gets crossed up on his assignment, leaving his man at the rim for an uncontested jam. Now it's Warren Central's turn to pound their chests a little.

But that's how it goes. In this game, nobody's rolling over because of one play. The only play that matters is the next one. And it's good— *so good*—to be back in the mix.

Warren Central finds their groove. They get Xavier so turned in circles that Coach Murphy has to take him out for a while. That means going to another freshman, Tony Harrison, who is way undersized—but at least he knows when to switch on screens. On our end, I keep us in it. A couple more Js. A nice drive and dish to Jones down low. A pick and pop for Reynolds.

Then it happens. With the score tied at 13, just a minute left in the first, Cox brings it up for Warren Central. He signals to his team like they're running offense. Then he stutter-steps at me and is *gone*. Like a sports car ripping past a hitchhiker. This time I don't have time to recover and meet him at the rim. Cox just curls around a late Jones challenge and scoops in a deuce. Plus Jones gets a silly whistle. Warren Central by two, at the line for a freebie.

The horn sounds while we shuffle toward our spots along the free throw lane. Probably Xavier coming back in for another go, I think.

"Derrick," a voice says. "Hey, Bowen."

I don't have to look to know the news. It's Gibson, subbing in for me. I trot to the bench but refuse to even look at Gibson on the way past.

When I hit the sideline, Murphy cuffs me on the back of my head. "Catch your breath," he says. He wants to make it seem like he's just getting me some much-needed rest, stretching out my breather over the quarter break. But anyone with an eye for hoops knows. It wasn't just fatigue that beat me out there.

As I sit and grab some water, Cox sinks his free throw to put Warren Central up three. Their crowd's feeling good now, the students

Kevin Waltman

jumping up and down. They get louder when, on his way up the court, Gibson mis-dribbles for a second and has to chase the ball down by the sideline. They think they've got him rattled—a short, white point guard seeing his first action. And there's a horrible part of me that flares up—I wouldn't mind seeing him fail. I swallow that bitterness down and make myself stand and yell to him. "You got this, Gibson. You good." But even as the words leave my mouth I can tell how unconvincing they are.

None of this bothers Gibson a bit. He even smiles a little as he crosses the mid-court stripe. Then he loops to the right wing to run an exchange with Fuller. Only Gibson doesn't give up the orange. Instead, he ducks his shoulder. He knifes into the lane. Then comes a step-back—just a *filthy* move—and he sinks a fifteen-footer.

The Warren Central crowd simmers down. Gibson trots back on D, clapping his hands in delight. He loves being on the road, feeling the heat of the other crowd. I have to respect that, at least.

Then he takes it next level. Just before Cox hits mid-court, holding up his index finger to say they want one shot, Gibson jumps him. At first, Cox tries to shrug it off. But when he crosses to his left, Gibson just rides him all the way to the sideline. Cox realizes they're losing valuable clock, so he tries going between his legs to shake Gibson. No luck. Gibson times it and pokes the rock away quick as a cat. Before Cox can even react, Gibson scoops the ball up and then it's flat-out quicks—there might as well be a cartoon puff of smoke where he leaves Cox. He's to the rim for a lay-in with jaw-dropping speed. He gives us the lead, then just puffs his chest out at the crowd while the clock runs out on the quarter.

Our crowd's so stunned they're slow to react, but when they do it's this high-pitched song of surprise and delight. The boys on the bench are just plain amped. As one, they leap up and start shouting at Gibson: *You the boss* and *That's what I'm talking 'bout* and *D-Train rollin'!* Gibson just bobs his head back at them, feeling pretty damn good about himself.

I stand and clap too. But there's something about his head bob that makes it seem aimed at me as much as anyone else. I recognize it because it's the same kind of look I used to give to Nick Starks when I was a freshman.

At least I get the bulk of the minutes. Problem is, when Gibson's running point, our lead balloons to four, six, even eight in the middle of the third. But when I'm in, Warren Central tracks us down like prey. So here we are with a couple minutes to go, nursing a three-point lead. I haven't fared any better keeping Cox in front of me, so Warren Central tries to solo us up. They just flatten out and let him go to work out top.

I concede a little space, dropping my heels down near the foul line. If he wants to rise up, I let him. I can still challenge from here. But it's not enough cushion. He blows by left. I can't do a thing to stop it.

There's still time to meet him at the rim, but Jones gets there first. Clean up top, but he bangs him pretty good with the body, drawing a whistle. Cox manages to spin in the bucket too. A chance to tie at the line. The gym roars to a fever pitch, their crowd sensing blood.

Jones nods, not complaining about the call. It's his fourth. We all look to the bench to see what Murphy's going to do. With two and change left, it seems like a no-brainer to stick with Jones, but it's his first crunch-time decision as a coach.

Kevin Waltman

Then we get a surprise. The ref holds up his hand, signaling that it's the fifth on Jones. Murphy, who was talking to Gibson on the bench, wheels around in disbelief. "It's just four," he says. He's not angry. It's like he's trying to direct a lost person how to get back to the highway. "That's only four."

Jones turns to appeal to another ref. He starts rattling off his previous fouls on his fingers, but then I see him stop. It dawns on him. He got a cheap whistle early in the quarter we all forgot about. The first ref is breaking it down to Murphy too. By this time the Warren Central crowd is clued in on our mistake, and they're heckling Jones pretty good with a *Sit down! Sit down! Sit down!* chant.

That's a killer. Senior big man gone in crunch time. And totally avoidable. If Jones had known he had four, no way would he have challenged so hard. That's on Murphy—it's a coach's job to remind his players in foul trouble. Jones doesn't say anything, but on his way back to the bench he gives Murphy a stare that speaks volumes—just in case anyone in the gym was doubting who should be held responsible.

Murphy does what he can. Instead of subbing in with Tony Harrison, he sends in Gibson, opting for small ball. Gibson saunters onto the deck and tells everyone to slide up a spot in size—me at the two, Reynolds at the three, Fuller at the four, Xavier at center.

I'm still shaking my head in disbelief—first we lose our big, then Coach slides me to off-guard—as Cox coolly drains his freebie.

Our ball. Tied. Instinctively, I clap for the in-bounds, but Gibson's right there. "Uh uh, Bowen," he seethes. "You running the two."

He walks it up, a little swagger to his stride. We run offense for a little while, nothing much happening. Everyone's a little too tight to pull the trigger, especially playing out of position. I figure it's time for me to ice it. So I break off a cut and flare out top, calling for the ball. Winning time.

That's when Gibson does the thing that makes me want to strangle him right there between the circles. The kid waves me down. "Flatten out," he says. "Stay wide." Thing is, I can't fight it. What am I gonna do, try to rip the rock from my teammate? So I set up behind the stripe on the right baseline, ready for the rock if I get a chance.

Gibson sizes Cox up, then darts left. It's all set-up. As soon as Cox moves his feet, Gibson spins on him, ducks his shoulder past, and scoops into the lane for a sweet deuce. Cox just shakes his head. In the front row, a few old-timers whistle like it's the baddest thing they've seen in years.

Gibson bobs his head like he owns the place. "Gotta get a stop," I shout. But he's all about that too. He may look like he's not paying attention, but when the in-bounds pass floats a little, he jumps it. Taps it away from Cox. Chases it down by the baseline. Then puts a no-look laser on me that almost catches me by surprise. I take a power dribble to the rim and gather. But when I rise I don't have that same old burst. Instead of an emphatic throwdown I have to try curling one in around the D. It rolls harmlessly off, but I get the whistle.

"Gotta bring the hammer on that," Gibson tells me.

I don't even respond. No way I'm giving him the satisfaction. Instead, I stroll out to the mid-court stripe and pull myself together. It's game one back from my injury and instead of feeling the flow, my head's full of noise. There's so much up in the air: late night texts from Jasmine, the schools relentlessly recruiting me, Mom about to

Kevin Waltman

burst with a baby. And now my back-up point guard showing out on me.

Fuller comes out to me, puts a hand on my shoulder. "You got this, D. Bury these and let's walk out of here with a win."

I turn to look at him. All last year, I tried getting him to loosen up, but now he's the one talking me down. I give him the best cocky smile I can muster, then head to the stripe. Once I get there, I remember the one good thing about a knee injury—lots of time to work on the form. That leather hits my hand and I feel it all come back—it's just basketball, the thing I do best in this world. I take my dribbles. Exhale. Bury the first.

The next one's easy. Straight bottom. And through it all—the mix-up by Murphy, my trouble corralling Cox, Gibson giving me static—we're gonna start the season 1-0.

I can live with that.

7.

D-train. That's the word everywhere. Hell, even Coach Murphy dropped that on the bus ride home. "No way I should have let Jones foul out, boys," he said. "I'll have to get an assistant to keep track of those things. But thanks, D-train, for bailing my ass out."

It seems to echo in my head even as I try to chill with my girl.

"You can't let that get to you," Lia says.

"You don't understand." She always says the right thing, but sometimes I resent her for it. I don't know why. "I'm sorry," I say. "I didn't mean it that way."

"It's okay."

Then we sit there in silence for a while. We're taking in a late Sunday breakfast at a diner on College, the place an even mix of churchgoers and neighborhood folks and hungover college kids. At the next table, a white hipster with his hair mashed up sighs over the crossword. Recently, my friend Wes has started to complain about the invasion of white people into what he calls "our blocks." Who knows where he's getting that put in his head, but he talks like he's the first person on earth to notice. But to me, if it's just diners and second-hand stores, they've got just as much reason to drop their dollars as anyone else. But our basketball courts? That's a different story. It's just not right. And what I keep turning over in my head is this—*Why? Why is Darryl Gibson even enrolled at Marion East? Why would a white family have moved to our district?*

"You want to catch a movie later?" Lia finally asks.

"Sure," I say. "What's playing?" She pulls out her phone to check some listings, but then I remember that tonight's a sit-down with Coach Murphy and my folks. "Ah, forget it," I say. "I can't tonight."

Lia's thumb freezes over her phone. We've been here before. She doesn't want to act all fragile, but she's not thrilled about coming second to basketball. "What is it this time?" she asks.

"I've *got* to figure out when to make official visits," I say. I try to sound tired out by the whole thing, letting her know that if I had my way I'd be with her instead. "Most guys have already made all their visits. And, I mean, I can make it down to Indiana any time. But Alabama? *Clemson?* Those are some hauls."

Lia nods. But she's not buying the poor-me act. "Then why don't you choose places closer to home? There are plenty of schools in Indiana and Kentucky, you know." She starts to scoop up another bite of waffle, then puts it down. She shoves her plate away. "I think I'm done," she says. If I didn't know any better, I'd think she meant *done* with more than breakfast.

"Lia, I know it sucks, but…"

She places her hands palm-down on the table. Leans toward me and smiles. "I'm not mad, Derrick. I get it. This is your *life*, you know?

I don't even *want* you to go to a stupid movie instead of doing this. It's not that at all."

We get up to leave. That hipster looks up from his crossword to inspect us. He gives a little laugh to himself, like he just knows all about everything. I can't help it—I bump his chair with my hip. He practically jumps in alarm. "Sorry, man," I say, but I grumble it like I'd just as soon crack his skull as look at him. It puts him on the defensive, and he mutters something. I can't quite make it out because he's staring down at his table. But the tone is pretty apologetic—like he's sorry for looking at us, for coming to this diner, for even having the nerve to breathe.

When we get to Lia's car, she sighs before she starts the engine. It's a cool but bright morning, and the sun has baked some heat into her car. It's uncomfortable without the air on.

"You're not even going to say anything, are you?" she says.

"I thought you said you weren't mad." Now I'm the one sounding pissed. And I kind of am. I mean, if something's bothering her, she might as well come out and say it instead of making me guess. That's something I never had to worry about with Jasmine—that girl didn't hold back.

"I said I'm not mad about you bailing on a movie," she says. Then she fires up the car, angrily, like she's ready to rip out into traffic and play chicken with the next truck she sees. "But have you ever thought about where *I'll* be next year? Does it even cross your mind? Have you ever thought about staying closer to *me* or letting me visit a campus with you?"

"Lia," I say again, but I don't have an answer. Or, really, it's not the answer she'd want to hear.

Kevin Waltman

Problem is, my not saying a word is the same as giving that answer. At least Lia takes it that way. She squeals from the parking spot and accelerates as fast as she can. She runs up on the bumper of some old bucket and whips out into the next lane. That earns a long honk from a car she cuts off. She just flips him off in the rearview mirror. "Fucking asshole," she says. But she's not looking at that other driver.

It's supposed to be fun. For other guys, it's a wave of cash and girls. Like the universe is rising up to meet every desire you've ever had just because you can ball a little. Even last year, Coach Murphy got offered a load of cash to steer me to a particular school.

But that road is for other players. What basketball recruiting means for me is my family sitting at the kitchen table with Coach Murphy—going over brochures, talking academics, even discussing campus life. It's almost like I'm any other prospective college student. Last time I talked to Wes he told me I was straight up crazy for not taking what was out there. "Grab what you can get when you can get it," he said. "Guys from our neighborhood don't get ahead by just playing it straight, D. You're the one guy who's got a chance to tilt the game in his direction and you pass? Crazy, man."

I don't dare bring that up now. Truth is, Jayson and Uncle Kid lean a little more toward Wes' way of thinking, but they know better than to breathe a word of it in front of Mom and Dad.

Mom has a list of school rankings in front of her with my five options—Indiana, Clemson, Michigan, Marquette, and Alabama—all highlighted. She just goes right down the rows. "Michigan's the top-ranked school by quite a bit," she says. "Then Indiana and Marquette are really close." For her, it's all about education. And she's got a point—the scar on my knee is a pretty good reminder that you better have some schooling to fall back on.

Dad leans over and points to a school she missed. She glares at him, but then acknowledges that Clemson isn't ranked too far behind Michigan. I know why she conveniently skipped that—she's been pretty up front about not wanting me to play in the South. "Okay, Kaylene, but they're all top 100 schools," Dad says. "Can we at least admit that where Derrick fits as a basketball player matters too?"

"And location," Jayson says. "I mean, we're gonna be heading to D's games so we might as well go someplace good. I say Alabama in the winter's where it's at." Jayson's as transparent as Mom—all he cares about is the girls he sees on T.V. during football games, and he's been pretty outspoken that Alabama wins in that category. So this earns another glare from Mom. It's a withering look, seeming to say that if she weren't so heavy with baby she's lean over and smack some sense into him.

Dad starts in about some research he's done on quality of life in the various places. I try not to roll my eyes. They mean well, all of them. But I'm not going to make the biggest decision of my life based on a cost of living index, or a magazine's rankings, or how hot co-eds are.

Finally, Uncle Kid clears his throat. Everyone stops and looks at him. He treads lightly—after all, he's crashing here because he lost his old place due to sheer stupidity, so he's still a little suspect in Mom and Dad's eyes. He glances over at Murphy, who just nods at him. It's this little gesture that suggests they've talked some things over beforehand. "All this stuff"—he motions toward the print-outs Mom and Dad have made—"it matters, but you're trying to make this decision on paper.

Kevin Waltman

What we have to do is get Derrick on these campuses and let him feel his way around."

Now it's Murphy's turn. "All of his schools have offered official visits, and we need to get rolling on them," he says. "We need to think schedules instead of rankings right now."

All the schools want me to come when they have big games. And that's what I want too. I want to see what Indiana's like when they're gearing up for a top ten throwdown. What the vibe at Alabama's like when Kentucky's rolling into town. Of course, I've got my schedule too, so we start picking out weekends where we've just got one game, and then coming up with some times I could make mid-week trips.

Mom and Dad dutifully fold up all their papers and we get down to business. We nail down the Indiana trip right away, since that's just an hour down the road. We decide on the Syracuse game, which should be pretty hype. Then, over Mom's sighs of disappointment, we start figuring out when to hit up Alabama and Clemson. We have a game the same night Alabama plays Kentucky, but we can make it for their game against Florida. And then there's the Clemson trip—their game against Duke, the team I hate most. It lands right when we have an open Saturday. I'm all kinds of on it.

That leaves Marquette and Michigan, but I hold off for now. I'm not feeling those schools quite as much as the others. So we'll wait and see about them.

When we've got it all settled, all that's left to do is for me to contact the schools with the dates. Then they'll take care of the rest. It's only one step to making the ultimate decision, but I lean back from the table feeling better about things.

"You good with this, D?" Murphy asks.

"Sure," I say. I can't give Murphy much more than that. He's cool with it all, not pushing me one way or another. But the truth is I still miss Coach Bolden in these conversations. We argued plenty, but I trusted the old man. I'm not quite there yet with Murphy. Especially not after him talking up Gibson the other night. "We'll see how it goes," I add.

Murphy nods, but I can tell something doesn't quite sit right with him. "That's all?" he asks.

"For now I guess," I say. Then I turn to Jayson and tell him we should go chill in our room. I don't really have anything in mind, but I don't want to keep on with Murphy.

But when Jayson and I get ready to jet, I see Murphy turn to Uncle Kid instead. "You got a second?" he asks. Uncle Kid, as surprised as anyone, snaps his head up from a Michigan mailer he'd been eyeing. Murphy just motions for Kid to follow him outside.

This I've got to see. So instead of heading down the hall with Jayson, I double back and peek out the front window. Kid and Murphy stand by Murphy's car and chat, standing there as easy as if they were discussing the weather or something. Then it hits me—maybe they're playing an angle. After all, Murphy did get a big offer last year. And when I was a freshman, Uncle Kid made a play for a job to get me to transfer to another school. Maybe now, with Coach Bolden out of the way, they think they can chase a payday. If they think that, though, they're in for a serious wake-up call from my parents—and me too, for that matter.

"What you think that's about?" It's Jayson, who's sidled up next to me.

Kevin Waltman

"Who knows," I say. "But I know Uncle Kid, so it's probably nothing good."

We check over our shoulders. Mom and Dad are still at the table, having their own conversation about schools. I'm kind of shocked they're not all up in Kid and Murphy's business. Maybe they're too obsessed over school rankings to notice.

"Let's hit it," Jayson says.

"Sure," I agree. There's nothing I can do about what's happening out there now. When we head down the hall, I peep at my phone. I'd had it on silent, but it's filled up with texts. Some from schools. One from Wes telling me to throw some green his way if I get offered some cash on my visits—a joke, I know, but a bad one. Two from Lia asking me to come over when I'm done talking schools. And one from Jasmine, still wondering when we're going to catch up.

8.

Against Richmond it's the same deal. My J is smooth as silk, but I can't get to the rim like I used to. All pull-ups in the lane. Then Gibson comes in and just rips past Richmond's guards like they're standing in sand.

If it weren't for the fact that Richmond's in a down year, we'd be in real trouble. Jones has foul problems again. Xavier can't remember his defensive assignment to save his life. And Reynolds and Fuller are forcing—taking bad shots, turning the ball over, gambling on the defensive end. It all means this—with two minutes to go, we're nursing a two-point lead. Richmond ball.

They've got a solid two guard, Randall Harrison. He's basically kept them in it, dropping 20 so far. Now, their coach barks out some orders to them from the sidelines. As a group, the players all look at him and nod. There's no secret though—everyone in this gym knows the rock's going Harrison's way. I've got their point out top, but while he motions to his teammates, I sneak a peek behind me. They've got Harrison flattened out on the right baseline. Their bigs are on opposite blocks. Again, no secret—Harrison's gonna come flying off those bigs

Kevin Waltman

looking for the ball. Easy enough to see, but a lot harder to check. But that's the job for Reynolds.

What I can do is pressure the ball enough to make a pass to Harrison harder. So I get up in their point's grill. He takes a step back toward mid-court and I jump with him. Flick for the ball once. Nothing there—just a move to keep the pressure on. For a moment, their guard looks uncomfortable. He switches the rock to his left and backs up again. I stay into him. His eyes flash a little, and I know that behind me the play is unfolding. He takes a step left, then goes behind his back to the right. It's a slow move and I jump to cut him off. I beat him to the spot, but I don't have the quicks to check his response—a little cross-over back to his left. He gets past me, giving him a free look at the play. He finds Harrison right in rhythm on the opposite baseline. There's no hesitation from Harrison. He grips and rips, burying a trey to put Richmond up one.

Their crowd gets *loud*. I see some shoulders slump on my teammates—doubt creeping in. I clap for the ball and Reynolds inbounds it to me. As I bring it up, the Richmond crowd starts stomping and clapping in rhythm. They can taste it. I take a glance to Murphy to see if he wants a special play, but he's got nothing. He looks a little frozen by the situation, really.

Well, if the coach doesn't know what to do, I do. Get to the rack.

I don't even bother setting my man up, I just power into the lane with my right. When their bigs see that I'm not waiting around to run offense, they jump to me. I take one last power dribble, plant, and rise up on their center. He doesn't have time to gather his legs, so he's got to reach a little.

Turns out that reach is enough to check me. He meets me a foot from the rim and flat-out caps me. The rock ricochets off my elbow, then glances off his knee before rolling out of bounds. Their crowd *howls*. It's still our ball, but that was an emphatic rejection. Their big just hovers beside me, scowling. He doesn't even need to talk trash. That stare says it all. He owns me.

A year ago I would have flushed that thing, no problem. But now I'm going to have to get used to my limitations.

I'm about to signal the out-of-bounds play when the buzzer sounds. Gibson saunters between the lines. Reynolds takes a couple steps toward the sideline, thinking that we're going with me and Gibson again for the stretch run. But Gibson waves him back. Then he points at me.

"I got it from here," he says.

It makes me want to scream—louder than all these Richmond fans combined. Lord, I'm a senior! I've taken us to the state finals! And Murphy's taking me out in crunch time? I know I've hit a rough patch, but this is a betrayal. You just don't do a player this way. I don't even look at Murphy as I walk past.

"Keep your head in it," he says. "Just catch your breath and I'll get you right back in."

Keep your head in it. It doesn't matter what's going on in my head—I can't help the team win with my ass on the bench. And the truth is my head is going to some bad places anyway. The worst thought a player can think flashes through—if Murphy's going to play me like that then I don't care if we win or lose.

We won. Not because of Gibson's heroics. Certainly not mine either. Mostly because of Richmond being a mediocre team. They lost track of

Kevin Waltman

Fuller on the in-bounds—bucket, with a foul to boot. Then they did the unthinkable—when Reynolds offered a little false pressure on the in-bounds, their big man stepped across the line. Turnover. Then they just kept on fouling us.

I got back in there, sunk some freebies, but it didn't seem as sweet as wins normally do. Even on the bus ride home, there was some chatter but not the hype atmosphere you'd think. Hell, we're 2-0 with both wins coming on the road, and we're not sure if we're actually any good.

Whatever. It's Monday after school and time to get things straightened out. I jet to the gym as soon as the bell rings. Gotta have a sit-down with Murphy. I've cooled since Saturday night. I know better than to go in guns blazing. Like it or not, he *is* the coach. I've got to give the man some respect. But I've also got to let him know he has to respect *me*. After all I've given this school I deserve better. He said again after the game that he was just giving me a last breather before winning time—but any fool knows that should come with five minutes left on the clock, not two.

Just thinking about it gets me boiling again. I make my way down the hall and put my hand on that thick wooden door to the locker room. I take a few deep breaths first—get my emotions under control.

Then I push that door open and walk on in. Only to find I'm not the first one in to see Murphy. Instead, there's Uncle Kid, a whistle around his neck and a rock tucked in his right elbow.

They both turn to see me, surprise on their faces like I've just caught them sneaking from a store with their arms full of stolen goods.

"Hey, D," Kid says. He saunters over and extends his hand, trying to act nonchalant. I accept his handshake but don't say a word. Instead, I just turn my gaze to Murphy. I raise my eyebrows, waiting for an explanation.

Murphy tries to smile like it's all good. It comes off as weak, like a kid trying to act cool when he's busted in the hallway without a pass. "Tell me, Derrick," he says. "Can you name a single person in this whole city who knows more about ball than your uncle?"

Well, yeah, I want to say. There's like every damn body in the Pacers organization. And the whip-smart coaches over at Butler. And last I checked Joe Bolden still resides in Indianapolis even if he isn't a coach anymore. Instead I just say, "Nah, I guess not." Besides, I can see where this is headed—the secretive conversations, the whistle on Kid's neck? It clicks now.

"Then what better man to ride shotgun on our bench?" Murphy asks. "I've got my hands full as head coach. I need some help. So Kid's my man." Then, as if to defend his decision, he starts rattling off Kid's cred—a Marion East grad, a serious baller in his day, a man who knows his way around Indy hoops.

I nod, but to me it means two things. First, it means Coach Bolden is never walking through that door again. I knew he wasn't coming back, but this kind of seals it—hiring Kid, a guy who went round and round with Bolden back on the day, is like defacing Bolden's house. But I also know this: now I've got an ally on the bench. I might be lacking some trust with Murphy, but at least my uncle will have my back.

I've still got my doubts. For as long as I've known him Kid's taken any good situation and screwed it up. Just last year he was set up with a job, hooked up with the finest woman he's ever been with. And

Kevin Waltman

he sabotaged it. Got himself twisted up in an unemployment fraud scam. That's why he's still a full-grown man slumming rent-free at our place.

But whatever. Kid and hoops. Nothing wrong with that. I step forward and give Kid a quick forearm thump on his chest. "Like old times," I say. "You and me running things on the court. Like when we balled out on the Fall Creek court when I was a pup."

That makes it good all around. As the two of them laugh at my comment, I suddenly realize both Murphy and Kid were a little iffy about how I'd take to the news.

The door swings open again. Fuller and Reynolds file in. Murphy and Kid stiffen up, preparing to officially share the news with the team. I head to my locker and start getting ready for practice. So much for my talk with Murphy. Can't sweat that now though. After all, there's one thing I learned from Kid all those years ago on the blacktop—when things are breaking wrong between the lines, the only thing to do is to get back after it harder than ever.

I have to admit, practice hums a little better. With Kid on the scene, there's less room for Xavier and some others to fool around. And Murphy can put more of his attention on the back-court. Right away he spotted a flaw in Reynolds' game. He pointed out that his step into his shot is real long—it takes him more time to get the shot off, but it also flattens him out and leaves him firing line drives. Like always, Reynolds bristled at the advice, but after two minutes of work he started finding bottom a little easier and everything was gravy.

Murphy even cracked on Gibson a little. Three straight times

Gibson drove hard middle when the play called for a reversal baseline. Three straight times Murphy corrected him. "Man, you're so amped to show everyone that you're the great *D-Train* that you only do one thing," he said. "Drive, drive, drive. Instead of D-Train I'm going to start calling you One-trick Pony if you can't mix it up a little."

Gibson pouted some, but give him this—you can't keep the kid down long. He bounced back after a minute and made some slick plays.

It all meant that I didn't get to interact with Kid much. Oh, I'd hear him now and then, barking at the bigs about how to box out. I even heard him tell Xavier that if he had a little more heart and a lot less lip he might get his name in the record books for rebounds some day.

But now we're all on one end, the ones against the twos, doing some early prep for White Station, a tough outfit from Memphis. We head there this weekend for a day tourney. Evansville Harrison will be there too, but we won't play them. Instead they get top billing against Tennessee's reigning state champ. Still, it's a chance to show out in a spotlight.

Kid's in charge of the twos, and he does his Kid thing—he huddles them up and gets them amped like they're about to rock Game 7 of the NBA Finals. And, hey, maybe *that's* been what's missing. Murphy's had to adjust to his head coach role, but nobody's stepped in to do his old job of getting guys pumped. Kid's a natural. "Remember," he shouts at them as they step back onto the court, "only way to flip your jersey and run with the ones is to *beat* the ones. Ain't nobody gonna give it to you."

Hearing that kind of talk gets me hyped too. And when I glance at Fuller and Jones, I see that fire in their eyes. The twos gonna come at us? Bring. It.

Gibson strolls out toward me. He starts clapping his hands, rallying his boys. Then Murphy bounces the rock my way. "Ball's in," he says. I grin at Gibson. He glares back. Oh, it's on.

I pop the rock to Reynolds on the wing and we run O. The twos know every move we want to make. Still, I carry out my fakes. I take a couple hard steps like I'm going to down-screen, then cut away from the ball to set a cross-screen for Fuller. Gibson jumps the play. He squeezes his body between me and Fuller, throwing off our timing. Fair enough. But if he's going to do that, then I'll improvise. I spin and seal him on my back, then cut straight down the lane, hands extended. But by the time Reynolds sees it, the lane's crowded. Besides, Gibson's got a hand on my hip, holding me back on my cut. It's a cheap move. He knows Murphy and Kid are too busy watching everything else to catch a quick grab. But when I take the bait—swatting his hand away—of course they see *that*.

"Clean it up, Derrick," Murphy snaps.

I just grunt in response and keep on. But before I can get my hands on the rock again, Jones gets free on the block for an easy deuce.

Next possession, Gibson gets right back to it. He grabs. Holds. Jumps plays because he knows what's coming. It's nothing new. Second-teamers have been doing this since basketball was invented. Still, that doesn't make it any less irritating. And this time it's made worse because we don't get a bucket. Xavier gets his first touch and chucks a bad one—a fadeaway from deep right baseline—that barely catches iron. While the second team grabs the rebound, Gibson gives me a quick shove. Nothing dirty—just enough to get me on my heels so he can create separation for the outlet. He catches at the hash and the only thing that stops him from a run-out is Murphy's whistle. "Bring it back," he calls. "Let the ones keep working offense."

But Gibson just grins from ear to ear. Everyone in the gym knew that was a run-out. And only I know he had it because of that push.

On and on it goes. It's not like I'm getting stopped cold. I've got four inches on Gibson. A few times I just rise up over him to show him who's boss. But I can't get the offense humming the way I'd like. And every time we get slowed down—a cut gets bumped off course, a reversal gets denied—Gibson seems to swell up a bit more.

Finally, I've had enough. Forget about rising up for mid-range Js. There's only one way to put a pest like Gibson in his place. When I flare baseline for a look, I don't even think about a jumper when the leather hits my hands. I rip it to the rim. Only I can't get the whole way past Gibson. That missing burst again. I push on into the paint anyway. I've got the size to muscle one up on the glass. But as I go up, Gibson gets another cheap one on me—he pins my right arm to his chest, then flops. He pulls me down, but it looks like I've charged into him.

Or at least it looks that way to Murphy. "That's a charge, D," he says. "Turnover. Let's start it again—and this time try to stay within the offense."

This time, I can't help it. It's that last dig about staying in the offense that sets me over the top. Hell, *no team* puts up points if they can't just break down the D once in a while. But that's not what I respond to. "Charge?" I yell. "Gibson pulled me down. A blind man could see that."

Kevin Waltman

Murphy rocks back on his heels. "Now, Derrick," he says. "I didn't see it that way. But even if you're right, you've got to play through a bad call now and then."

A bad move by Murphy. To even acknowledge my complaint is a sign of weakness. Bolden—or *any* coach worth his whistle—would have had my ass running stairs before the last word was out of my mouth. I glance around. Xavier and Jones are having a private little laugh off toward the baseline. Reynolds has his shorts sagging so far he's about to trip over them. Rider, relegated to third-string point, is just staring into the rafters like there's some movie playing up there. And then there's Gibson with his snarky little smirk. This is not a tightly focused team. And that's on the man in charge.

I scoop the ball up from the baseline and head back out top. I give a little sneer toward Murphy, testing him. No reaction. So I press the issue. I turn toward Kid. "You could see it, right?" I shout. I point at Gibson. "Foul's on him, right?"

Kid clears his throat. "I didn't really have an angle," he says.

"Oh, come on, Kid!" I shout. "You were right on top of the play!"

Kid's face darkens. It's the expression he gets when my mom hints a little too forcefully that he needs to move out of our house. "Let's just play ball, Derrick," he says.

"Whatever," I say.

"That's enough. Let's play." It's Murphy now, but he's got no real throat behind it. Instead, it sounds like a gentle suggestion.

We go another twenty minutes without incident, then Murphy calls it for the day. All I want to do is get the hell out of here, maybe get some time with Lia. I'm thinking about the quickest shower in the history of basketball when I feel a presence beside me as I walk to the locker room—Kid. Scowl on his face.

Used to be, I'd back right down from Kid. He was always the big man on the court when I was playing, the guy who was better, the guy who knew more. Not anymore. Not after seeing him fail in a million different ways. And besides, with my extra height he can't even lord his size over me these days. "What?" I snap.

"You want to apologize?" he asks.

A few of the guys give us some looks as they file past. Truth is, as much as I want to open it up on Kid, I don't want a scene. That's not a good look for a senior leader. So I lower my voice. "Man, I don't see where I'm the one who should apologize."

Kid rolls his eyes. "Fine," he says. "Be a stubborn son of a bitch." He points way down to the opposite baseline, where we were playing. "You don't think I saw what Gibson did on that play? Hell, I been seeing guys pull out that garbage since before you were born."

"Well then, why didn't you say so?" I say. That comes out a bit sharp, and guys stare again. But they keep moving toward the locker room. They're probably thinking this is just a family thing. Which it kind of is.

Kid sighs. He shakes his head at his shoes. "D, this is my shot. You see that, right? I could actually *be* a coach. Something more than a guy who sloshes beer in dirty mugs at a dive bar. But it ain't gonna happen if everyone thinks I'm just doing this because you're my nephew. So I *can't* take it easy on you. I *can't* just jump to your defense. Who'd respect me if I did that?"

I want to shout right back at him that nobody respects a guy who rolls over for some scrub who just transferred here. So much for having a man in my corner. But he has a point. I relax my shoulders and nod. Give Kid a little backhand to his arm to let him know we're cool. "Okay, man. It's just…" But I don't know how to finish that sentence. I don't know what it just *is*.

"Can I say something, D?" Kid asks.

"Sure."

He takes a deep breath. Then he launches in. "That play down there"—he points to the baseline again—"it shouldn't matter what Gibson does. A year ago you'd have been swinging from the rim while he was still trying to catch up to you. It's the knee."

My back stiffens. My mouth goes dry. I do *not* want to hear him start saying my knee's not good. Hell, that may be the truth, but I don't want to *hear* it.

Kid holds his hands up in defense. "There's nothing wrong with it," he says. "The only thing wrong is you don't trust it." Now he leans in toward me like we're in on some shady secret. I can smell a day's worth of coffee on his breath. "It's there. The burst. You can't see it, but I do. When you're just in the flow, not thinking about it, you snap off a cut like nobody's business. Or you top out going for a board. It's only when you want to rise up for a dunk that you hold back. I can see it on your face. You just don't trust it yet. But it'll come."

Maybe. That's what I think. Maybe it'll come. I know more than ever there are no guarantees. "Thanks, Kid," I say.

Then we head to the locker room. Static squashed. Except I'm in for one more surprise. "You gonna miss that cash from tending bar on weekend nights?" I ask. "'Cause I *know* Marion East isn't laying heavy green on an assistant coach."

"Man, some things are more important than money," Kid says.

"How's Wes working out down there anyway?" I ask, checking on my old friend.

That stops Kid in his tracks. "Wes? That boy hasn't shown up to work in almost a month."

Wes being a fool again. That one hurts. Talk about not being able to trust something.

9.

Here's the thing you learn about hoops—you have to keep plugging. As a freshman and sophomore, you think the whole season hinges on every game, on every play at every practice. Now I know there's always another game coming. Always one more play to make. The next shot's always the most important one.

So we scrape along. Gibson eats some of my minutes. Murphy tries playing us together at times, which just means Gibson freezes me out and Reynolds sulks at losing his spot. Xavier alternates between being a young beast and looking like he's never played organized ball before. But we win. We knock off White Station by getting some late stops. We come home for a win over a tough Cathedral squad. Then we follow it up with a smooth win over a struggling Michigan City team.

At 5-0, we should be feeling good. And some guys are. Xavier struts around the halls at school like he's the second coming of DeMarcus Cousins. And Gibson acts like he's the sole reason we're undefeated. But when we were in Memphis, I saw what true excellence looks like—Evansville Harrison. Man, those guys had it humming.

They won by sixteen over the best team in Tennessee. Cruised to it. They're sitting at 7-0, and nobody's come within single digits. And their point, Dexter Kernantz, has taken it to another level. If Gibson thinks he's got quicks, he should take a look at Kernantz. The kid is dropping nine dimes a game. And he's become a true stopper on the defensive end.

Every day at practice I try to tell guys this. "We've got to get better if we want to compete for the whole thing," I say. But Xavier just smiles and shakes his head. Gibson smirks at me like I'm the one holding us back. Even Murphy's riding too high. He keeps calling us his "undefeateds," pumping up egos even more.

Maybe Coach Bolden rubbed off on me too much. Maybe I've come to think if a team's having too good of a time then they're doomed for disappointment.

And then, with a few minutes left in a Wednesday night practice, my man walks through the doors. Not Bolden. But my old teammate Moose Green, Xavier's older brother. He pushes open double doors at the end of the gym and just stands there, waiting for everyone to notice him. It doesn't take long. Kid breaks into a big smile and shouts, "There he is! The legend!"

Moose tried walking on at Ball State a couple years ago. Then, when that didn't work, he transferred to Southern Indiana. But last I heard he got suspended for an "undisclosed reason." And one look at him says he's not exactly stayed in playing shape. He's stretching the seams of his winter coat, and his belly's pushing over his belt pretty good. But when he hears Kid call out to him as "the legend," Moose's chest puffs out and he squares up his shoulders. Forget playing weight.

Kevin Waltman

The guy still looks like he could hop between the lines and dominate the paint in his street clothes.

"I hear you boys were getting a little big-headed over a few wins," he shouts. "Even though you all saddled with my sorry-ass little brother down low."

Everyone laughs except Xavier, who coughs into his hand but lets loose an audible *asshole*. It's just one brother giving another one some grief. Xavier smiles then and trots off the court to bump fists with his big brother. "Get out here and I'll show you who's boss now," Xavier says.

"Shiiiiiiiit," Moose says. Laughs all around again. And it's this that's truly been missing. There's no real spirit on this team, no brotherhood. Everyone's feeling good enough about things, but mostly they're feeling good about *themselves*.

Moose saunters toward the court. He sees a stray rock and stoops gingerly down to pick it up. Then he takes one rhythm dribble and flies from about 22 feet. Money. That sends him strutting around the court nodding his head. "I *still* own this place, you hear?" Then he turns to Murphy. "Man, I wish you were running this show when I was playing. You woulda let me fire from range like that."

Murphy laughs. He picks up another ball and bounces it cross-court to Uncle Kid. "Let 'er rip," he says. And Kid does, burying his shot as cleanly as Moose did his. That lets Murphy turn back to Moose. "Anyone can knock down a J with nobody guarding him. Even an old man."

Now it's Kid's turn to get mock offended. He starts yammering about how he could still run anybody in this gym—and that gets him shouted down by every other warm body in the place.

After a few minutes of that kind of mess, Murphy tries to get us back on track. It's no use, of course. I mean, guys fall back into drills, but there's no focus. It's the kind of thing that would have had Coach Bolden stomping holes in the hardwood. But Murphy just gently pleads with us for a while before calling it a night. Not twenty minutes ago I was feeling good—Moose's energy infecting me the way it always did when we were teammates. But now I can't help but feel like we're gonna get our asses run on Friday night.

The phone's filled up again. As I leave the locker room I check it. Texts from Lia all but begging me to come over late when her dad leaves. A message from Dad reminding me that he's working late so I need to help Mom at home. And another message from Jasmine saying she's going to be back home this weekend, so we should "hang." That word, *hang*, sticks out like it's a text from a friend. Then again, I remember what it meant to "hang" with her back when we were in the middle of things.

"Checkin' all the love from schools, huh?"

It's Moose, who's lounging in a folding chair by the side of the court. Waiting on his little brother, I guess. I tuck my phone away and walk over to him. He stands and gives me a big hug and a few thumps on the back. "Long time, Moose," I say.

He just points back to where I stashed my phone. "For real," he says. "You got the wolves still howling for you."

I laugh. "You could say that." I explain that I've narrowed to my five, but that other schools still chase me. I guess until I ink that letter of intent, there's no real reason for them to stop. And something tells

Kevin Waltman

me that some schools won't stop even then. "The way I'm struggling to get my burst back, you'd think they'd ease off."

Moose shrugs. "Aww, they know you're the real deal. You're dropping what? Nineteen a game? And you're not all the way there yet?" I smile. The big man's spitting some truth. Maybe I get too hung up on what I can't do that I miss all the things I am doing. Moose strokes his chin, which now sports a goatee Coach Bolden never would have let him have, like he's deep in thought. "I wanted to talk to you about that anyway," he says.

"If you're here to recruit me to Southern Indiana, save it," I say. That coaxes a laugh from Moose. He knows that even if he owned the paint here for years—and even if my knee never gets back to full strength—my trajectory's lifting me way over Division II hoops.

"Naw, D," he says. "But, you know, you get to college and you learn some things." I figure he's about to drop some school knowledge on me, try to shake up my world view. But it's not nearly as deep as that. "You got to get that paper while you can," he says. He looks away for a while. Takes a deep breath. "You know why I got booted? A DUI. That's it." I want to tell him that a DUI isn't exactly jaywalking, but I let the man make his point. "Meanwhile, our star got caught boosting laptops from dorm rooms and they just made him sit the first half of a single game. But me? I'm gone. Scholarship and everything. Now, if I were getting ten rips a game, it'd be different. But it's not about being fair, man. You just watch. That knee of yours? I know it's gonna get better. But something else happens to you and they'll just throw you out. They're all the same, man."

"You know it's not like that," I say.

"Oh, really?" Moose gets a smirk on his face like I'm being naïve. "Look, D, I know your parents are straight shooters. And I know Coach Bolden was old school. But this is *you*, man. Ain't none of them ballin' out. This is *you*. And I'm telling you, you got to get paid while you can. Squeeze those schools for all they'll give."

"All right, Moose," I say. I reach out to give him a fist bump. Instead, he grabs my hand. He gives me this meaningful look like I best listen to him. So I tell him I'll think about it. Then another text sounds on my phone—a nice excuse to make an exit. As I head out, we both promise to get together over Christmas break.

When I walk out the door, I feel torn. If that's the line Moose is running, I don't want to hear it. But I also know he might be putting some truth on me.

Mom's feeling it tonight. She's on the couch, exhausted and uncomfortable, when I come in. Jayson's already holed himself up in our room with the excuse that he's got to rehearse lines. That leaves me in the firing line. "Derrick!" she snaps as soon as she hears me. "Get me a drink of water. There's a pitcher on the table."

I do it before I even set my bags down. But when I hand it to her, she takes one sip and scowls at me. "Ice, Derrick. Ice."

So I hustle back to the kitchen. Get the ice. This time Mom thanks me and lays on the praise, telling me I'm sweet to take care of her. But just as I start to set down my bags, she's got another request. "I haven't even had a chance to read the newspaper," she says. She points back to the kitchen table. "Your dad always hogs it." So I get that for her. Then it's the remote, which Dad left in his chair before he left.

Kevin Waltman

Then it's a bowl of potato chips. Then more water. I swear I've run more sprints in the first fifteen minutes back home than I have in a month of Murphy's practices. But I don't mind. I mean, it's my *mom*. And every time I feel that little twinge—like, *poor me having to do everything*—I remind myself how much she does for me. I'm not even talking back when I was in diapers. I mean even now. Trips to the doctor. Summer leagues. Late nights consoling me after losses. What's a few trips to the kitchen?

"Any day now," she says.

"Any day what?"

For all her exhaustion, she about leaps off the couch. "My due date!" she yells. "What the hell else is coming that's so important?"

"Sorry," I mumble. She just shakes her head at me and reaches for the newspaper. I look at her then. Really look. She's immensely pregnant, and I don't know how this feels like a surprise to me, but it does. I mean, I've known that we've got a baby coming. That's been pretty clear since the summer. But somehow it's always been this vague thing off in the hazy future. Something to look forward to down the road a ways. Not, like, a *baby*. Right *now*. In my head I start to compare it to how when you're in a game, crunch time can sneak up on you— *bam*, out of nowhere it's a tie game with a minute left. Then I think for a second about how Mom might react to my comparing her pregnancy to a basketball game. Probably not the best way to think about the baby.

Then I hear her sigh. Well, not a sigh exactly. It's this sound Mom makes that starts as a sigh and then descends into an angry grumble. I've heard it for years, but since she's been pregnant it's become a more common part of the soundtrack at our house.

Usually it's because of something Jayson or I do. Or she just walks into the living room and sees Kid on the couch. But this time it's the newspaper. More violence on the near East side. Two teenage boys dead. Two more in custody. "I'm supposed to raise another child in *this?*" She backhands the newspaper so hard it flies out of her hands and flutters to the floor. She stares up at the ceiling, maybe waiting for God to answer her question.

"It'll be okay," I say. It's the kind of thing people say to you when you're upset. And it doesn't work any better on Mom than it would on me.

"Lord, Derrick, you *know* Wes is headed in that direction. What saved you? Luck? What's going to save Jayson? What's going to save this baby?" She places a hand gingerly on her belly. But she's just getting started. "Three kids. What were your Dad and I thinking? We should have been more careful. I mean, three kids? Who has three kids? Poor people, that's who. And we're gonna be poor for the rest of our lives."

She stops herself then, like she remembers suddenly that I'm standing there. She apologizes for talking that way in front of me. She insists that Jayson and I are the best things that have ever happened to her and that the new baby will be a miracle, too. But I can see the worry still lingering like a shadow over her face.

Money. I know it's not everything, but that's a lot harder to believe when you don't have enough paper to go around. The math is easy. If I played it right, I could score $50,000 to ink a commitment. With Kid needing a place, Wes needing cover for his debts, and my parents needing some scratch for the baby, I can't pretend that kind of cash isn't sorely needed around here.

Kevin Waltman

"Mom," I say. "You know there are ways to get ourselves in better shape, right?"

She narrows her eyes at me. "Boy," is all she says.

Immediately, I rush to the defensive. "I'm not saying we should, Mom. I'm just saying we *could*. Just to get us over the hump."

Rage flares in her eyes, but then her hands shoot down to her belly. Maybe the baby kicked. Or maybe she's just trying to keep her emotions in control for its sake. With a great effort, she props herself up with one arm. Then she inches up until she's sitting. "Look, Derrick. I'm not going to lie. We could always use more money. Who couldn't? But we're not going to sell you to get it."

"It's not really like that," I say. "It's just getting a little payday." I realize how I sound. Just like Moose—*get the money while you can*. Or like any talking head on T.V. who insists that "getting paid" is the greatest thing on earth, no matter the cost.

Mom squinches up her face. It's the look she used to get when she had bad bouts with morning sickness. "So you're saying that shopping my son around to the highest bidder isn't selling you? And, what, we're supposed to trust a coach whose first move is to break the most basic rule there is?"

Somehow, I've been put in the position of defending something I didn't even really believe. Or maybe I do. I mean, why shouldn't I get paid? If I go somewhere and we make a run to the Final Four, you bet that coach is getting a bonus. And you bet that school is raking in the T.V. money. And you bet enrollment jumps the next year. How am I not due a little more than a scholarship and some meal money? But I don't dare say any of that. Not if I want to live through the night. "I know," I say. "It just seems like money's the one thing that could solve a lot of problems around here."

My mom softens. "It wouldn't hurt. But some college educations and some dignity would go a lot further in this neighborhood than any payout will."

And that's that. End of story. For now at least.

I head back to my room. Jayson's waiting on me. Big grin on his face.

"What?" I say.

"You a fool, D."

"You heard?" I ask.

He nods. I sling down my stuff and rifle through the mail Jayson's stacked on the dresser. More clutter from schools that I thought might back off.

"You're not a fool for wanting to get paid," Jayson says. I turn around so I can look him in the eye. He doesn't even flinch. "You're a fool for talking to Mom about it. You want to get some green, just get yourself some green. Don't ask permission."

10.

Jasmine has never looked better. And here's the thing—I *know* she
prettied herself up for me. No doubt, she can look fine rolling in a ratty
t-shirt and jeans, but when she puts on the real deal—a black dress
that's cut a little lower than I'm used to seeing on her, some earrings
that pop a little, even heels—she just floors me. Yeah, she's overdressed
for a coffee shop near the Butler campus, but that's how she rolls. So
when I walk toward her table—one near the window with the afternoon
light streaming in—I feel like I'm about to fall over.

I'm glad we're here. Not because I think Butler's anything special.
Oh, they act like it. And I guess you've got to give them credit for all
their March runs. But it's not my style at all. No, I'm glad we're here
because I know Lia Stone won't come within five miles of this place.
Probably doesn't even know it exists. Around us, the place swims with
white people. I mean, *really white*. There are a few scraggly-looking
souls, college kids trying out their hippie phase. Then it's all button
down and khakis. Or girls in oversized sorority sweatshirts. When
Jasmine and I were together, this made me crazy. Like she wanted to be

white. Or thought she was better than other people at our school. Now I'm just happy to be here—anywhere with her.

"Well?" Jasmine asks as I sit down.

"Well what?" I ask.

She rolls her eyes and smiles. "How have you been, Derrick? It's been forever." Instinctively, the hoops talk pours out of me. For so long now, when someone asks me how I *am*, what they really want to know is how basketball's going.

About halfway through my explanation of where the recruiting process is, Jasmine's waves me off with both hands. "No," she says. "I mean how are *you?* I always figure basketball takes care of itself with you. I want to know if you're happy. How your family is. You know"— and here she gestures to the coffee shop around us—"the things people actually talk about."

I slump back in my chair and offer a big grin. "You know, girl, if I stood up right now and announced I was going to Indiana, I bet people in this place would start yapping about hoops pretty quick."

She smiles, shakes her head at me. She bats those eyes, her long eyelashes doing a number. "You know what I mean, Derrick."

So I get into all the non-hoops business of my life. The house packed to bursting. My mom flat worn out. Wes into more nonsense.

When I'm done she just looks at me and calmly says, "I miss you, Derrick." She makes it sound like it's a natural response to everything I just said, even though it's really out of the blue. And she says it matter-of-factly, like she just told me what she had for breakfast earlier or something. So even though it's a loaded comment, it doesn't come off like some declaration of love.

Kevin Waltman

"You too," I say. It's a lame response, but it's all I can think of. Truth is, if someone set me down with pictures of Lia and Jasmine and said *choose,* I'd choose Lia. At least I think I would. I mean, Jasmine and I tried and tried and there was always something that got in our way.

Our words seem to charge the air. Around us there's the hiss of a cappuccino maker, a forlorn sigh from a student staring at their laptop, an overly loud laugh between two men just coming into the place. Part of me wants to run to Lia. Part of me wants to get down on my knees and beg for Jasmine back.

Instead, I simply say "What about you? How's school?"

Jasmine wound up at Louisville. She said it was about staying close to home, but I know that was an excuse. And, look, it's not like Louisville's a lousy school. Hell, most Marion East grads wouldn't even get a look from a school like that. But Jasmine was talking the Vanderbilts and Dukes and Stanfords of the world. She had the *smarts.* So for her to land just a couple hours down I-65 is kind of like me settling to play at some D-II school.

And now, when I put the question to her, she looks down at her hands folded on the table. "Good," she says. "School is good." But she still won't look at me.

"What's wrong?" I ask.

"Nothing," she says, annoyed. "I said it's good."

I reach across and touch her wrist. She jerks back like I've electrocuted her. "Easy, Jasmine," I say. "This is me you're talking to."

She relaxes then and starts to talk. Or, really, she tries to. I can see her start to explain, but she stops herself short a few times—she opens her mouth and it's like the words are stuck there. She looks away again.

She shakes her head. Then she looks back again, squaring me up with her eyes. "College is hard, Derrick," she says.

"Aw, come on. You always rocked straight As. I know you got this."

She shakes her head again. Angrily this time. "Straight As at Marion East doesn't mean much, it turns out. It didn't exactly translate to the test scores I was hoping for last year. And at school I feel like everyone else came from a different planet. Like they've got all this knowledge I'm still scrambling to pick up."

I stare at Jasmine, trying to detect just how bad things are. Is this her just venting a little about some hard work? Or is she really getting swallowed up? If Jasmine were to fail, it would somehow kill a part of me. It's like everyone who leaves Marion East with a little velocity just crashes back to earth. Kid's playing career flamed out. Moose's didn't go much further. Now Jasmine? Maybe if you grow up here, it's just fate working against you.

"It's nothing," Jasmine says. "I'll be fine."

Somehow that makes me believe her less. My mom talks about it all the time—kids who do well at city schools have a big wake-up call waiting. Just because you're the best student out of a bunch of bad ones doesn't mean you're going to crush it in college. I just thought Jasmine would be different. Maybe it will be the same with me next year. Maybe for all the popping stats at Marion East I'm going to find out I'm not really cut out for big-time ball.

"So what kind of grades are you talking?" I ask.

She stiffens on the spot. Her lips pinch down like she's tasted something bitter. "I said I'll be fine," she says. "Let's just talk about something else." She pauses, then raises an eyebrow. "Like, you know,

Kevin Waltman

you and Lia." An icy feeling runs through my veins. Like when you're between the lines and you suddenly realize you've been caught flat-footed on a back-door play. Jasmine bringing up Lia? I don't know how to handle that. Of course, Jasmine can see that all over my face. She laughs, loving that she can put me on the defensive that easily. "Derrick, come *on*. It's *okay*. I'm your friend. You can tell me about the girl you've been seeing for, what, a year now?"

Somehow, her saying that we're friends makes it seem like we're still something more than that. Jasmine's always had this ability to tell me one thing and make me think another. But I play it straight and talk to her about Lia. Things are smooth enough, I explain, but when I start to say how there's a little static about me taking off somewhere far away for college ball, Jasmine perks up. It's like she senses an opening.

"Do you remember that party where you met her?" she asks.

Again, she gets me racing. She's talking about me and Lia, but it's really a comment about me and Jasmine. At that party last year, I chatted up Lia for a second, but I left with Jasmine. We were still hooking up now and then, and that was the night we came as close as we ever did to sealing the deal. *Do I remember that night?* Lord, what I remember is Jasmine's breath hot in my ear and the feel of her body pressing against mine.

"Uh huh," I say.

"Those were good times," Jasmine says.

Then we stare at each other in silence for a while. She brings her coffee mug up for a sip, but she never breaks eye contact. Damn. Even the way she drinks coffee is sexy. And officially, right at that moment, I feel pretty sure I'm breaking some unwritten rule with Lia.

"I miss those times, to tell you the truth," Jasmine says.

"You mean you miss being with me?" I ask. Just asking that feels like swimming further out into murky waters.

Now Jasmine leans back and folds her arms. She cocks her head and inspects me. I realize she's finally got me where she wants me. I blinked first, said something that could only be interpreted one way. "But you're with Lia," she says. "I don't want to get in the way of that. It's just…" and then she trails off, letting me fill in that blank with my imagination.

I want to just run off with Jasmine. Grab her hand, head to the car, and do about 150 miles per hour down to her dorm room in Louisville. But even as I imagine that, I know what would happen— somewhere along the way, she'd cool down, re-think things. She'd let me get only so far. And there it is—*that's* what she wants. That control. Of me. For the first time ever, Jasmine has something in common with a baller. She just wants to get back to the good old days when she was on top of the game. I hate thinking it about her, but I know in my heart it's true. She doesn't want me back because of me. She wants me back just to feel like her old self again. I'm just here for her ego, now that it doesn't get stroked by an A on every single paper she writes.

"Well, you're right," I say. "I got Lia now."

It's not what she was expecting. In fact, she leans forward like she expects me to say more. And when I don't, she wilts a little. She's too tough to break down or beg, but I see her shoulders slump ever so slightly. I hear the distance in her voice when she changes the subject.

All that energy sparking the air between us? Gone. Our conversation gets cold faster than her coffee.

Kevin Waltman

Lia can sense it, I swear. The texts say it all.

Good luck.

Oh, we gonna get after it. We owe these kids.

Yep.

That's it?

Yep.

Biggest game of my life and that's it?

Yep.

You just messin with me?

And then silence. The only thing happening on my screen is the clock changing minute by minute. Like a chump, I check the bars. Power it off and on. Like there's got to be something—anything—the matter other than my girl Lia suspecting me. I'm sitting on the bus, wondering if anyone could have seen me with Jasmine and reported to Lia.

"Trouble with your phone?" It's Fuller, sitting across the aisle.

"I got some kind of trouble," I answer.

"Oh," Fuller says. He sees right through me. Anyone could. He rattles out a knowing laugh, trying to sound all wise. "Woman trouble is the worst kind of trouble."

I just laugh at him. "Man, do you hear yourself sometimes?"

"What?" Fuller throws his palms up, truly confused. When we were sophomores, this drove me crazy. He just doesn't get how to play it cool. But now I love it. Hell, I'd take a roster full of Fullers right now instead of the mess we've got.

I shake off his cluelessness and point to my phone. "I didn't even *do anything*," I say. I lay it on thick, echoing the lament of just about every guy who's ever had a girlfriend mad at him.

It draws a laugh from Fuller. He edges over in his seat, then leans halfway into the bus aisle. Behind him, I see the south side of Terre Haute sliding past. We're on 41 now, barreling south for our showdown with Evansville Harrison. There's an old mall that looks like it was built a hundred years ago. And then it's that same dreary stretch that every middle-sized city has. The chain restaurants that need paint jobs, the second-hand stores. There's a turn for the fairgrounds and then a sign for the federal penitentiary. I bet Marion East has sent more guys there than to Indiana State, the college that's just a few miles behind us.

"You ready?" Fuller asks. "Gonna take down Kernantz?"

"I'm not even sweating that," I tell him. It's a lie, but I don't want anyone to know different. "It's five-on-five, remember. I'm more worried about getting our five playing together."

Fuller's chest swells out. The kid loves some teamwork talk. "Sounds good to me," he says.

We bump fists, our hands meeting right in the middle of the aisle. When I look up, I see Uncle Kid peeping in our direction. He gives me a wink. I know what this means. I've seen it about a million times on the blacktop. He feels pretty damn sure we're gonna show out tonight.

It takes half a quarter for all that feel-good vibe from the bus to evaporate. Evansville Harrison controls the tip. On his first touch, Kernantz just rips it right to the rim. I'm left reaching at air while he knifes into the lane. Jones comes to help, but Kernantz just shovels it to their best big—Scotty Sims—for a nasty jam. On our first possession,

Jones gets it in his head he's got to match Sims bucket for bucket. When he gets a touch at seventeen—obviously out of his range—he launches, clanging back rim.

The rebound ricochets out to the elbow, where Evansville Harrison grabs it. They outlet to Kernantz. I'm back to slow him up, but Reynolds made a deadly mistake. He lunged at the rebound and now he's trailing his man by a good ten feet. Two-on-one, with Kernantz handling. I've got no chance. Kernantz pushes it right at me until I have to commit. Then he just drops one over his shoulder to their off-guard for another easy deuce. 4-0. And their crowd sounds as loud as a jet taking flight. As I bring the ball up again, I hear it—there's a slight mocking tone to their cheers, almost like there's an undercurrent of laughter. They think they're gonna blow us right out of the gym.

So I try to shut them up. When Reynolds comes to the wing, hands extended for the ball, I just wave him down. Kernantz isn't the only big-time point guard in the state. And it's about time for this crowd to get a rude reminder. I muscle right, getting some contact with Kernantz. Then I spin back middle, sealing him off so I can glide into the lane. I've got some room, so I take a power dribble to gather myself. The bigs come, but I just rise right up—and I get some lift, but about two inches less than I used to. Instead of a throwdown, I try to scoop one in around Sims and it just scrapes iron.

They rip and run again.

This time we get back, but they just let the offense click. They're a unit, for real. The ball zips around faster than a hockey puck. After a few reversals, Fuller gets lost on a back-door. Kernantz sees it, feeds it, and it's another bucket right at the rim. 6-0.

That prompts a timeout from Murphy. When I trot to the bench, my neck and ears burn with anger. And shame. I should know better than to get caught up in some macho showdown. That's the kind of thing I used to do as a sophomore—until Coach Bolden broke me of it. I realize, as we slump down onto the bench, that that's what I'm expecting—some of Bolden's old wrath. Instead, Murphy cuffs me on the shoulder and says, "Good take, D. It'll fall next time." Then he turns to Gibson and tells him to check in. "You've got Kernantz. Let Derrick slide to the two. Reynolds, you're out for a couple minutes."

That earns a huge huff from Reynolds. I look at Murphy, waiting for his response. But none comes. I even look to the back of the huddle at Kid. Maybe he'll step in and remind Reynolds how to act. But he's only a week into the job. It's not his place.

Of course, the Gibson-Kernantz matchup goes how you might expect. Gibson has no damn chance. Sure, Kernantz can't just blow by Gibson with his first step, but Kernantz has been *around*. He's got moves on moves. And after a couple minutes we're staring at a 14-3 hole. We're also staring at each other in the time-out huddle again, searching for answers where there aren't any. While we sit, Kid and Murphy have their own private huddle a few feet onto the court. I see Kid gesture angrily toward the defensive end, like he's personally offended by how we're getting whipped.

On the bench, there's some serious grumbling.

"I need some damn touches," Xavier says.

"*You* need some touches?" Jones gripes. "You don't even know where to go on offense."

Xavier scowls right back at Jones.

Kevin Waltman

"We can't win anyway if we can't get some stops," Fuller says. This is about as pessimistic as he gets, so he throws in a "Come on, guys!" as a little afterthought.

Meanwhile Reynolds still sulks for being benched. He's got one foot in the back of the huddle, but he's angled away from us like he can't bear to look.

I try not to let it get to me. I let the other guys bellyache and try to focus instead. I look down at my kicks. An 11-point hole? Normally that's nothing. A good run erases that. But against Evansville Harrison? On the road? We'll have to play out of our minds the rest of the way to have a chance. I glance toward our stands, but I know I'm not going to see my people. Mom's due date is in two days, so she's not exactly making road trips. And Dad and Jayson aren't going to leave her on her own, for sure. While I'm glancing around, I feel Gibson staring at me.

"Kernantz is a freakin' jet," he says.

I have to grin a little at that. At least we understand each other's pain.

Finally, the coaches make their way back into the huddle. Kid stands, arms folded tight across his chest, while Murphy kneels in front of us. One glance around and he can tell guys are about to go off the tracks. "Easy," he says. "Take a deep breath." Then he looks over his shoulder, points up at the scoreboard. "There are no easy fixes for that," he says. "But here's the plan. First, let's get our heads on straight. We've cruised all year, so a spot like this will tell us what we're made of. Let's rise to it. Second, let's be a little patient on offense. They're gonna have a hard time checking Derrick at the two-spot, so let's work through him some more. And on defense?" He pauses now. We're on pace to give up over a hundred in a high school game. Our problems on that end are about as hard to solve as crime in the city. Murphy takes a deep breath before giving us his solution. "We're going zone. Two-three."

Zone. Somewhere back in Indianapolis, Coach Bolden just felt a chill in his bones.

Their scoring slows. To some it might even look like the zone works. But it's like slapping a Band-aid on a gunshot wound. Evansville Harrison is a supremely talented team, athletic as hell, but they're also experienced. So they're not going to fold because of a flimsy zone. Instead, they work the ball around. Reversals. Duck-ins to the lane. Overload a side to test the zone. On most trips, it ends with Kernantz finally knifing between two defenders, making the zone collapse. Then he'll either zip a bullet out to a shooter or squeeze a nifty pass to Sims. Either way, they get a ton of good looks and bury most of them.

I'm the only thing that keeps us within shouting distance. With Gibson running point, I don't have Kernantz in my jersey everywhere I go. It starts with a mid-range J when I just use my size to elevate over their guard. Then I get a run-out for my first dunk in longer than I care to remember. Then a put-back. Then a deep three.

By mid-third I'm flat *rolling*. When I drop another three—this time freeing myself with a slick step-back—even some of the Evansville Harrison fans *ooh*. And lord knows these stands are filled with college scouts. If nothing else, maybe some of those schools that cooled on me after my ACL will kick themselves for it.

But none of that matters. I'm not wearing a Marion East jersey to impress people in Evansville or coaches from schools I'll never go to.

Kevin Waltman

I'm here to *win*. It just so happens that right now the best way to do that is to drop bomb after bomb on these fools. So I do. A leaner in the lane. A turnaround from the shallow wing. Then, with the clock racing to zeros on the third quarter, I flare off a Fuller screen. Gibson puts the rock on me, but I catch it *deep*—twenty-five feet, at least. Do I have the range? Ha. Everyone in the gym knows the shot's wet as soon as it leaves my hand.

When it drops, the horn sounds on the quarter. Our bench erupts. Even Reynolds rushes onto the court pumping his fist. I glance at the scoreboard. We're still down, 60-54, but for the first time since opening tip it feels like we might close that gap.

"That's the *truth*, D," Jones shouts. I'm so amped I don't even know what I say in return. All I know is that I can't wait to get back between those lines. Murphy's talk is just noise to me. Even when Kid tries to get my attention, I shake him off. He gets it—he's been in this kind of zone before, back in the day. I just stare at the court. And when the horn sounds to break the huddle, I practically sprint back out there, like a pit bull released from its leash.

It's Evansville Harrison's ball first. The momentum's shifted just a little our way, so they spread the offense out. No hurry. A few dribble exchanges out top. A half-hearted look to the post before another few reversals. It's way too early for them to go into a true stall, but burning thirty seconds off the clock settles everyone down. It's like someone snapped the burner off a pot that was about to boil. Except for me. I've still got the fire in my belly.

And when Kernantz gives it up to their two, I jump him. It's breaking zone principles, but now's not the time to worry about that. I hound him out to the hash, then stay into him as he backs up further. I'll chase this kid all the way to the Ohio River if I have to. He panics. He waves once, frantically, for Kernantz to come bail him out, but his savior's all the way on the opposite baseline. He picks up his dribble, and that's that. I clamp down, and all my boys behind me jump the passing lanes. The crowd senses trouble and rises in an anxious roar— screams of *Pass it!* and *Call time!* blending together.

In the end, he just gets a five-second call. I was hoping to pressure him into a bad pass, a steal, a fast break for us. But when that whistle blows on the five-count, I hear Murphy stomp his foot from our bench. He shakes both fists in front of him, intensity flashing across his face. For the first time, he seems like the fire-breathing coach we've needed all along.

Behind our bench, the entire Marion East crowd—a small, faithful group that made the trek to Evansville—rises in unison. And for a second their noise bullies the home fans back into their seats. As Gibson brings the ball up though, Kernantz starts gesturing to the crowd. He raises his hands over and over, begging them to get back on their feet. And what Kernantz says, the fans do. Suddenly, they roar back to life and drown out our fans.

Me? I love it. The fact that the supposed top guard in the state has to beg his crowd to get loud means we've tilted this game back in our direction. Time to strike.

Gibson starts into the offense. I widen to the right wing, then sprint for the opposite baseline. My man glides past a Jones screen and chases me out to the perimeter. With the way I've been shooting, he doesn't want to give me any look from three. Gibson sees it. He

Kevin Waltman

pump-fakes my way, selling it perfectly. My man lunges, all but spilling out of bounds. I slip past him, receive a laser from Gibson. Then I hit attack mode.

I power dribble into the lane. See the bigs coming. And I pull up. Since I've been fourteen, this would have been a time to explode right to the rack. But not anymore. Instead, it's a tough in-between look. As soon as I float it up there, I know it's off. A scraper. An easy board for Evansville Harrison.

When they outlet to Kernantz, I expect him to go for the kill. Just rip it right to the rim. Instead, he slows in the front court and waits for his teammates to join him. He circles it back out top while we settle into our zone. Then he looks right at me and grins. Some of the crowd sees it, and they howl. Just like that, he's back in control again. Of the rock. The game. The whole damn gym.

They run another thirty seconds off the clock, but in my heart I know what the end result is going to be. And, eventually, it comes. Fuller gets pinned on a screen and Kernantz flies free on the baseline. He's got about a week to set and fire.

Bang. We're back to a nine-point hole and our fans are back in their seats.

What I want most in the world is to grab that rock and attack the rim again. But what would I do when I get there? I can't just rise up on people anymore. I may be filling up the stat sheet, but if I can't put one down in someone's grill, I'm just not the same player.

The game slips away. The lead swells to 11. To 15. Then, when Murphy pulls the starters, it gets ugly. At the final horn, the scoreboard reads Evansville Harrison 84, Marion East 62.

Before I head to the locker room, I stare up at that score. I stare so long that when I blink the image leaves an afterglow on the inside of my eyelids.

"That's what happens when one guy tries to play savior," someone says.

Before I look, I know who it is. Gibson. "They put me at the two-guard," I tell him. "That's a scorer's spot." Then I step to him. "And in case you didn't notice, I shot us back into the damn game."

He sneers. "Shot us out of it too."

Before we can escalate, Kid's on us, a hand on each of our backs. "We gotta talk, we'll talk, but not in front of them." He nods toward some lingering Evansville Harrison fans. They're full of themselves, enjoying the fact that the beat-down we just got has spilled over into in-fighting. "Keep it in the locker room," Kid says, and he gives us another nudge in that direction.

11.

You make your own luck. That's what my folks always say. And it's a pretty good basketball slogan too. No excuses. You can't gripe about a bad call or a tough roll on the rim. *You make your own luck.*

So I look around Wes' place—the first time I've been inside his digs in almost a year—and it looks like he's made some terrible luck for himself. The majority of the house is a disaster. Unread mail stacked on chairs. Dust an inch thick on counters. Cracked windows in the kitchen. A scratch zig-zagging down the television screen. Garbage cans overflowing with fast food bags and napkins.

Wes' mom was never exactly stable, but last year she fell apart. And now it looks like she's gone altogether. Wes senses what I'm thinking and sighs. "Man, my moms is having a rough time. She's got this new guy. He lives down Central, I think. She crashes there most of the time, but he's no good for her." I want to ask what exactly *no good* means, but the subject seems to make Wes bristle. Without saying another word he shrugs his shoulders and heads to his room.

His space is spotless. Like the calm at the center of a hurricane. But even here, the change is clear. When we were runts, his walls were covered with posters of jazz giants—guys I didn't recognize but who Wes knew of through his dad. Now the walls are still slapped with posters, but it's all gangsta rap nonsense. The kind of thing Wes used to laugh at.

And it's not that I'm too good for a little hardcore noise. With Wes though, it's like he's trying a little too hard to be like the guys on his walls.

Then there's his closet. It's perfectly ordered. Every piece in place like a museum exhibit. Only now there are lots of oversized coats and baggy jeans, everything red and black. It's a lot of expensive stuff, way out of the range of someone who's supposed to be paying off a debt. One peek in my closet and a person would see all the potential places I'm headed. A look in here shows a kid going nowhere.

"So how's work?" I ask. I play like I don't know, just to see if Wes will come clean.

"Eh," he mutters. He rubs the back of his neck like some overworked factory hand. "It's a grind, but what you gonna do?"

Seeing Wes lie so quickly kills me. And it's practiced and slick. Where's the guy I used to hang with? The kid who always told my parents everything at the first suspicious look because he could never think up a cover story? "Stop it, Wes," I say. "I talked to Kid. I know."

This is all the room Wes needs to get worked up. "Then why you playin' me that way, D? You got something to say, then up and say it."

My instinct is to get up in his grill, give him a reminder I've got about a full foot on him. But I've tried that before. I've tried pressuring and pleading, anything to get his head back on straight. But now I look at him and I know it's too late. The simmering anger in his eyes? The lip

Kevin Waltman

curled in defiance? The who-gives-a fuck attitude? These are things Wes used to practice. Now they're who he really is.

My phone goes off, but I silence it. I point to his closet. "At least man up and tell me where you're getting the scratch for clothes like that."

"Man up?" Wes shouts. "Like you know anything about being a man. Got the whole world kissing your ass 'cause you can shoot a goddamn jumpshot."

"It ain't like that," I tell him. I'm about to remind him how much sweat I've put in. The countless hours on the blacktop and in empty gyms and in film study. Never mind rehab. Never mind pre-season conditioning. Everyone thinks ballers just win some kind genetic lottery. They can't see all the work that comes before someone's a star. But before I can get that out, my phone rings again. And again I silence it.

"What the fuck ever," Wes says. He shakes his head. Somewhere in there, I can tell he's regretting acting this way even as he does it. But he won't back down. He gestures wildly toward his window. "You ever look around these streets, D? I mean really look? It's not exactly easy to get ahead, D. Not if you're born this deep in the hole."

It's an excuse. A lie people around here tell themselves when things go wrong. It's no different than when Jayson and I were little kids and we'd scream *It's not my fault* when we broke a toy. At least that's what my parents would say if they heard me talking the line Wes just gave me.

Though he's got a point. I know that much. Even my parents, if you pinned them down on it, would concede it a little bit. *These streets* is right. There are worse places to be born, sure. But there are a lot better places too.

Wes glares at me for a few more seconds, daring me to say something back. When I don't, he huffs in disgust and turns away. He looks out the window like he's also taking inventory of our neighborhood. I know the deal. A murder rate a million times higher than the rest of the city. More high school dropouts than college graduates. Foreclosures. Repossessions. Dealers. Bangers. I mean, my house is a success story—and we've got an uncle crashing there who's been busted for unemployment fraud, and my parents barely scrape by each month. My parents are also pretty fond of pointing out that if people up in Hamilton County think the world is so fair everywhere, then maybe they ought to boot their pampered kids out of their mansions and send them to Indianapolis schools for a while. *We'll see how fair fair is*, Mom says sometimes.

"Wes," I say. He wheels around and I can see that there's water welling up in the corner of his eyes. He blinks it back, screws his face back into that tired, tough expression.

"What?" he snaps. "What you want to tell me ain't been told me before?"

"Wes," I repeat, but I'm at a loss. What I guess I'm thinking is that you have to *believe* in something other than the blind lottery of this neighborhood. You have to believe that you can rise above this muck, even if the real truth doesn't back you up. I mean, in hoops if you don't believe—you lose faith that the next shot is falling, that you'll win the next game, that things will get better—then you're dead in the water. I stare at my shoes for a long time. "Nothing," I say. And then I keep watching my shoes as they leave Wes' room, then pick their way through the disaster of his living room, then head out the door and land

Kevin Waltman

firmly on the sidewalk. How many times have I walked this stretch of pavement between our houses? I take a sharp breath of mid-December air. I try to will the door to open behind me, force Wes to tell me to wait up. I turn back and look. Nothing. Just the blank brick of that run-down house.

My phone rings again. I dig it from my pocked and shout, "What?!"

"Damn, D," Kid says. "Answer your phone! Get your ass to the hospital, boy." When I don't say anything for a few seconds, Kid answers my unasked question. "Your mom's in labor!"

PART II

12.

Basketball's a crazy thing. When I was little it seemed like the calendar was broken up into two sections—basketball season and the bland, brutal months without hoops. Then, when I got good, it took over the whole year. Camps and summer leagues. Individual workouts. AAU. Pretty soon, there was no offseason. And once recruiting started? Oh, the NCAA might mandate some dead periods on that stuff, but from my end it feels pretty relentless.

Basketball is all there is. For years now, I've lived it, breathed it. I wake up thinking hoops. Go to bed visualizing greatness. Everyone I meet—*everywhere*—asks hoops first. To separate me, Derrick Bowen, from D-Bow, that player between the lines, is impossible. And I don't even want people to. Who I am as a person is who I am as a player.

Then you get plopped down in a brown chair in the waiting room of a maternity ward. You watch your uncle pace back and forth in front of a window that looks out onto the parking lot. You watch the sky outside that window darken and fill with flurries. Your little brother passes the hours with his face buried in his phone—texting, surfing, playing a game that has the most grating music you've ever heard. Your dad sprints back and forth with updates. He instructs you to call relatives to keep them posted. Every time he comes into the waiting area, he loses a little more color in his face. His eyes look a little wider and more frantic each time. And then the updates stop. It goes from every half hour to nothing. Brutal silence for hours. Just the hum of hot air in the vents, the rhythmic clop of Uncle Kid's feet on the hard floors, the blip-blip-bloop of Jayson's phone.

Basketball is nothing.

At some point, Kid starts in on the coffee. Without even asking, he fetches some for me and Jayson too. And without thinking twice, we drink it. It's dark, tarry stuff. Jayson tries his and almost gags. That affords me and Kid a brief laugh, but it doesn't last. The sound echoes around the cavernous waiting area, and it almost spooks us. Earlier, the place hummed with nurses changing shifts, families coming to visit new mothers. Now it's just us. The sky outside has long been dark. We all return to sipping our coffee—even Jayson who squints at the bitterness of every sip—and we don't say a word. What's to say? We each know what's running through the others' heads. Nothing but bad thoughts. We got here at 1:00, and now it's nearing midnight. No news from Dad in five hours.

I stand and pace now. I work the same patch of carpet Kid did earlier. Back and forth, back and forth. I look out that window. A car passes now and then. The headlights cut through more flurries. I try not to let those bad thoughts take over. I decide that Mom and Dad, both exhausted, simply fell asleep before Dad could race down here to tell us the news. Or that they're just taking their time, having a couple hours with their newborn before sharing the news with the world. But I can't keep it up. Those both seem like ridiculous explanations to me. I stop pacing and look out the window again. At the far end of the parking lot, I see a man walking. His hood is pulled tight around his face. Even from here, I can tell he's freezing. He walks one way, stops. Goes back a few rows of cars. Then he looks around, lost. He fishes in his pocket and presses a button on his keys. Once, twice, then a third time. He's standing under a light post, and I can see clouds of warm air come from his mouth as he curses to himself. He can't find his car. About six rows away, I see the taillights of a minivan blink when he presses the button again. He looks around. Perhaps he heard the bleep of the car, but he's still not sure where. I think about going out to help him. Maybe the blast of cold in my face would do me good too.

Just then Kid's at my side, a new cup of coffee in his hand. I accept it, even though the last one left a sour, burned taste in my mouth. I glance up at the clock. Past midnight now. Officially a school day. I can't imagine going to Marion East in a few hours. Not because of straight fatigue—I've made plenty of first bells after late nights back on the basketball bus. But because it just seems like a different world entirely.

"D?" Jayson asks. Kid and I both turn to my little brother. He's still sitting in that same chair, phone in one hand, Styrofoam cup in the other. He looks up at us, so much worry on his face that he looks like he used to when he was four, his lips trembling on the verge of tears.

There's no staying silent now. Kid's the first one to him. He insists everything's okay. Gives him a playful punch on the shoulder.

Kevin Waltman

Jayson nods, but then looks square at Kid. "You're just saying that."

Now Kid looks at me, like I'm supposed to step in and save the situation. I start to mutter around, but I have no idea what to say.

Luckily, I don't have to say a word. At last, Dad comes shuffling down the hallway. We all rise and step toward him, eager. But he looks so bleary, so out of it, that we stop in our tracks. We just assumed that he was coming to tell us good news. Things could go the other way.

Dad rubs his eyes. "You all want to come back and meet little Grace?" he asks.

Now we spring into action. We dump the coffee cups in the trash. We dowse our hands with the hand sanitizer stationed on the wall. We practically race past Dad to go back.

"Hey, easy. Easy," he says. "Your mom doesn't need a circus back there."

We simmer down and then Kid asks, "Does Kaylene want me back there?" It's a fair question. Of course Kid would be here to keep an eye on us if nothing else. But he and my mom have never exactly been tight. And she might not want to see the man who's still crashing in what's supposed to be the baby's room.

Dad puts a hand on Kid's shoulder. "Kid, you're family. And Kaylene loves you. Remember, the day she stops getting tough with you is the day you know she's done caring."

Kid chuckles a little at that. We continue on down the hall. We're halfway to Mom's room before I realize Dad's never actually said that everyone's healthy. I hang back a second to talk to him. "Is everything, like, okay, Dad?"

He smiles. "Everything's perfect, Derrick. Absolutely perfect." He leans toward me a little bit, like sharing a secret. "But listen. Whenever you hear somebody talk about how *tough* some athlete is, remember this. There's never been a man who lived that's as tough as your mother."

I don't need the details. But I get what he means.

Up the hall, Kid and Jayson are lingering by Mom's door, waiting for us. We catch up, and then Dad puts one hand on the door. With the other, he pats the air as if to say, *Keep it calm*. He pushes that door open. Then we walk in and I see my little sister.

We are one right now. That's not always the case. We fight. We bicker. We get on each other's nerves as much as any other family. But right now? We're one. We all gaze down at Grace in Mom's arms, the rest of us in a semi-circle around the hospital bed. People speak, I know, but nothing really registers. There's just Grace. She's a wriggly, trembling little thing, her bits of hair still slick. Once in a while, she'll peer out of those tiny eyes, but she only looks toward Mom. She's got some lungs on her too. Her cries come in short, loud bursts that echo in the cold room.

Finally my mom looks up at us. It's like breaking a spell. We all suddenly realize where we are again. Her eyes seem tired, as they should be, but they're wet with happy tears. And despite her fatigue there's a life to them that I haven't seen in a while. "Well," she says, "what do you think of Grace?"

Dad looks up at us too. Jayson, Kid, and I kind of pull back, not knowing who's supposed to answer. The delay is not the right move. "Don't everyone speak at once," Mom snaps. It's like our silence has insulted her newborn.

"She's perfect, Mom," I say. And it's easy to say because she is.

That pleases Mom. She bends her head down to look right in Grace's eyes. "She is, isn't she?" Mom says. Then she lifts Grace up a little, extending her toward me. "Want to hold your little sister, Derrick?"

I'm suddenly not so sure. I mean, yes, of course I want to hold my sister. But she's so tiny. So fragile. I feel like if I hold her wrong, I'll break her.

Dad can see what's going on. "It's okay, Derrick," he says. "You can hold a baby tonight and still be a baller tomorrow. Just be gentle."

So I pick her up. She squirms her little arm free from the swaddle. I have to tuck it back in before she scratches her face. And there we are. Me and my little sister. Her eyes seem unbelievably big. It's like they bore right into me. All of a sudden I get something. This— holding a baby, taking care of a newborn—requires a lot more out of a man than anything on the court will ever do. All that locker room talk about manning up, about being a big man with the honeys. It's just noise. Real men, I realize, can take care of things. And I'm just the big brother. That's a whole different deal than being a daddy. But when those eyes look up at me, full of mystery, I get some idea of the massive responsibility that my parents have on their hands.

Grace blinks a couple times at me, then unleashes her little baby howl. When I look around—eyes wide like a freshman who's forgotten the offense—my parents both laugh. "Just pat her," my dad says. He motions in the air to show me how. I try it just like he suggests, but Grace just cries louder. That draws even more of a laugh from my mom. I want to be able to comfort Grace, but the more she cries the more I get nervous. The back of my neck feels hot, like somehow I'm failing an important test. I glance toward Jayson, make a slight offering to him, but he wants no part. He retreats three full steps toward the door, like a crying baby is a live grenade.

Like the star coming to bail out a scrub, Kid glides toward me, hands outstretched. I ease Grace into his arms. Kid starts to pat her just like Dad showed, but he holds her up closer to his face. He coos to her and mutters little phrases about how wonderful she is and how much he loves her. In seconds, she's quiet. In a minute, she's asleep.

"The natural," Mom says. She shakes her head in amazement.

I can tell there's a story behind this. "What do you mean?" I ask.

"You don't remember?" Dad says. I shake my head. "Well, of course you wouldn't from when you were a baby, but I thought maybe you'd remember from when Jayson was born."

"What?" I say.

Mom jumps in now. "Kid's the baby whisperer," she says. "Any time we couldn't get you or your brother settled, we'd call up your uncle."

Dad snaps his fingers. "Like clockwork," he says. "You wouldn't think it to look at the guy, but there's not a soul in the world can put a baby to sleep like Kid."

I *do* take a long look at him. Dad's right about Kid. Usually, there's a jittery quality to him, like he's on the verge of something bad. But holding Grace seems to calm Kid. Maybe he's more in his element now than he ever was on the court. Maybe it's hoops that got his head all twisted up with the wrong things. Maybe he should have been a family man like Dad all along. Just for a second, I get this glimpse of an

Kevin Waltman

alternate story of Kid's life. One where he stops doing what he thinks will make him seem tough, and he does what's in his heart instead.

Then he eases down to the couch, still holding Grace. "Gracie girl," he says. "You good. Kid's got you." He kisses her on the forehead. It's like the rest of us aren't in the room at all.

13.

Somehow, there's still school today. There might as well be fog swirling down the hallways for as much as I can focus. I drift from period to period. All I can think about is Mom's long labor last night. Of little Gracie—already, she's Gra*cie*, courtesy of her Uncle Kid.

Outside of the American History classroom, I'm still sleepwalking. Then I feel something along the small of my back, trailing down toward the top of my jeans. I practically leap out of my shoes. Hell, if I could get that kind of vertical on the court, I'd be rolling.

"Lord, D. It's *me*," Lia says. "Where's your head?"

I explain to her. As I start telling her about my little sister, somehow it makes it all more *real*—like as long as the news was just within the family, it was like a dream, but now it's a true thing out in the world. I smile as I talk, but Lia doesn't. When I finish, rather than saying congratulations or anything like that, she looks pained and shakes her head. "What?" I say.

"Derrick, were you even going to *tell me*?" she says, her voice rising into a half-scream at the end. "I'm your *girlfriend* and you couldn't even text me last night?"

Kevin Waltman

Before I know it, I'm rolling my eyes. That sets Lia off even more. She gets ready to shout at me, but then she just crosses her arms across her chest, pinches her mouth shut, and looks away.

When she gets this way, I get all twisted up too. I'm torn between wanting to get down to beg forgiveness—tell her she's the best thing I've got going and that I can't imagine my world without her—and just turning away and leaving her there cold. Neither reaction would really seem like a lie. But I try for middle ground. I take a deep breath and try to explain. "It was super late, Lia," I start. "At first I didn't call you because everyone was rushing around like the baby was coming any second. And then it took forever, and I kept thinking I'd text you once I knew everything was okay, and then it took even longer, and…" I trail off. She's not having it. Suddenly the notion dawns on me—maybe I won't be the one to end it. Maybe *she's* through with *me.* "I'm sorry," I say. It sounds tired—probably because we say that to each other as much as anything else.

"Whatever," she says. We look at each other for a few seconds. We're only a couple feet apart, but we might as well be on opposite sides of the Grand Canyon. "Am I just wasting my time, Derrick?"

"What do you mean? We're just, like, in a weird place, but it always gets better."

She looks away again. "It's not that. God, it's not even about last night." The bell rings for us to get to class, but neither one of us flinches. Lia thinks for a second, trying to find the right words. "I just feel like a big part of you is already gone. And I'm not invited."

Maybe she's right. Maybe the reason I can't figure out how to respond to Lia is that in the back of my mind I keep seeing myself next year. I'll be on some campus with the swirl of college around me. And when I picture that, Lia's not there. Maybe that's what's wrong with our team too—I've got one foot out the door. But I can worry about that later. Right now, Lia.

"You've got nothing?" she huffs at me, angry at my silence. She shakes her head and starts to storm down the hall.

"Lia, wait," I call. She stops, but she only turns around halfway. Her arms are still folded across her chest. "I go down to Bloomington for my official visit this weekend. My family's gonna be all baby all the time, so why don't you come with me instead?"

Lia lights up. It starts in her face with a smile. Then her arms unclench and she practically bounces to me. She hugs me tight, and I can feel all her curves pressing against me. Just like that, it's all back— that heat between us, that breathlessness. She feels it too, because she whispers in my ear, "I will make you *real happy* you just said that." She squeezes a finger into one of my belt loops and gives a little tug as she says it, just in case I'm not sure what she means.

Damn. When she gets like this, my heart starts racing so fast. I feel like ditching the rest of the day to take her up on her offer right *now*. And that gleam in her eye tells me she'd probably be down if I suggested it.

That's all good. I've been through enough things with girls to know sex doesn't cure problems, but it's good to know we can still get to each other that way. So, riding that high, I head into next period. I'm late, get a leer from Mr. Hasbrough, but I don't care. I got scholarship offers. I got Lia Stone. And as I sit, I try to color in those images I have of my future. I imagine the two of us exploring a college town

Kevin Waltman

together—walking to classes, hanging at parties, having all the private time in the world in athlete dorms. I imagine texting her as I'm on my way home from a road trip. Instead of waiting until the next morning to see her at school, she could just come to my place right then. Let herself in with her key. It could work.

There's just one problem. That thing I just suggested, her coming with me on a visit? I was like a guy who panics in a half-court trap and flings the ball up for grabs. It's about the worst idea anyone's ever had.

If some high majors backed off because of my knee, it's not stopping other schools. The offers keep coming. I'm not just talking scholarships. Mostly it's cold hard cash. But these schools know what's up—Kid sits me down and tells me he got offered a place. A much needed one since he's relegated to the couch now that Gracie's here.

"It's not like they were dangling some mansion in Meridian Hills out to me," he says. "Just some two-bedroom place on College. But," —he looks out our window as if verifying something—"a hell of a lot nicer than any place around here."

I shake my head in disbelief. "Who offered?" I ask.

"Does it matter?"

Jayson practically springs off the couch. "Hell, yes, it matters," he says. His volume stirs Grace in her swing—it's a rickety old thing Mom's co-worker gave her, so squeaky I'm surprised Grace can stand it. But it's the only thing that keeps her calm. She's such a crier that even Kid's had trouble soothing her since she's been home. Jayson shifts quietly, then leans forward and whispers. "What if it's a place that balls out? What if it's better than some of the places D's looking?"

"That's not the way we're playing it," I tell Jayson. I'm standing, too nervous before a Friday game to sit.

Now Jayson flops back on the couch, exasperated. He keeps his voice low, but points back toward Mom and Dad's room where they're getting some shut-eye. "According to them," he seethes. "But, man, you know they live in some old-fashioned world. Look around us. We need some *green*. And all these schools are holding it in their hands."

Kid nods. If anyone understands the need for some hand-outs, it's Kid. He's sitting in Dad's chair though, and it's like he takes on that role for a minute. He rubs his chin thoughtfully, offers Jayson a patient smile. "Look, Jayson," he starts. "Look at me. You want to see where short-cuts get you? I'm a grown man who sleeps on a couch." Amazing. When I was a freshman, Kid was the one trying to work a deal for me to transfer to Hamilton Academy. Now he's the one lecturing Jayson.

Jayson sneers. "It's not about you, Kid," he says.

Kid pounces on that. He leans forward. "Exactly." He points to me. "It's about Derrick. This is his call, nobody else's. And if he's on board with playing things straight, then that's how we're gonna do it."

Jayson huffs and looks away. He's cooled it on the attitude lately. Probably because when Mom was pregnant, he knew better than to mess. But he still gets this way now and then. Last year he got himself all turned around because nobody was giving him attention. Even now he'll hint pretty hard that people ought to come out and see him perform on stage the way they come see me between the lines. This is more than that though. He really thinks it's ridiculous that all I'm getting out of this deal is a scholarship. Across the country guys with half my skills are getting cars, stacks of cash, whatever they want. And there it is again—that nagging feeling that maybe Jayson's right. I think back about what Moose told me when he visited practice. Part of me wants to turn to Kid and, like Jayson, demand to know what school was dangling the goods. Couldn't hurt to know. But I don't.

Instead, I turn to Jayson. "I get it," I say. "Probably when I was your age, I figured the pay day was the thing." I'm about to explain to him that it gets complicated fast. That even as a freshman I turned down that transfer to Hamilton Academy. And I've learned the easiest path isn't the best. But Jayson's not having it.

"Oh, save it, D," he snaps. "You want to yap about how you know hoops better, fine. But don't give me that *when I was your age* shit."

The first cry sounds like a slap of a hand on a table, short and sharp. We think for a second maybe that's it. But then the second one comes, lower pitched but more pained. And then the floodgates open. Grace wails. Her arms and legs flail in the swing as if she's in terrible physical pain.

Kid's off the chair and over to where Grace is stationed by the kitchen table. "Shhhhh," he keeps saying. He stops the swing, but can't get her unbuckled. All the time, Grace keeps crying.

Mom emerges. I hear her stomping down the hallway. She turns the corner and heads for Grace. She taps Kid on the shoulder and he backs away from the swing. Then she smoothly dips down, unbuckles Grace, lifts her shirt and lets Grace nurse. She does this all in a moment, deft as a point guard shaking three defenders and then dropping a dime.

Grace stops nursing every second or two to let out another cry. Mom glares at us. Maybe she heard Jayson too. He rises from the couch and shrugs, refusing the blame. He heads back to our room and closes the door hard—not so hard that it's an obvious slam, but there's just enough force behind it to make a nice thud.

That sets Grace off again. Mom's face pinches down in sleeplessness and anger. It's all she can do not to scream too.

We tip against Ft. Wayne Snider in an hour and a half. In the morning I'm heading to Bloomington for an official visit, but I've got to take my girlfriend with me. Grace's cries rise in volume, and I feel the tension rise right up into my shoulders and neck. It's like everything's about to crack into pieces.

Right out of the gate, we're down a half dozen. Some of it's because Xavier picks up two quick fouls, and Murphy has to pull him. But mostly it's because we're all playing like a bunch of strangers.

Jones tries to play hero, firing a few up from out of his range. Both scrape iron harmlessly. Reynolds lets his attention drift. He runs the wrong sets on offense time and again. He gets in the way of a post feed, then bumps into Fuller, who would have been open on a back-cut. Fuller huffs at that, then proceeds to take out his frustration by jamming an elbow in his man's chest—a quick offensive foul and another turnover.

When I glance over at the bench, I see Murphy rise and walk toward Gibson. I know what's coming next, so I decide to do what I can before Gibson checks in. I pick my man up full court, dogging him all the way up. He handles the pressure, but I hope my jump in intensity feeds my teammates. It seems to at first. Fuller and Reynolds get out into passing lanes. Our bigs keep their feet quick and cut off post entries. But it doesn't last. I stay after it, but after a few ball rotations our pressure wanes. It's like we're out of shape or something, unable to stay at full tilt for more than fifteen or twenty seconds. I pressure my man into a bad dribble pick-up in the corner, but instead of clamping down, Reynolds lets his man drift free for a look from range. He buries it, of course.

Our crowd moans and settles back in their seats, while the Ft. Wayne Snider faithful roar. I clap twice for Fuller to give me the in-bounds pass. When he does, I race it up. Murphy's almost on the floor telling me to call time-out. Instead, I power past him and into the front-court. The defense is back, but in my heart I know we need something—a quick three, a run at the rim, a hoop-and-harm. I get to the hash mark and cross over, turning my man. Then I rip the rock behind my back to turn him again—a move he flat can't handle. I'm past him and headed toward the lane, all the big men converging. And that's when I know it—I can't do it. I mean, *maybe* I could get a leaner around them, but the days of me rising over guys for a dunk are gone. I zag back baseline and keep my dribble alive. I spy Jones trailing, but he's just running into the teeth of the defense. And then my man clamps back down on me. Then a double comes, and I'm trapped in the corner.

I spin toward the ref and call time-out. Surrender.

At the bench, Murphy gives me a long look. "You saw me, right?" he asks.

"Yeah," I huff. "I thought I had something."

Murphy takes a long look back at the court, like he's wondering what I saw that nobody else in the gym could see. "Well, catch some air," he says. It's cheerful, like he's telling me to help myself to some lemonade. Then he points at Gibson. "In for Bowen."

"Absolutely, Coach," Gibson says. It comes out all military precision, like he's the most obedient player ever to suit up.

A twenty-five point whipping. It was sixteen by half and never got closer. Brutal.

I know what to do afterward. Shower it off.

And then I hit it. No hash-it-out session with Fuller, no big heart-to-heart with Murphy, and certainly no we'll-get-'em-next-time chat with Gibson. I towel off, put on my clothes and coat, and I'm a ghost.

What matters to me is all out ahead. We've got a Saturday night off, so I'm off to Bloomington for my official visit. I'll go early, check out the town. Make myself at home. Think about what it will be like next year when I'm suiting up for a Big Ten power and my old teammates are still getting run by second-rate schools from Ft. Wayne. *To hell with them*, I think. They can't even show up and get after it? Then I'm already gone.

Outside, the cold air fills my lungs, gives them a quick burn. Most of the cars have already emptied the parking lot—just some leftover fast food bags drifting around in the wind—but the Friday night traffic is ripping by. I look around and suddenly realize I was in such a hurry to get out the door I don't know where I'm headed. I don't want to go home—listening to Grace howl isn't exactly going to soothe me from this loss. I can't go to Wes' house anymore—besides, he's probably out peddling weed for some crew again. I absolutely do *not* want to hit up a party or burger joint with any of my teammates.

But I know what I have to do. Talk to Lia. I pull out my phone to text her. When I look though, there's a message from Jasmine. It's long—a novel by text standards—and it's an apology for how things went down last time. All she wants is to see me again when she's in town next weekend.

I want to believe her. Then again, I wanted to believe this senior season would be a magical run. I delete her text and mash one out to Lia. Let the past go, I figure. Just move forward.

"D!" I hear. "D, wait up."

I want no part of waiting up, not for anyone. But I know the voice. It's Kid. I could leave a coach hanging, but not my uncle. I watch the traffic rumble past as I wait for Kid. So many times I've come out of that gym into the Indianapolis night—usually after wins, but after my share of losses too. Every time I've been thinking only about my next game *here*. Nothing ever felt like the end. Even the last games of seasons just felt like a pause since I knew ball was kicking in again soon enough. But now? I look back at Marion East looming behind Uncle Kid as he comes my way. It feels like it's all about to disappear for good.

"D, you gotta get it together," Kid says. He's half out of breath from hustling after me. A far cry from playing shape.

"Me?" I say. "I put up eighteen and eight boards. Don't know how much more I can do for those guys."

Kid looks up at the sky and shakes his head. "Come *on*, Derrick," he says. "You been around the game long enough to know stats don't tell a thing. Man, you got to be a teammate to those guys. You got to be the senior leader. You got—"

"What the hell do you think I'm trying to *do*?" I shout. Anger flashes across Kid's face. He knows I'd never talk to another coach like that, not even Murphy. Right now I don't really care. I just keep on, same volume. "I can't guard Xavier's man for him. I can't remind Reynolds of the offense every damn possession. I can't give Fuller skills he'll never have. And, hell, Jones is a senior too. Why can't he step up and lead?"

Kid stares at me. The white puffs that formed between us as my breath hit the cold drift away on the wind. "You done?" he asks. I don't even respond. "Jones? You want him to step up and lead? Is he the one getting high major offers? He been a four-year starter? It's your job to keep this team together and you know it."

"Well, if it's my team then how come I'm getting run to the bench at the first sign of trouble every night?" I shout. And there it is. The real source of the tension. Kid knew it already. But now it's out there for real. Every time I see Gibson at that scorer's table, it makes me want to burn my uniform.

"That's how you feel about it?" Kid asks. Again, I don't respond. He knows my answer. Behind me, a car lays on its horn and some drunk passenger hollers at us as he passes. Just more noise. Kid gives them the finger—but he waits until they're well clear, too far past us to see and start up real static. Then he turns back to me. "You ever think that Gibson has something to add to this time? Or that—"

"He can add something more than I can?" I shout, interrupting him again.

This time Kid's had it. "Hey, just slow your roll, Derrick! I'm trying to *talk* to you."

"As my coach or my uncle?"

"As your *coach*," he seethes. "Because right now if I was just your uncle I'd whip your ass." He and I both know his days of being able

Kevin Waltman

to whip me are long gone, but he's plenty heated up. So I don't press that one. "Now listen. You go on down to Bloomington tomorrow. But while you're there think about how long they'd stand for a guy who bolted on his teammates after a loss. And think about how maybe Murphy's giving you some extra minutes of rest so your knee doesn't blow again. And think about how many offers you'd have left if it did."

We stare each other down for a few seconds. To people passing, it probably looks like two guys about to pull on each other. I've seen standoffs like this. In this city, both guys are usually strapped. But for us it's just a family squabble. Or a coach-player disagreement. Both, I guess.

My phone goes off. The sound breaks the spell. I gesture like I'm about to get it, but look at Kid for permission. He nods, a way to say *go on*. As I fish it from my pocket though, I'm suddenly aware that we're not alone in the parking lot anymore. Up by the door, more guys are filing out—Gibson, Fuller, Reynolds. I wonder how long they've been lingering there.

But I don't wonder long. The text is from Lia, telling me to get over there in a hurry. She probably thinks this is going to be a good thing.

So I bolt. Kid can yap all he wants. Truth is I'm going places those other guys can never go

The game went poorly, but it's got nothing on this showdown with Lia. She got right up on me when I walked in the door, but that cooled. Real fast.

"You have got to be kidding me, Derrick," she snaps. "You spring this on me the night before?"

"It's just a terrible idea," I say. I start to run down all the reasons again—we won't have any time together, I'll be caught up in basketball stuff, her father will find out she's spending the night with me and lose his shit. But Lia's not about to hear it all again.

"Go to hell, Derrick," she says. "You just want to be free of me so you can go down there and hook up with some college skank."

"Lia, you know that's not true," I say. "Look," I start, but there's nothing left. I've explained all I can. I knew it would go over this way. I knew it was a chump move waiting until the last minute to tell her she couldn't come with me to Bloomington. But I also know it's the only way. "We're gonna be okay," I say. I step toward her.

"Step the fuck back," she snaps. But she's the one who retreats. She bumps into the coffee table by the couch and the old lamp in it trembles, throwing crazy shadows around the room. Lia holds one hand out in front of her, fingers splayed, as if she's fending off an attack. The other trembles by her temple. "Do *not* try to touch me right now."

We stand in silence. The heater kicks on, rattling the walls with its effort. Like every other place around here, Lia's house feels like it's one piece of bad luck from falling apart.

"Go," she says. "I know you want to. So just go."

14.

Alone. There's something about being alone in the car. For a while, I let
the stereo thump, pushing it as loud as it will go without ruining Dad's
speakers. But then, once I get free of the city and Indiana opens up—
long, flat stretches of farmland—I snap the music off. There's so much
noise everywhere in my life that it's suddenly nice just to get a little
quiet. Around me, Hoosiers are on their way to wherever their Saturday
takes them. I see them sipping coffee behind the wheel, the heat
steaming up. As I get nearer to Bloomington, it seems like half of them
have Indiana gear on, some of them even with little IU flags attached to
their antenna.

Finally I roll into town. I don't have to meet with the coaches
for an hour yet, so I swing through campus. I try to imagine myself
here. Walking these blocks. Hanging with teammates. The retail places
all advertise Christmas sales, and tinsel snakes around the downtown
streetlights. The place is hoops crazy too. Everywhere I look—pizza
places, laundromats, bookstores—I see Indiana banners and posters.
And students. They're huddled against the cold as they walk, some of

them with books clutched tight to their chests. Others look bleary and hungover, trudging past the bars where they must have tied on one last night. Somewhere in the distance—maybe a couple blocks over in student apartments—someone's blaring the IU fight song.

It's certainly a different make-up of people than what I see at Marion East. They're white, mostly, but there are plenty of other races mixed in. So it's something else that makes them seem so different. Then I get it—I see a couple walking down Kirkwood, a tall, angular white guy in a thick sweater and leather jacket, next to an Asian girl who's decked in jet black. They're sharing a laugh about something. They stop in front of a bar called Nick's, sitting squat and dusty and looking like it's been there for five-hundred years. They gesture toward the window, then laugh again—to me it's like they might be laughing about something that happened there last night, or just as easily about some philosophical concept I'll never understand. The difference is they—and all the other students around them, even the guys who look like they woke up in their own puke—look more mature. It's like they come from another planet where everyone graduates with honors and wears designer clothes and has money falling out of their pockets. I get an icy stab of panic that wherever I go, I'll be the outsider.

A turn takes me past some student housing. The places look old, ready to fall apart. But even here, it's not the kind of decay that I recognize from my blocks back home. Instead, it just looks like a never-ending parade of parties have taken a toll. There are couches sagging on front porches. Empty kegs floating in garbage cans. Once in a while there are some places that look like someone is taking care. A potted plant or two on the porch. A fresh coat of paint. And, in every drive, cars that I can only dream of—SUVs and Lexuses and even a Benz. And here I am puttering in my dad's old beater. It's not lost on me that all it would take is one phone call to a less principled school and I could be behind the wheel of something a lot nicer too.

Then I turn a couple more times, and I see it. Assembly Hall. For anyone who's grown up playing hoops in Indiana, it's sacred ground. Gray, massive, dropped down in the middle of expansive parking lots. Scattered around it are more places I recognize from T.V.—the football stadium, the practice fieldhouse. But those places are just like satellites in orbit. Near Assembly Hall, there's already action. The ESPN trucks are set up, workers milling around. I know that inside, the Game Day crew is about to fire up their show—Jay Williams and Jay Bilas and Rece Davis hyping the game tonight. In the lots and along the streets there are already students filing toward the arena, hoping to get their faces on screen. There are also guys selling tickets, hoping to turn a buck on the big game. They stand patiently or sit in fold-out chairs, waving a fistful of tickets. Once in a while someone stops to negotiate with them.

I've got time, so I circle the arena a couple times, soaking it in. All of a sudden, when I swing back past those student houses, I'm not so intimidated. Sure, they may come from different backgrounds. Sure, they've read some books I haven't. Fine. Ain't nobody going to come cheer for them when they ace a history exam. Nobody's gonna shell out tickets to watch them shop for clothes. But come next November, if I'm in a cream and crimson uniform? Oh, you bet they're gonna be flocking to Assembly Hall to see me suit up. It's a nice way to remember that hyped recruits don't need to worry about "fitting in" like some other scared college freshman.

Finally it's time. I wheel the car into the spot they told me to look for. There, in a bright red Indiana coat, is some grad assistant waiting on me. He rushes up to the car to shake my hand, and then he's chatting a mile a minute as he walks me to Assembly Hall. He's just talking about how juiced the town is for the Syracuse game tonight, but it's on. The hard sell's started already.

We walk down a ramp that's tucked away from all the action. The wind whistles overhead as we descend. Then he unlocks a big metal door and waves me in. There, smiling like he just can't wait to see me, is the Hoosier head coach. One look and I can tell the guy's as pumped as anyone else in Bloomington. He extends a hand and tells me it's great to finally have me on campus.

We start walking toward the coach's office. We pass pictures of all the All-Americans—Cheaney, Isaiah, Alford, and more. Framed team portraits of the championship teams. Old SI covers with Hoosiers in action. The place just oozes tradition. But then he stops mid-stride. "You gotta see this, Derrick," he says.

He reverses course and we wind around a dark hallway. On both sides I see doors, some labelled as training rooms, others blank and mysterious. As we continue walking, an anxious buzz fills the air. We round the corner to see the scene—we're still tucked away from sight, with the stands towering above us. They're already filled with fans. On the floor, the Game Day show is counting down to air time. That iconic hardwood is polished to a high shine. The white image of the state, with a red IU in the middle, gleams at center court. Directly above that, the scoreboard pops with clips of great Indiana players doing their thing. I recognize vintage Isaiah, and more recent clips of Oladipo and Yogi

Ferrell. At either end, the banners sway. Huge, crimson reminders of the hoops tradition here—five national championships, twenty-one Big Ten championships.

As I'm soaking it all in, I peek over at the head coach. He just nods at me. He knows how impressive it all is. Truth is, all those banners are like huge weights on his shoulders too. He's got this legacy to live up to. No matter what he does, it won't be enough to satisfy some fans. Those national championships all belong to other coaches, most to Bob Knight. But to me, Knight's just a story, some legend that's mostly made up. And as far as I can tell from the stories, I'd like playing for the guy standing next to me a lot more than Knight.

Then again, there are those banners.

Before I can think too much more about it, the telecast goes live. On cue, all the fans gathered burst into cheers, as if instead of the ESPN crew between the lines, they just saw the Hoosiers bury a buzzer-beater. The T.V. audio's pumped in through the sound system. I hear Rece Davis' voice cutting crisp and clear through the crowd noise. "Welcome to Bloomington, Indiana and Game Day! College basketball is built on tradition, and the two programs we'll see today—Indiana and Syracuse—have plenty of it. Everyone here remembers the matchup in 1987 for the national championship. And in just a few short hours they'll get it revved up again here in Assembly Hall." Then he looks out at the crowd, laughs, and turns to his cohorts on the set. "Looks like some of the Indiana faithful have it revved up pretty good already on a Saturday morning."

The coach squeezes my shoulder. "Enough to get you a little amped?" he asks.

I just smile.

"Wait until game time," he says. "This place. Derrick, I'm telling you, this place will be over the top."

Then he leads me down the hall again, so we can hit the stairs up to his office. I know it's my first official visit, and I've got a number of other schools to see. But right now? Advantage Indiana.

I don't want to get swayed on my first official visit. That's like proposing to the first girl that kisses you. But, man, Indiana has it cranked *up* today.

I sit right behind the bench and soak it all in. The coaches whipping the guys into a frenzy. The chatter of the refs trying to cool tempers. The smack the players are laying on each other. And all the sounds of hoops—the crisp cut of kicks on hardwood, the rhythmic pulse of a dribble, the sweet rip of a shot finding bottom.

Indiana's a slight favorite, but the game starts out tight. And when Syracuse pushes out to a six-point lead midway through the first, you can kind of feel the energy seep out of Assembly Hall. Suddenly, all those students who were liquored up and crazed for the game settle back into their seats. The upper deck is silent and semi-dark. It almost feels like nobody's up there. The biggest noise comes from down the sideline, where the Syracuse bench and small crowd howl and bellow.

At the next timeout, the head coach gets right up into his guys. He doesn't berate them. No—he's all positive energy. But he is big-time intense. "This is still ours for the taking," he shouts. "We need some shots to fall, that's all. And, hey. We have way too good of shooters not to have that happen!"

Kevin Waltman

They break huddle and I can tell the players respond. They keep the chatter up as they stroll onto the court. I can't hear them, but even I can read lips enough to know they're sprinkling in some spicier language than their coach used. As soon as the ball's live, there's an extra zip to Indiana. The crowd must sense it too, because they rise and start to urge the players on.

It doesn't take long. They run a dribble exchange out top, then a simple overload of the zone—but Syracuse is slow to react. It gives a wide open look from range, and Indiana buries it. Bang. Right back to a three-point game. And the crowd responds. Immediately, they remember why they're here—national television, top twenty showdown.

From there, it keeps rolling. Another three. A turn-and-face from the foul line. A hoop-and-harm in transition. Yet another three. In between Syracuse calls a timeout, but they just flat can't hang. Their coaches work themselves into a lather, encouraging, screaming, bullying the refs. But it's no good. One by one the heads of the Syracuse players start to hang down in doubt.

The Indiana run gets broken up now and then by a Syracuse bucket. But the onslaught is pretty relentless. Again a three. A drive right to the rim. A leaner off a ball-screen. And one more three at the buzzer.

At halftime, Indiana's taken that six-point deficit and swapped it out for a 51-33 lead. The arena is flat pandemonium, the sound rolling in waves down from the rafters. Beneath it, Syracuse sulks to the locker room. Indiana sprints.

That's when I remember. I'm supposed to follow on in to the locker room. Part of my official visit. I jog across the court, and I feel it—the noise has died down a little, but as I step across that iconic center court, I feel the cheers sweep down over me. It's almost like it's for me. *Me.*

And that's when I realize. This whole thing. This decision. Where to go next year. It's not about what my folks want or what Jayson thinks I should do. It's not about some advice from Moose or some guilt trip from Lia. And it's absolutely not about anyone else in the Marion East locker room. This is all about me. Nobody else.

I had no idea a visit would be so exhausting. I wind my way back north, the sun quickly sinking on a cold Sunday night. The rest of the visit was a blur.

I went out to a party with the players. Pretty dope. They were playing it cool with me around—no drinking, had me back by curfew. But I saw enough to know how out of hand things could get. It was a house party, wall-to-wall with absolutely killer girls. I didn't push my luck—they were interested in players on the roster, not one who might suit up in the future. And besides, with me having to head back to my host's place by curfew, there's only so far I could get. And I wasn't about to hook up and prove Lia right. I couldn't live with myself if I did that.

The players steered me away from any booze, but I know what's up. The later the night got, the more worked up some of them got. I know that more than a couple weren't just riding some post-game high.

The message was clear. I might not be able to indulge now, but come to Bloomington and it's all there for the taking. Then again, in the back of my head I could hear my mom griping about such behavior. So the Saturday night scene I'll have to keep to myself—maybe let Jayson in on a few details.

Kevin Waltman

But today it was non-stop. They had me back-to-back-to-back in meetings. Coaches. Academic advisors. Tutors. Campus tours.

The place was pretty chill on a Sunday, but it still gave me a taste of what life might be like off the court. I'd never seen any of the campus outside of filler shots during game telecasts, but it was pretty tight. The day was cold but sunny, so students were still out. They filed into the big limestone library and powered past on bikes. They lingered in the open spaces between buildings and by these limestone archways that served as an entrance to campus. Laughing, talking earnestly, just hanging.

The hall where I met with the advisor, though, was as silent as a cemetery. The building looked ancient, intimidating. When I got inside, there were long shadows cast across the marble floors. I looked up to see these dark oil paintings of very serious looking men in their academic robes. The advisor sat behind a small wooden desk. Behind her, tacked to the wall, was every kind of information imaginable—graduation rates, a list of majors, employment statistics. She didn't even need to look at them. She could—and did—rattle off every good academic feature of Indiana without so much as blinking. I should have been impressed, but I walked out of there feeling a little off.

It was better when I checked in with some players for lunch. But even then, I was still a little out of place. They didn't mean to, but they couldn't help cracking inside jokes—things about coaches or girls or even classes. They took me to Nick's, the place I'd passed just the day before. It was clear they were royalty in there. The place was covered in IU pictures, some of them from so long ago they were browning with age. The waitresses kept checking on us every two minutes. When I spotted a few of them talking excitedly with each other, I could tell they weren't just providing good service—they were trying to clock some time with the players.

After that it was more chats with coaches. My chance to ask questions about the program. About how they see me fitting in. About anything at all. But by that time I was so worn down I could barely think of a thing to ask. That didn't seem to bother the coaches. They were more than ready to go on and on about how Indiana's the best place in the world.

Then it was time to go. Which puts me here, in the car, motoring back to Indy. The sky's growing dark, the weather turned from sunny to bitter. Flurries kick up. They whip across the flat, open spaces on either side of State Road 37. They're too light to stick anywhere, but you can just feel the cold settling in.

I wait until I get past Martinsville to stop for gas. By then, the only place is a run-down station that looks like it hasn't been cleaned since 1945. Before I fill up, I go in just to stretch my legs. There are newspapers still on the stand, a picture of the game yesterday front and center. The guy behind the counter looks up once at me, then just returns to the magazine in front of him. He grunts to acknowledge my existence. I scout out something for a snack, but everything looks way past its expiration date. So instead I grab a Coke from the back. I hand my money to the guy, but he still doesn't even make eye contact with me.

As I walk back to the car and start the pump, I think about how much different that guy would have acted if I'd have been among the players on the front page of those papers. But I'm not. I'm still just a recruit. And the more I think about it, the more I realize I'm a little unsettled after my visit. Everyone was cool and hype. Everyone was excited. But *of course* they were. They just whipped up on a top twenty program. They got the front page, the attention, the love. *They* did that. Not me. And while the Indiana offer is still on the table, the more I think about it, the more I realize they were pumped for all of *that*, not for me. Nice? Sure. But in retrospect if feels like they were going through the motions a little. Like, *Here's this guy we've offered, so we gotta be nice and everything.* But it's not like they need me. And maybe now, post-injury, I'm a safety recruit for them. A guy to add depth. An in-state talent who might still become something.

The wind whips through the gas station lot. Stings my face. There's not another building in sight. The cars fly by on 37, racing north and south. There's a lot of places I could go too, all kinds of possibilities in front of me. But right now I feel every inch of the distance between me and that uncertain future.

15.

Gracie howled all night long. And, man, for such a tiny thing she can make some big noise. That cry reverberated through the house. Sometimes she'd settle just long enough so I could drift back close to sleep. Then a cry would pierce the night again. Jayson, a few feet away, kept muttering curse words every time it happened. Then he'd sigh and flop around on his bed, sometimes covering his head with his pillow to try to drown out the noise. I kept sneaking peeks at my alarm clock, tracking how many hours of sleep I was losing.

Finally, at about 3:00, I got out of bed. I didn't know what I was going to do, but I sure couldn't keep lying there wide awake. As soon as I opened the door to the hallway, a big cry from Gracie met me. Then I heard a sound in the kitchen—someone opening the refrigerator. When I went out, I saw it was Kid, fixing himself a late night feast.

He turned around, silhouetted by the refrigerator light. He squinted for a second, then saw it was me. "Hey, D," he whispered. "Little trouble sleeping?"

I nodded.

"Can't imagine why," Kid joked.

Kevin Waltman

Then he pointed to the kitchen table and told me to sit. For a minute, the house was quiet except for the low rustle of Kid fixing some plates. I thought, maybe, that I'd just fall asleep right there. I lowered my head on the table. Maybe I did drift off, because when I looked back up, Jayson was joining us.

"This is ridiculous," he muttered. "I've got school in a few hours. Play rehearsal after that. I need some damn sleep."

"You?" I said. "Shit, Jayson, try being on the road all weekend and then coming home to this."

"Shut up the both of you," Kid shout-whispered. "There's no sense in trying to one up each other on your grievances. Just be thankful you're not the ones trying to get her back to sleep." He tilted his head toward the back of the house, where my parents were likely about to lose their minds. Then he slid three plates on the table, each one stacked high with chips and a massive sandwich—ham, tomato, lettuce, multiple cheeses, mayo. He fetched some glasses from the cupboard and poured us all tall glasses of milk. They seemed to glow in the moonlight peeking through the window. He sighed and sat beside us. "Remember this. The mama and daddy got the hard job. For guys like us it's just an excuse for late night eats."

Then we dug in, none of us talking. If there's such a thing as sleep-eating, I think we were doing it. Only we'd pop our heads up every minute or two when Grace started crying again. Finally, as we finished, a firm hush settled over the house. Somehow we could all sense that she'd gone to sleep at last. Kid looked at each of us with his eyes wide. "I swear if either of you makes a noise on the way back to your room, I'll kill you my damn self."

We stifled a laugh, then delicately put our dishes in the sink.

"What's wrong with Grace, anyway?" Jayson asked. "I mean, is she okay?" Now that he had a full belly and some peace and quiet, he'd grown concerned.

Kid shrugged his shoulders. "She's fine. Baby's cry, man. And maybe she's got her days and nights confused."

"That can happen?" Jayson asked.

"All the time," Kid whispered.

"How you know all this? How come you're so good with babies?" I asked. I mean, it's one thing to hear Kid hold forth on hoops—the guy played. But all this baby knowledge keeps coming out of nowhere.

He shrugged again, then looked away sheepishly. "Ah, a long time ago I was hooking up with this woman who babysat for, like, a thousand kids. Dating her was like living in a nursery. After a while, I kind of liked helping her. I was good with the kids. Then I realized I liked them more than I liked her, and…" He trailed off. "Anyway," he said, "maybe we should go get some sleep instead of having me reminisce about some ex."

"Amen to that," Jayson whispered.

Then we shuffled silently back to our rooms. For a moment, it was almost nice. My eyes burned from lack of sleep, but there was a camaraderie with Jayson and Kid I hadn't felt in a long time. Part of me wanted it to last, like there was some spell we were under that made us nicer to each other than usual.

But now, at practice the next day, the spell sure is broken. And Kid's feeling the weight of that missed sleep too. I can see it his eyes,

Kevin Waltman

bloodshot as when he used to come around the house scrounging breakfast after a long night throwing down drinks.

I'm hurting. Head pounding. Legs heavy like I've just run ten sets of arena stairs. Maybe this *is* what it feels like to be hungover. If it is, I know I've made the right choice to stay away from booze.

"Let's go! Let's go! Let's go!" Murphy shouts. His shouts aren't angry, really. Just more enthusiasm. But right now enthusiasm seems like an obscenity to me.

I lace up my shoes and try to stretch out my legs, taking extra care to be sure there's no tightness around my knee. Then I trudge to the court. Usually, even at practices, I can't wait to hit those boards. But not today. Part of it's the fatigue from last night. But part of it too is the same old tension waiting there—Gibson trying to show me up, my teammates slacking and sulking.

Out on the court, guys are already messing around. Xavier's hoisting twenty-footers. Reynolds is trying to bank in threes. Even Fuller's in on the circus. He's flipping up hook shots, each one clanging off back iron. I walk right to him. "You gonna break that out against West Lafayette Friday?" Fuller laughs, trying to shrug me off. Even then he looks impossibly serious, like his version of nonchalance is something he's rehearsed methodically in his mirror. So how is this guy, the most straight-laced teammate I've ever had, goofing off at practice? I basically ask him that, and I remind him that by the end of last year we were tight. We swore we'd run the table this time around.

"Well, *I'm* here, Derrick," he says, "just waiting for my teammate D-Bow to show up." He stares at me then, as defiant as Fuller can get.

Before I can respond, Murphy claps a few times and asks guys to come to center court. They do, slowly. Xavier chucking up three more shots before he gets one to fall and then decides he'll join us at last. Murphy doesn't blink. Drives me nuts. When Xavier finally arrives, Murphy smiles at us all. "We're gonna run fives to start out," he explains. "But we're mixing it up."

Then he drops the hammer. Gibson's running point. I bite my tongue, but inside the alarms all go off. My heart thumps in rage. My vision blurs. Gibson at point? For *real*? I have busted my tail for this school. I stayed here when I could have bolted to cushy Hamilton Academy as a freshman. I reined in my game as a sophomore. Hell, I went under the knife as a junior. And now *Gibson at point?*

Murphy's still talking, but I've blocked it all out. Until I hear my name again. "Bowen?" Murphy says. "You with us?" I nod, but he can tell I haven't been listening. He repeats that he's sliding me to the two guard. He rattles off all the reasons—I can be our first scoring option, I can get looks with my polished jumper, I can get fast break points when Gibson pushes. He makes it sound exciting, like we're little kids he's going to take to the arcade. Whatever.

At least I'm still in the starting five, I guess. What Murphy doesn't say—but what we all understand—is that Reynolds is heading to the bench. And he doesn't contain his anger like I did. He mutters a *bullshit* just loud enough for us to hear. Then he walks toward the baseline in disgust. On one hand, I feel him. The guy's come a long way since he was a scrawny freshman, and it's because of some sweat he's put in. He knows he'll still get his minutes subbing at the two and three spots, but that's not the same as being a starter—which he has been since last year. On the other hand, I've had about enough of his attitude.

"Now come on, Reynolds," Murphy says. It's pleading—the tone a weak parent takes with a brat. He walks after Reynolds, then meets him at the baseline and puts a hand on his shoulder. He explains patiently how Reynolds can still be a force for us, but Reynolds is leaning away the whole time.

Once they've done yapping, it's time to run. The rest of the squad seems like they don't really give a rip either way. They're still just going through the motions. No urgency. You'd think we were already off for Christmas. Except for Gibson. That kid can't contain his bounce. "Time to get it rolling," he says to nobody in particular. He bobs at mid-court, switching the rock back and forth between his legs, waiting for everyone to get set. Then, once we're live, he smacks that orange and attacks. He rips it past Malcolm Rider, the poor, lost back-up. Kicks it to Fuller in the corner. Then he cuts my way, setting a solid screen on Reynolds. "Go, Bowen!" he shouts. "Get it, get it, get it!"

I just don't have it in me to *get it* today. I make my cut at half speed. It's still enough to get open. When I receive the rock from Fuller, I know I could attack the rim. Instead, I just float up a little fade-away. It goes front-rim-back-rim out. A tough bounce.

"Come on, D," Murphy chirps. "We can get a better look than that."

I trot back on defense, pretending not to hear. Instead, I make eye contact with Uncle Kid. I sneer and shake my head at him, like *Can you believe this joke we've got for a coach.* Kid's lids still look heavy from a lack of sleep, but that shakes him from his stupor. Only instead of meeting my look with sympathy, he scowls at me.

"Murphy's right, Derrick," he says. "You can get that look any time. Work for something better."

Lord, I can't trust anyone.

Meanwhile, Reynolds has darted ahead. He's open on the far baseline. It takes the second team a while to recognize it. So I decide to take out my frustrations a little. I flip that switch *on*. It takes me just a few strides to get from the hash to the opposite baseline. The ball arrives ahead of me, and any fool can see Reynolds is jacking that thing up. He catches and sets. Rises.

And I explode toward him. I could pluck his shot from mid-air if I wanted to, but I've got my own point to make. So I jack-knife that thing out-of-bounds, spiking it toward the bleachers that are pushed back against the gym's wall. The ball thumps off those bleachers, then ricochets back toward the court like a pinball.

That one draws a few whistles and shouts from the boys. It doesn't undo the indignity of getting switched the two spot, but it feels good. In fact, the elevation I got on that one felt like how it used to be—like I can just hang out in mid-air, disregarding those laws of gravity the other mortals on the court have to obey.

Kid catches me at my locker after practice. I'm in no mood for some serious talk, but apparently he doesn't care.

"You gotta get that head straight, D," he says.

I unlace my kicks and lean back in my locker. "I'm straight," I say. "Just tired after last night." I've already had this kind of lecture from Kid once. I'm in no mood for an encore.

Kid folds his arms and takes a step back. "You and I both know this doesn't have anything to do with last night," he says.

"Then what?" I pop. "If you know everything, explain it to me."

Kevin Waltman

Kid leans toward me. I can smell the coffee on his breath. But more importantly I can see a little anger in his eyes. They're still bloodshot from that sleepless night, and they seem to burn a little. He doesn't raise his voice to embarrass me, but he lays it out in no uncertain terms—if I'm going to act all hurt about Murphy switching things up, then I'm not the player he thought I was.

"Cut the shit, Kid," I tell him. I don't raise my voice either, but I know I can be more blunt with my uncle than I would be with any other coach. "You know my ticket's as a point guard. I'm not getting all those offers to run at the two."

Kid nods, but he's not letting me off easy. "Or," he says, "you could pull your head out of your ass and realize that you've got a chance to really use that jumper you've spent four years perfecting. Or that a lot of schools just love a guy who can drop twenty a night from the two spot."

Behind Kid, teammates eye us. They can't make out the conversation, but they aren't idiots. They know what's going down. I catch Fuller staring at us and he looks away fast, like he's suddenly in a hurry to hit the showers. A couple lockers over from him, I see Jones and Xavier whispering to each other. Then Xavier laughs. Maybe it has nothing to do with me, but it doesn't help my mood one bit.

The only person missing on the scene is the one I'm actually angry at—Murphy. In my heart, I know he's the one I need to be hashing this out with. But Kid's the one in front of me. So I take it out on him instead. "What do you know about it?" I seethe. "You had a chance to go to high majors back in the day, and what? You blew it and wasted your skills at JUCO."

Kid just closes his eyes. I immediately regret what I said. I wanted to sting him, but bringing up all his old failures is over the line. He shakes his head. Then walks away. As he does his shoulders slump with all that old weight—his broken career, his mistakes, his wrong turns that have left him dead-ended.

I should call him back. Apologize. I know this. But I finish unlacing my shoes and hit the shower instead.

Murphy's right about one thing. They can't check me at the two spot. Free from the responsibilities of directing the offense, I can just hunt my own shots. I get it loose early and keep it rolling. A three from the right baseline. Another triple from the wing. A shot-fake and go for a pull-up. A mid-range J from the elbow. Another triple from the top of the key.

And on and on and on. By the break before the fourth, I'm already pushing 30. Every time it's looked like West Lafayette might pull away, I ring the bell again. It's like I'm keeping us in it single-handedly. But that's the problem—it's just me. Everyone else is struggling. Gibson has about a hundred assists from feeding me, but the box score's gonna look real ugly in the morning for everyone else in a Marion East jersey.

In our huddle, heads are hanging.

"Come on," Murphy urges. "We're only down four. Let's go!"

For once, I jump in with the same enthusiasm. "Coach is straight," I say. "We can take these guys."

Fuller nods, trying to get his spirits into it. But everyone else just looks on with dead stares. It's been that way all game long, like the more buckets I pour in, the more everyone else resents me. When Reynolds has subbed in, he's been as bad as when he was a lost freshman. Jones spent the first quarter griping about getting more touches. Now he's just jutting his chin out in a pout. Hell, even Kid won't look my way—hasn't said word one to me since our go-round in the locker room earlier in the week.

Our huddle breaks for the fourth. I sprint out to the court. No use hanging with my teammates if they're just going to drag me down. Alone at mid-court, I gaze around the stands. I know somewhere out there, Lia's watching. But things have been pretty brittle with her too. And my family didn't make the trip. Jayson had play rehearsal and Mom and Dad didn't feel like packing Grace in the car seat just to hear her howl the whole way up I-65. It's strange. All around me is the buzz of a game. The West Lafayette band is finishing up their fight song, the other players are shuffling out of the huddles. The fans are settling in for the stretch run. But in my heart, I feel *over* this already. Come next year, I might be back in West Lafayette, but it'll be to take on Purdue on national T.V. instead.

Fuller finally steps to me, breaking my little trance. "Let's take these guys, D." He's not exactly amped as he says it, but at least I know I can count on Fuller to give it his best run.

"Damn straight," I say. I gesture toward our teammates. "Let's get these guys *going*."

Fuller raises his eyebrows and shrugs. His gesture suggests that he has no idea how to do that. Well, I do. Just keep getting after it myself until they have no choice but to jump on this train. I give Fuller a quick fist bump. Then it's time.

Our ball first. A bucket here and it's a one-possession game. Fuller bounces it in to Gibson, and he walks it into the frontcourt. As soon as Gibson nears the top of the key, he spots the difference. West

Lafayette has gone zone. Gibson backs up a couple dribbles and signals us to go into our zone offense.

I stifle a smile. Our first look on the zone is a beauty that Murphy installed for just this scenario. I cut hard to the perimeter, calling for the ball. Fuller sets his feet to screen the man with baseline responsibility. But it's all show. I spin and sprint for the rim. Fuller back-screens his man instead, and Xavier walls off the defender in the paint. And there it is—an easy run to the rim for an alley-oop. My knee might not be 100% yet, but I could handle this one on crutches.

One problem. Gibson fakes the lob to me, then just watches while I soar, uncontested, toward that rim. When I land, Gibson's still holding the ball out top. He stares at me for a beat, then whips a pass to Fuller on the wing.

A freeze-out. Unreal. I don't know if that was Gibson's choice on his own or if some other players got in his ear, but that's unacceptable. It's all I can do not to storm out to the top of the key and demand an explanation.

Instead, I cut toward Fuller. It's breaking the offensive set, but at this point who even cares about that? I clap a couple times for the rock and Fuller gives it up. He cuts to the other side of the court, emptying out some space for me to work. I put the ball on the deck with a hard dribble right. The whole zone jumps with the move—all eyes on me. I rip it between my legs to my left and knife toward the lane. Again the D jumps. The other perimeter guys sink down. The big steps up. The defender on the opposite baseline sinks into the paint. All it takes is a little head-fake like I'm going for a pull-up—all the hands fly at me. And I'm gone, spinning back baseline. The big man comes to challenge, but I rise from about twelve feet.

Kevin Waltman

At the last second, I duck under the big's arm and shuffle a pass to Xavier. I put it right in his paws. All there is to stop him is that undersized defender coming from the opposite baseline. Easy as it gets.

And Xavier boots it. The pass skips right through his hands and lands harmlessly out of bounds.

I can't help it now. I stomp my foot and clap my hands. "Come on!" I shout. "That's gotta be a deuce."

Xavier just huffs once, almost scoffing at me. He spins and trots back on defense. I watch him go, trying to burn a hole through his jersey with my stare. Then it's Jones piling on. "He probably didn't expect it," he sneers. "Ball goes up every fucking time you touch it."

That's it. Forget it. I'll play out the string. Get mine. Then peel off the Marion East colors off for the last time, ink a letter of intent, and *get gone*.

But right now, it's West Lafayette bringing it up. They feel our tension and feed off it. Unlike ours, their offense hums. Guys communicate. Look for open teammates. Soon enough, Xavier gets himself turned around and his man slips to the rim—and unlike Gibson, their point guard puts the rock in the right place. It ends in a dunk, plus a cheap foul on Jones.

There's a whole quarter left, but we're as done as a team can be.

16.

"It should always be this easy between us," Lia says.

We made up. In the best way there is. Now, in the aftermath, her house seems silent. Her dad's gone again, giving us all the time we need to do all the things we want. In the space below her door, I see the light change rhythmically—their Christmas tree lights blinking in anticipation of the holiday. I know that not far away, my dad and Jayson are attending the Christmas Eve service, as much an escape from Grace's crying as it is a religious rite. Kid's who knows where. He's been a ghost since we had our run-in. And Mom? Well, she's on Grace duty. That's a rough Christmas Eve.

The heater kicks on at Lia's. It's like the noise breaks our little spell. She slides away from me, running her hand down my chest and stomach as she does. Lia sighs—this sexy little sound that about gets me all revved up again. She senses it and laughs. "Cool your engines," she says. "We got all night if you want. Dad always stays out forever on Christmas Eve."

She's trying to tease me, but that last line had a little touch of hurt to it. It makes me imagine her when I leave here—stranded all alone, vulnerable in a bad part of the city. Lia deserves better than that. Everyone who lives around here deserves better than that. I relax for a second, stare up at her ceiling. Above us, there's a brown stain on the ceiling, I guess from where there used to be a leak. It's not big, just a splotch I never noticed before, but it gives me the feeling like this place might fall down around Lia someday. I'm filled with regret for the way I've treated her. It's not like I've done her dirty—haven't cheated, never even raised my voice at her—but I can suddenly see why the idea of me zooming off to college without her is tough.

"Lia," I say, "I wish you could come with me on these visits. I never meant I didn't want you there. It's just not the way it works, though."

"Save it," she says. She shimmies back into her jeans and then pulls a sweatshirt down from her closet. It's some ancient Colts gear, frayed at the wrists and about ten sizes too big for her—and somehow it's the sexiest thing I've ever seen her in. "I'm not looking for apologies," she tells me. "We're past it already. Or didn't you notice?"

I smile. There it is. More than anything else, that little edge to Lia—flirting, challenging—puts us right again. I gather my stuff to get dressed and then head to the living room where Lia's already getting us set up on the couch with some snacks and drinks. She's got a big blanket ready too, wearing it around her shoulders like a cape. I sit on the couch and then she nestles in beside me. At first we're side by side, but after a couple minutes she lifts her feet up onto the couch. Then she lowers her head to my lap. I think maybe it's go time again, but Lia senses my excitement. She shifts like she's uncomfortable. "Rub my shoulder," she says. "I need some attention."

I do as I'm told while she flips around with the remote. Everything is Christmas cheer on the tube. Santas. Angels. Miracles. I don't believe in that stuff anymore, but right now anything feels possible. All that hoops tension evaporates. Most of the time it's hard to separate my life or who I am from what's going down on the court, but this moment with Lia makes me wish I could do it more often. Just be a regular guy. Just be eighteen. Chill.

Lia moans real soft while I rub her. She's acting like she's found something interesting on the tube, but I know we're headed back to her room soon enough. She reaches down and runs her fingernail along my leg—from the inside of my calf up to just above my knee, then back again. "That feels nice, D," she says.

We just keep it like that for a while. Touching each other, trying to hold onto the magic. I keep biding my time, trying to figure out just the right instant to bend down and kiss her neck, try to take this back to the next level.

Instead, it's Lia who changes it up. "I know it's your decision," she says. "And I know nobody takes their girl with them on visits. But would you mind just at least talking it out with me sometimes?"

"Sure," I say. "That's cool." I so don't want this conversation now. Hell, I don't want to talk about anything ever again.

"It's just that maybe I could help you make a decision. You never know."

I don't say anything to that. I just keep rubbing her. But beneath my touch I feel Lia's shoulder tense back up. Her hand stops moving along my leg. Soon, she raises back up from my lap. She lowers the volume on the T.V.

"I mean it, Derrick," she says. "I need that much."

"You got it," I say. "Whatever you want." But I can tell it doesn't satisfy her. And I bet she can tell I'm just trying to say whatever I can to be done with the conversation.

Christmas isn't what it used to be. And I don't mean we don't get fun stuff and get all hyped about Santa and wake up at the break of dawn to rip open the presents under the tree. No. That's been gone for years. I mean, this time nobody's even in a good mood.

Mom and Dad sit on the couch, Grace tucked into Dad's arm. They both look half-dead after another night where they got just a few hours of sleep. At this point, Grace's cries don't keep me up—I just kind of register them for a few seconds and then go right back to sleep. But Mom and Dad are *hurting*.

Uncle Kid? Last year he was throwing around all his ill-gotten dough, fixing me up with choice Pacer tickets. This year he's fidgeting, embarrassed that all he could afford were some gift certificates for me and Jayson. Plus, he still can't look me in the eye. I tried when I saw him this morning. Gave him a *Sorry, man* and a *Merry Christmas*. But he just said *Yeah* and shuffled past me to get a cup of coffee.

At least Jayson isn't in a *bad* mood. He's just kind of neutral. He organizes his small stack of gifts in the corner. Then, when nobody seems up for anything else, he reaches for the remote on the table. "Shhhh," Mom and Dad both say in unison. When Jayson looks their way, they both point to Grace sleeping. "Well, do you mind if I just chill in my room then?" he whispers.

Dad waves him on in permission. Which means I'm stuck out here with everyone else. Sure, I could go back too. But I don't want to crowd him on Christmas morning. I head for the kitchen. Instead of a big Christmas feast like some people have, we've got a cooling pot of coffee and some donuts Kid bought yesterday. In the fridge, there are fixings for turkey sandwiches. That's about it. I close the fridge again and grab a donut. I sit at the kitchen table. It seems wrong somehow. All of it. I guess maybe when I make it to The L I'll be styling all the time. Serious blow-outs on holidays. A personal chef instead of stale donuts. But who am I kidding? I'm back to being bumped from the point guard spot at Marion East—just like I was a freshman again. If I can't even run the one-spot here, then how am I ever gonna make it to the NBA? Even if the schools offering me still take me as a two-guard, I'm too small—even at 6'4"—to run at two in The League.

I look out the window and see some Christmas snow falling. It starts to stick on the roof of the house next door. Their curtains are drawn, but I bet behind there, things are better. I've never thought that about any other house on the block before. But here? Kid's still icing me out. So are my teammates. My parents are too sleep-deprived to even notice. Even my girlfriend is cold on me more often than not. This is not the way a big-time baller is supposed to live.

And there's the answer—maybe I'm not the big-time baller I thought I was.

I plop the half-eaten donut on the table. I decide to head back to my room after all. As I pass through the living room, Mom and Dad and Kid look up at me briefly. But before I'm even past them, their eyes lower again, returning to their silent thoughts.

When I open the door to the room, Jayson startles. He's back at the closet, but on my side. He spins around and crosses to his bed, where he's got his gifts spread out.

Kevin Waltman

"What you doing over there?" I ask.

"Nothing," he says, trying to shrug it off. "I'd lost one of my shirts and thought it might be on your side." A lie, I know. Jayson is so adamant about things staying on the right side that he'd throw a fit if a piece of lint from one of my sweatshirts dropped on his half of the closet.

"Jayson," I say, softening my voice so I don't sound angry. "Christmas morning seems like a funeral out in our living room, so can we at least be cool with each other?"

Jayson looks like he's going to keep on with his charade, but then he smiles. "Yeah, D. That's no joke of a Christmas out there. Straight out of a movie. I bet they about to bust out the carols any second." He laughs a little, shakes his head at the idea.

But in the end, I still need an answer for why he was in my stuff. I point back to the closet. "Come on, Jayson. Just tell me."

His gaze drifts back toward the closet too. Then he hops up on his bed. He wads his sheets and pillows—already in a messy tangle—between him and the wall so he can recline on them. "Honestly, D, I was going through all your old letters from colleges."

"Why you doing that?" I ask.

Jayson shakes his head, like it's ridiculous I don't know. He stares at me, as earnest as my little brother ever gets. "Man, I know I act like I don't care sometimes. I know I get all twisted up about the attention you get. *All that.* It's just show. Sometimes when I can't sleep because Grace is crying I lie here and dream about where you'll end up. So I was just going through that old stack, thinking about the possibilities."

It shocks me a little, the notion of Jayson spending that much head-time on where I might go to school. It's almost sweet. But instead of telling him that I just say, "Some of those possibilities have dried up, I guess. And who knows. If I can't run point, maybe the schools I'm visiting will pull their offers. I'll wind up taking some scholly from, like, Valparaiso."

Jayson pops up on his bed now, suddenly angry. "Don't say that, D!" he shouts.

I hold my hands out to my sides. "Why not? It's the truth. You think schools won't pull out? Why you think that mail slowed way the hell down after I tore up my knee last year?"

Jayson squinches up his face and shakes his head. "I *know* that, man. I know this game's a dirty business. I'm not dumb. I mean don't say that stuff about you not being able to do whatever you want to do. You want to ball out, then ball out."

"It's not that easy," I say. Now my voice is rising in anger too. "I don't get to decide the lineups. I don't get to magically make my knee better. I don't get to wave a wand and get my quicks and burst back."

"That's excuses," Jayson says.

I reach down and roll up my pant leg. Real slow and methodical. Then I raise my knee toward Jayson. I run my finger up and down the scar from my surgery. "Tell me how that's some excuse I'm making up."

Jayson doesn't even pause to look. "You know what my theatre teacher says?"

"Oh, this will be good."

"He says that the way you make it happen on stage is to actually *believe*. The real actors aren't even *acting*. They *believe*, D."

I can't take it anymore. I practically scream at him, "And what's that got to do with my shitty senior season?"

He screams right back. "The court's a stage too, D! You *know* that! And you have to believe."

Then silence. Except for one thing. Through the door, down the hall, around the corner to the living room. It starts as one muffled cry, then escalates. It's the biggest of Grace's cries. The one where it seems like she's bawling so hard she can't even catch her breath. It comes in waves—*wha-wha-wha-wha-whaaaaaaaaaa.*

I sneer at Jayson, shooting blame at him.

"Don't put that on me," he says.

I cross to the closet and grab my coat. Time to make some kind of escape. Where to, I have no idea. But somewhere I don't have to hear my little brother lecture me on Christmas morning. Somewhere I can ignore the fact that he might be talking sense.

17.

It's Christmas break here at Clemson too, but the place is pretty amped. That's because Duke's on the slate tonight. I sensed the coaches kind of wanted me here for a more winnable ACC game—maybe Georgia Tech or Wake—but I figure I might as well see the place when it's hype.

Their arena's just been remodeled, and it's looking shiny as a new coin. The place gets packed pretty quick. Even the student section is filled with kids coming back early to campus to heckle the Dukies.

Beside me, my dad yawns. He checks his phone for a text from Mom. All trip long, she's been hitting him up with Gracie news—some of it about cute things she's done, but mostly guilt trip texts about blow-out diapers and long crying jags. Now his phone must be clear because he shoves it back in his pocket and turns to me. "What do you think?" he asks. He sounds bored, but I know it's just the fatigue hanging over him.

"I think a place like this just needs a jolt of D-Bow to set it right," I say.

He smiles. Almost laughs. For him, maybe it's just good to see some of my old cockiness come through for a second. He thinks about what to say, but all he offers is, "Eh, maybe." But he's not sold. He knows for all the energy in this arena, Duke's still strutting between the lines as a fifteen-point favorite. So maybe he thinks I'm talking that way because we're right behind the Clemson bench, so close to the action that I can hear the coaches talk up the players. They're doing a sales job, too—trying to talk their boys up a bit. It's not brash, not anything to get them over-hyped, but they keep telling the players they can get this one. I know how that goes. Underdogs can get themselves all worked up for an upset, but sometimes a little doubt creeps in right at tip.

The truth is, I don't care too much about the outcome of this game. Would I love to see them hammer Duke? Hell, yes. I'd root for a prison team over those guys. But even if they lose, all it means is I can step in next year and lift them up.

I also want a place I can get better. That can happen at Clemson. It's one thing for some McDonald's All-American to go to a place like North Carolina for a year and then bolt to the NBA. Half the time, they're no better walking out of Chapel Hill than they were walking in. But I've seen the kids at Clemson. They improve. Like K.J. McDaniels—guy went from a four-point per game freshman to a lottery pick. Or Rod Hall. By the time he was a senior he was one of the best points in the ACC. I get a few years learning the ropes from these coaches, there's no ceiling on me.

I don't walk through any of that with Dad. He's too tired to hear it probably. It's also just something I want to hold back for me. I'll talk academics, campuses, all that with my parents—but things I *feel*, which in the end is what it comes down to, I can't ever really explain to anyone else.

By the time I'm done thinking all that through, it's tip. The ball goes up, and right out of the gate Duke does what Duke does. It doesn't get ugly, but all the energy's out of the arena by the second T.V. timeout. *So what*, I think. Maybe next year this time Duke will come to Clemson and get an eyeful of something new.

Mom doesn't want to hear it. She's been against Clemson from the get-go. Even more dead-set against Alabama, where I'm visiting in a month. She knows better than to think that racism starts when you head south across the Ohio River. One glance around our neighborhood can teach you that it's not like black people have it easy up here. But she has this built-in distrust of those southern states that won't fade easy.

In the end, I just told her that I wanted to at least keep Clemson on my list. That even if it didn't have all those banners hanging in the arena like Indiana did, I liked what was happening at Clemson enough to keep considering it.

Grace was asleep in Mom's arms, so she didn't do much more than huff at the notion. But now, in our room, Jayson lays into me.

"Your boys got *run* by Duke," he says. He's right. Clemson fought like crazy, but they still lost by sixteen.

I shrug. "They stayed with them for awhile," I say. "Would've had a chance if the refs didn't hand things to Duke like they always do."

Jayson laughs. "Oh, here it comes. Whining about the refs. That's what it's going to be like if you go to Clemson." I wad up a dirty shirt and throw it at him. He dodges. Then he gets a little more serious. "For real, D? You're thinking about a school in South Carolina?"

"Yes, for real," I say. We've got practice in an hour—our last tune-

Kevin Waltman

up before the season starts ripping at us again—and I'm in no mood for distractions.

Jayson doesn't exactly care. "Everyone got the rebel flag on their t-shirts? Rocking mullets?" He laughs as he says it, but there's a touch of sincerity there.

I sigh. "I didn't see a single rebel flag on campus, Jayson. They all but banned them, I think. And if you think there are more mullets in South Carolina than there are in southern Indiana, you crazy."

He lays back on his bed. He picks up a script for a school play, thumbs through a couple pages. A few times he focuses on the page and mouths some words he's trying to memorize. Meanwhile I'm just chilling. Trying to clear a little head space before diving back into hoops.

"It's just, you know, Clemson's a long ways off," Jayson says. That script lies beside him now, and he's sitting up again. "I mean, what, I'll get to see you play just a few times a year?"

This is a legitimate point. Forget the state Clemson's in—that distance matters. As things have grown more crazy around here—Dad getting sick my sophomore year, Kid getting in trouble again last year, Gracie arriving now—I've suited up a few times without my family in the stands. But if I go to Clemson? That would suddenly be the norm. Guys do it. All the time. And, I mean, if the dream comes true—I make it to The League—I've got no say in where I go. So if the Blazers draft me it's either move everyone to Portland or just have them watch me on T.V. Part of growing up, I guess.

"I know, man," I say. "But even Marquette and Michigan are a few hours away. It's not like you'll be in the stands every game there, either."

Jayson smirks. "D, I'm not sweating that. I just want you to go someplace where I can visit you and hook up with college girls." I roll my eyes, but Jayson leans forward to double down on his nonsense. "For real, now. Those southern girls as fine as I hear? I need to know it, D."

I play it straight. "Christmas break, Jayson. Students were gone. Nothing but the band in the stands."

Jayson sulks at my response. Then he cocks his head and squints at me sideways. "Level with me, D. You saw some specimens, didn't you?"

I can't take it anymore. "Are you *serious*? You talking to me about *specimens*? You do know that if Mom ever hears you talking like that. she'll ground you until you're thirty-five, right?" I wait for a second, then lean forward on my bed to whisper like I'm sharing some secret code. "But, yeah, Jayson. Those southern girls are all that."

"I knew it!" he says, practically popping off his bed with excitement.

Then it's time for me to head to the gym. I start packing my bag while Jayson sinks back into his manuscript. I take a quick look around the room. The LeBron and Steph Curry posters. The mess of Jayson's schoolwork on the floor. The tangle of his X-Box cords in the corner. I didn't think I'd spend my senior year still sharing a room.

"Catch you later, Jayson," I say.

He looks up from his script. "You still here? Get on out and give me some quiet."

"Shut up," I say.

We're both messing, and we both know it. Still, just to be sure, Jayson glances over at me and puts his script down again. "D?"

"Yeah."

Kevin Waltman

"Before you go on to college, just take care of business at Marion East, okay?"

"Most definitely," I say.

Taking care of business is going to be a lot more work than anyone thinks. We've got a trip to play Muncie Central tomorrow. And if we don't tighten it up fast, they'll make us look foolish. We're a complete mess now.

Most of last year was wasted because there was a gap between me and the rest of the team. My fault? Their fault? Didn't matter. We couldn't get ourselves on the same page. It wasn't until I blew out my knee that we figured out how to be teammates again. And here we are, right back in the same place.

The shift of me to the two–guard just means I can score just about any time I want. In a lot of cases, I'll still have an inch or two over the other team's two. That's even true at practice. That inch I gained in the off-season gives me a slight edge on Reynolds, and I've got a year of bulk on him too. So I just wear the kid out—flares to the stripe for three, rises from mid-range, duck-ins to the post, even some rips to the rim.

Every time a shot finds bottom, I can feel Reynolds get a little hotter. He mutters obscenities under his breath. If a teammate shuffles over to give advice or tell him to hang in there, Reynolds just spins away in anger.

Murphy and Kid don't say a word. They just crank the offense back up so we can prep for Muncie Central. "Again," Murphy says.

But to everyone else, I'm the bad guy. They feel for their boy

Reynolds. Or they're like Jones and Xavier—they liked it a lot better when I was running point and looking to get them shots instead of hunting my own. Even Gibson seems angry at me. In live action, he'd have double-digit assists by now. Instead of caring about that, he seems to hesitate every time he looks my way. If I pop free on the perimeter, he'll wait just a split second before getting me the pill. I know he sees me in rhythm. He's just waiting to give Reynolds a chance to close. Doesn't matter. Even if Reynolds has solid position, I just throw a quick move on him—jab right, then blow by left for a leaner—and it's a bucket again.

Maybe Murphy finally senses the static. He cuts the offensive drill short and flips the squads so the ones can work on D. Right away, the tension between me and the rest of the team becomes more evident. On offense, I could still take over every time I touched leather. On D, you always need communication—and I'm not getting it. Checking Reynolds is usually not a problem, but today I need my head on a swivel. I get blindsided by a back-screen. Then, when I sense a ball-screen coming to one side, I hedge—but nobody tells me the screener slipped to the other side, and I get a face full of chest. Meanwhile, Reynolds gets a free run at the rack. Even he can bust out a nasty throw-down with that head of steam. He woofs about it pretty good too. "That's what I'm *talking* about," he says. "Ain't nobody gonna check that." Most of that's meant for me, but he cuts his eyes toward Murphy too. Reynolds still hasn't forgiven Murphy for exiling him to the bench.

I take the opportunity to turn to Xavier. "How 'bout a little talk?" I say. It was his man setting the ball screen, so it's on Xavier to let me know what's up.

Kevin Waltman

"Whatever," he says. He turns away. I grab him by the wrist to stop him. He yanks it away, but I squeeze. "Son of a bitch, let me go!" he yells. His arm is slick with sweat, so finally he pops it free from my grip. When he does, the momentum makes his hand flail about an inch from my chin.

"Watch yourself!" I say.

Xavier puffs out his chest and gets in my grill. "That's on you!" he yells.

I try to bring it back to hoops. "Yeah, but me getting cracked on that screen is on *you*. You've got to *talk*."

"Yeah, well you do enough yappin' for everybody," Xavier says. A lie. I've done my trash-talking in the past, but I haven't said word one today. "And you sure as hell take enough shots for everybody. Same as always. Just like my brother said."

Now *that's* enough. Griping about me hoisting shots is one thing—every second-tier player has always felt that way about the leading scorer. But dragging in his brother Moose? Not cool.

"You're so full of shit," I tell him. Up until now, guys have been content to let us hash it out on our own near the sideline. But this draws people over, hands extended to grab us before things get real, everyone saying *Take it easy* or *Let's cool it.*

Xavier's not having it. "You telling me I don't know my own brother?! Moose said if Coach Bolden didn't rein you in, you'd have jacked twenty shots a game." He looks around, arms extended. "And wouldn't you know it. No Bolden and it's D-Bow taking every damn shot."

I can't contain myself. Even with Fuller pulling me back from my right side, I reach out and push Xavier with my left. *Hard.* I catch his shoulder, but it's enough to pop him back a step.

Xavier rears back like a wild animal. He tears free from Murphy and Kid, who've stepped in way too late. Xavier raises his right hand and it hovers in the air for a second like a sledgehammer about to fall. That pause gives me just enough time to dodge when that fist flies.

Fuller's not so lucky. Xavier swings right past my chin and catches Fuller in the nose. Fuller crumples on the sideline, hands held to his nose.

The gym, which was reverberating with shouts two seconds ago, falls silent. We all huddle around Fuller, staring but paralyzed. Finally, he makes a sound. Just a long, low, moan. Then I see a thin trickle of blood ooze between his fingers. At that sight, Murphy finally springs into action. He snaps his finger at Kid and sends him off for a bag of ice. Then he kneels by Fuller and talks to him a little. He leans down so he's just a few inches from Fuller's ear.

"You gonna be okay, man," he says. It's almost a whisper, maybe a prayer. Murphy has to know he's lost control of this team now—if he ever had it to begin with. "You gonna be okay," he repeats. "Let's just take a quick look." He puts his hand over Fuller's and gingerly inches it away. When we get a look, everyone recoils. Fuller's nose is mashed and bent, an arc across his face where there used to be a straight line. It's cut where Xavier's fist landed, but blood also seeps out of his nostrils. It pools on his mouth and chin.

"Awwww, damn," Reynolds says, pretty well summing up what we all feel.

"That bad?" Fuller wheezes.

Nobody responds, which is answer enough.

I'm fuming. At Xavier. At Murphy. But mostly at myself. I feel almost ill, a burning in my stomach. *Anyone but Fuller*, I think. The one guy who never tried to do anything but be a good teammate. And here he is writhing in pain on the floor.

"Happy now, D-Bow?" Xavier asks.

It's a cheap shot. Cheaper than the swing he took at me. I just walk away. Straight to the locker room. Forget Xavier. Forget all of this.

I think about those stupid slogans the school posts on the walls. Strength in the hive? In this place, you better just look out for yourself.

18.

He appears like a ghost. I'm about a block from the house and he materializes out of the steam rising from a grate. I don't even see him until he's just feet away from me. When I do, I leap back. Around here, there's no telling when someone wants to punch your ticket.

"Just me, D-Bow," he says.

He flips back his hood and smiles. Still I have to squint to believe what I'm seeing. "Nick?" I say.

"You damn straight." He extends a fist. I meet his with mine. Then we stand there, not knowing what to say. Nick Starks! It would be less shocking to see Paul George step up at this point. My freshman year, Nick and I went at each other pretty good. He was the senior point guard, and I was the freshman who wanted to change that. Never mind the whole Jasmine thing. That season started with her cozied up to him, but it ended with the two of us setting off sparks. So it wasn't a big secret that Nick Starks and I were not exactly fans of each other. I didn't buy him any graduation presents, and he hasn't been sending me any long letters home from college. Now here he is, hanging on Patton.

Kevin Waltman

"What the hell you doing here?" I ask flat out.

He grins. I used to hate that cocky smile of his, but now, after three years, it's a nice blast from the past. He points south for a second. "I was down at Jasmine's house, trying to check on her. Thought I'd walk up here and see what the word was with you." I squinch up my face. Jasmine's not mine to be jealous about, but still. Nick notices. "Aw, drop it, D. I ain't trying to get with her. You know as well as I do ain't nobody gonna get Jasmine settled down for a long time."

I laugh a little at that. Then suddenly I realize something. Whatever noise Nick and I had between us, it's all gone. We're not two dogs fighting over the same bone anymore. We're just two vets of the same basketball team kicking it on a cold evening in the old neighborhood.

I unclench my hands. Take a deep breath. I realize half my tension isn't even about Nick. It's still that I'm worked up over the fight with Xavier at practice.

"Well, you want to get out of this cold?" I ask him. He nods, and we step toward my house. Then I remember that when I open that door, Grace will probably be crying too loud for anyone to think, let alone catch up on old times. So I slap a spin move on the pavement. "You up for hitting Sure Burger?" I ask him.

"Cool with me," Nick says.

A few brisk blocks later and we're in the warmth of Sure Burger, the smell of sizzling burgers and piping hot fries thick in the air. The early dinner crowd squeezing in, everyone stomping slush from their feet. Nick squeezes into a table by the window, both our chairs rocking unevenly. We start into our food right away, like now that we're settled in we have no idea what to talk about. But that doesn't last long—we've got that one pure thing in common: hoops.

"You check the Indiana game last night?" Nick asks.

"Oh, yeah," I say. "They got after it again. I'm telling you, they got a chance to win the Big Ten."

Nick talks over a mouthful of cheese fries. "Always gotta watch out for Sparty." I nod, like Nick's just dropped Gospel on the room. We go on like that for a few minutes—scarfing down grub, talking about this team out west or that highlight reel jam from the other night.

Then, all of a sudden, Nick places both hands palms-down on the table and leans toward me a couple inches. "Time to get down to it," he says. "I didn't come see you to yap about college hoops." I lean back, trying to re-establish the space between us. I knew I shouldn't have trusted Nick. But he just plunges ahead. "Man, I stopped caring about college hoops the day my scholly got yanked at Ball State."

"They pulled your scholarship?" I say. "I didn't know that." I hang my head for a second. It's like there's some huge gravitational pull in our neighborhood. Nobody can get free. My parents could have, but Mom got pregnant with me. Kid could have, but he got himself dragged down by nonsense. Jasmine should have—maybe she still can—but college is knocking the wind out of her. Moose is back. Now Nick. He had a chance to ball at the college level. Get a free education. And now what? A job back home. Even that's a false promise. Guys who get jobs here can't make ends meet, end up tangled in some game. Then it's prison or grave.

Nick balls up a napkin and throws it on his tray, like he's trying to dismiss the topic. "Started having problems with my feet. Broken

Kevin Waltman

bones, some messed up stuff. I let it out that they'd been hurting me in high school and all of a sudden they started talking some pre-existing condition crap. Pulled the scholly like that." He snaps his fingers. "It's a dirty business, man. Ain't no way I'm getting back into school without a scholarship, you know. So there goes my ticket." Then he shakes his head, disappointed, maybe, that he even got into all that. "But like I said, I don't care about college hoops. Only school I care about is Marion East. That's why I'm here."

He looks at me, eyes wide, like now I'm supposed to say something. All I can think of is that here he is—three years out of high school—still sweating Marion East, and I'm still on the roster and I barely give a shit. I can't say that though.

So, in my silence, Nick takes a breath to continue. I think for a second that he's about to drop the same line on me that Moose did. Here's one more Marion East grad flamed out, one more voice to tell me I better get mine while I can. Instead, he says, "You got to get that team going, man. I been coming to the games. You got the talent, but you're all pulling in different directions."

I laugh at that. "Nick, you don't even know."

Something in the way I say it tips him off. "What happened?"

There's no point in trying to hide it. If he's hanging around these blocks again, he'll know soon enough. So I launch into it. The long drama of Murphy losing control of the team. The static between me and everyone else. The daily grind of having to fight Gibson for alpha dog on the squad. His freezing me out. Xavier losing his cool. And then Fuller crumpled on the floor, blood dripping from his nose.

Nick hangs his head, then shakes it back and forth. He looks so mournful it's like I told him he just lost his grandpa. "No no no no no," he mutters. Then he looks back up at me and jabs his index finger in accusation. "Man, this is your senior year."

"Yeah, well," I say. "Get rolling for the playoffs, I guess."

Nick shakes his head again. "You know better than that too."

"Worked for us when you were a senior," I say. "We didn't get things figured out for a *looong* time. Then we made our run."

That draws a smile from Nick. I can see it all flicker across his face—our late-season tear, ending with Marion East's first Sectional championship in forever. Then coming within a heartbeat of going to State. "Yeah," he says. "We sure 'nough got after it." Then he stabs a fry into some ketchup, eats it while he reminisces about our glory days. It's cool, but I realize that's not who I want to be in three years. Not here, looking back to when things were good. These Marion East years are always going to be special to me, but I don't ever want them to be the best years of my life. Even if I don't end up balling out in The League, I want to get clear of this place. I want to *make it.*

Nick looks up at me again. There's still a grin on his face, but it fades slowly while he stares. "Once we got it figured out, we had a helluva team," he says. "But you know the only regret I have from high school?"

I just shrug.

Nick taps his chest. "Me," he says at last. "I regret how I acted around you, trying to keep you down instead of being your teammate. Look, D—" he relaxes his shoulders, trying to empty out all that tension young guys have to carry around with them. "You're right that we got after it in the end, but I keep wondering if it couldn't have been even better. What if you and I had got on the same page from the jump? What it we even just squashed things between us by Christmas? Maybe instead of looking back at a Sectional title, we're walking around as State champs instead?"

"I feel you," I say.

"No," Nick counters. "I don't think you do. Man, you got all this ball out in front of you. But someday—maybe four years from now, maybe fourteen years from now—ball's gonna end. And *believe me* you don't want to be sitting around thinking you could have had a better career if you didn't get yourself all tweaked over some bullshit noise with a teammate." His voice rises toward the end, and out of my peripheral vision I see the two guys at the next table pausing to listen. But Nick's not done. "Besides, no matter what you think of guys like Xavier and Gibson, in their hearts I bet they want to win every bit as much as you do. I mean, that's what I found out about you when I was a senior."

I take a long drink of my Coke. Then I swirl the ice around in the cup. Set it back on the table. All that stuff Nick just put on me makes plenty of sense, but am I gonna let him have the satisfaction of knowing it? "You done with the lecture?" I ask.

He rolls his eyes. "Come on, Derrick. I'm trying to help you out, brother."

Now I lean forward, jabbing my index finger at him this time. "You ain't my brother," I say. "You're just the guy who was in my way when I was a freshman. And now you're just clinging to glory days."

Nick's jaw drops. He looks about like a girl who's just been dumped. But then the anger comes. He slams his hand on the table, jostling Coke from his cup. "You as stupid now as you were then," he says. Now it's not just the guys next to us staring. The whole restaurant cranes necks to check the action at our table—some of them worried that some violence will erupt, some of them probably hoping for it.

"Nick, man, I'm clowning," I say. He stops where he is, not trusting me. "I thought you said you shouldn't get all worked up over what some noise with an old teammate."

He's still fuming, I can tell. That chest is rising up and down in anger, and his whole body seems tensed as a dog about to attack. But he sits. Shakes his head again. Mutters a few obscenities at me to get it out of his system. "You *always* gotta make things difficult, don't you," he says.

"Maybe," I say. "But how 'bout you tell me how things could go easier."

Nick takes a long look at me, checking to see if I'm for real. Behind him, everyone else whirs slowly back to their business. And then Nick launches in again, back into lecture mode. I sit and take it.

Standing here, finger hovering by the doorbell, I truly regret listening to Nick. It's not that I'm out of my element. Just a few blocks away—Ruckle and 32nd. But I'm not sure I'm ready for what's on the other side of that door.

But I promised Nick. So I press the buzzer. At first, there's nothing—no sound of someone approaching, nobody hollering that they'll be there in a sec. Around me, the night's getting cold, and I figure that's that. Head home before the freeze sets in, before the streets get dangerous. I'm just about to spin and head back up to Patton when

Kevin Waltman

the door opens with a gentle *whoosh*. The man of the house—goatee, glasses, crisp blue button-down and brown cords—stands there, blinking. He seems surprised, like this is the first time anyone's ever come to their door. But he doesn't seem nervous—at least not the way any other white guy in the city would act on this corner after dark. "Derrick?" he asks.

I just nod in response. Behind him, I see his wife relaxing into a chair with a book and a glass of wine. Further back, in the kitchen, the son is clearing dishes. Even though I just saw him, for some reason I feel compelled to ask. "Is Darryl home?"

Mr. Gibson smiles. "Of course," he says. He's a little over-excited, like he's meeting Darryl's girlfriend or something. Then again, I bet I'm the first kid from Marion East that's ever been to this house. He calls over his shoulder. "Darryl, you can leave the rest of the dishes. You have company." Then he waves me in, shutting the door behind me.

The place is basically a library squeezed into a refurbished house. In their living room, bookshelves line all four walls. And it's not for show—you can tell that they're in constant use. On every row there are books missing, the rest of the stack tilting into the open spaces. In other spots, books jut out for easy access, bookmarks sticking from them. On every coffee table there are more books and magazines scattered—and they're not the kind of trashy mags that most people snap up in the checkout lane. No, these things look a little deeper. Instead of celebrities on the front, they've got pictures of serious-looking people—authors maybe or politicians. One even just has a picture of a prison on the front, the words *American Shame* written below it in blood red. For all that text scattered around though, the rest of the place looks spotless.

The walls look newly painted, the furniture is all dusted, the carpet is vacuumed and free of debris.

"Well," Gibson says. He's standing behind me, like he's been there for a minute watching me gawk at their place. "What you want?"

"Darryl," his mom seethes, looking up from her book. She's got big glasses that kind of take over her face, but behind them her mousy features seem over-stressed by how tightly her brown hair's pulled back in a bun. "That's no way to talk to a friend."

Gibson eyes me up and down. "Well, tell me when a friend gets here."

"Darryl!" his mom says again. Then she sets her book in her lap and addresses me instead. "I apologize for my son's horrible hospitality, Derrick," she says. "I promise you this is not the kind of manners his father and I try to instill."

"It's okay," I say. "Besides, he's right. I haven't been exactly a friend to him."

She shakes her head. "Yes, but you're in our home. It's his"—she tilts her head toward Darryl—"job to be the host." Then, as if deciding her son needs a demonstration, she leans forward and starts asking me questions. At first it's just about school. Subjects I like. Teachers that are tough. Standard parent stuff. Then she surprises me. "Have you decided where you'll play college ball next year, Derrick?"

"No," I answer. "I got it narrowed. But I haven't decided."

"Well, I've long been a believer that college athletes should get paid," she says. She glances toward the kitchen, indicating her husband. "Barrett wrote a long paper on it that should be published in the spring. You really amount to unpaid labor. And it *is* labor, sometimes more hours than what we would call full-time employment. Just another way the system tries to deny the poor what is rightfully theirs."

I about tell her that there are plenty of college athletes who come from way too much money to call themselves *poor*, but I'm late on the trigger. She keeps rattling on. "So I say if a university is willing to offer you money for your services, you are entirely within your rights to take it. Some might call that cheating, but I honestly believe it's some small piece of fair compensation."

"Jesus, Mom, the guy didn't come here for that," Gibson says. "Save it for your classroom."

At that, his mom bolts up out of her chair. "Now that's *enough*!" she snaps. She's still under control, but she's plenty worked up. "This attitude of yours is getting real old, real fast."

And now I know a couple things I didn't know five seconds ago. First, despite her frail features and meek face, Gibson's mom has some fire. And I know that it's one thing we have in common—our competitive spirit comes from our mother's side.

"Let's just head upstairs, Derrick," Gibson says. He shuffles off, shoulders slumped in self-pity. I follow.

His room doesn't fit with the rest of the house. It's not just the debris and disarray—that just looks like any teenager's room. It's that he's peppered his walls with pictures of ballers and rappers. The players I get—any self-respecting point guard is gonna slap some pics of Chris Paul and Derrick Rose on his wall. But the rappers? And not just any rappers—these walls are sporting Tech N9ne and Big K.R.I.T. I guarantee you, parents who read the stuff that lined those walls downstairs don't exactly have an appreciation for the artists lining these walls. All of it under the same roof of a white family on Ruckle and 32nd. *Crazy.*

"I'm sorry about my parents, man," Gibson says. "They think they've got to, like, prove to everyone how much they know about black people. It's stupid."

I just raise my eyebrows and point to a few of the posters on his wall. "You sure you talking about your folks?"

"Man, shut up," Gibson says. But then he laughs it off. "I been dealing with that stuff my whole life," he explains. "People saying I'm a wannabe and all that. But you tell me. When your parents got, like, twenty advanced degrees between them and they think it's a good idea to move to this part of town, am I supposed to listen to, like, Beethoven and shit?"

"Wait, what?" I say. "You mean your parents could afford to live somewhere else?"

"Shit," he says. "We moved here from Bloomington because they both got jobs over at Butler. But are we living on that side of town? Hell, no. They talk all this nonsense about refusing to live in a segregated world. But, man, look around. I feel pretty damn segregated, you know?"

I have to laugh at that. The kid's got a point. And I realize that he's got his problems just like anyone else. We look at each other and he just shakes his head, like explaining the situation just makes it more exasperating to him. "Whatever," he says, trying to change the subject. "Why you here, anyway?"

There's a sour tone to his voice, but I don't take the bait. He's already pretty worked up. I can't pretend like I've been welcoming to

Kevin Waltman

him. I've been lingering near his doorway, but now I take a step into the center of the room. It closes the gap between us, and Gibson suddenly seems pretty small. As if sensing it, he takes a few steps back, clears a couple old school papers off a chair, then points at it for me to sit. I go ahead and take a seat. "We got to get on the same page, man," I say. I offer it matter-of-factly, looking him right in the eye as I talk.

For a second, he narrows his eyes at me in distrust. The tension stays in his body. He grinds his teeth a couple times. Then he exhales. He rolls his eyes, but he starts nodding. "I know it, D. This whole mess between us is nonsense, right?"

"Right," I say. "We both want to win. I don't really care about anything else."

Gibson nods. He starts to pace back and forth in his room, getting worked up at the idea. "I know it. So do the rest of the guys on the team, but we have to show them how."

"Now you're talking," I say.

Then he stops and looks at me. It's like seeing me makes him remember how much he's resented me over the course of the year. His eyes narrow. "Look, I know we're never gonna be tight. But I'm never gonna freeze you out on the court again, okay?"

That's all I wanted to hear. But I know I've got to make some kind of pledge to him too. "Cool," I say. "And I won't squeeze off shots every time I touch it either." I want to add *even if I do have it rolling*, but I just leave it at that. No sense in taking a step backwards now. I offer him a hand. Gibson grabs it and pulls me in to hug it out. We give each other a few thumps on the back and then step away. "We good?" I ask.

"Yeah, we straight," he answers. He gazes around his room, then at me again. Neither one of us is sure what to do now. He lets that snarky smile creep across his face, but this time I'm not the target. "I bet if you want, my moms and pops will set you up with a nice long lecture about the exploitation of black people. They dish that shit out like other parents give out milk and cookies."

I laugh. "Yeah, I'll pass," I say.

Gibson smiles. "What I thought," he says. "I bet that's how their students feel too." Then we both bolt downstairs. Gibson ushers me to the door before his parents can even react. "Let's get after it at practice tomorrow," he says.

Then we're done. And as I zip my coat up against the cold night, for the first time in a month I feel like maybe we can make something out of this season yet.

When it's your own house, you can feel it the moment you walk in. That silence that's all wrong. If everyone's asleep or if the house is empty, that's silence too, but you know it's okay. This is different. It's like the silence of a grave. I walk in that door, see the coats hanging in the open closet. Shoe scattered on the floor. The chairs sit empty, same places they've always been in the living room. I scan across the room, toward the kitchen where there's a light on. My whole family—even Kid, who's all but vaporized since our falling out—sit quietly by the table. Dad's giving Grace a bottle, so even she's quiet, content to feed. When I step toward the kitchen, everyone looks at me. I don't know what it is, but judging by their faces, it's bad.

They glance now at each other, checking to see who should be the one to talk first. Finally Dad hands Grace gingerly over to Mom. Grace

Kevin Waltman

fusses for a second, but latches back onto the bottle and quiets again. Dad stands and walks to me. Behind him, I see Kid bury his face in his hands. Even Jayson can't bear to look now, instead staring off across the kitchen and out the window.

"We would have texted you," Dad says, "but this isn't the kind of thing for a text."

"What is it?" I say, getting more anxious with each second they don't tell me.

Dad puts his hand on my shoulder. He has to reach up to do it. But in that instant I feel like I'm five again, and Dad's calming me down from a tantrum. "It's Wes," he says.

"What?" I ask. In my heart, I know.

"He's been shot."

19.

It could have been a lot worse. Two inches to the right, and my boy would be a corpse. Instead, the bullet went clean through near his left shoulder. The nurse said Wes was awfully close to bleeding out. Even though I'm sitting just a few feet from him in his hospital bed, all I can picture is him on a cold Indy sidewalk, blood pooling around him. It happens almost every night in this city, but it's different when the victim is the guy you grew up with. Then it's not a number or a headline—it's a life hanging in the balance.

Outside Wes' door, an officer sat patiently. He questioned me pretty good before letting me in, but I know he's really just waiting on Wes to wake up so he can start investigating. Or maybe he doesn't even care. Maybe he's just following procedure, checking off items on a list before he can go home and forget about Wes just like this city forgets about everyone else who gets clipped.

Wes. My boy. We used to kill whole days together running around in the summer—playing hoops at the park when we were so little it was all we could do to heave the ball up to the rim, scrounging money from our moms and then burning through it on candy and hip-hop magazines, busting into vacant apartments and scavenging through what people left behind. Now here he is, his chest rising in ragged breaths. He's hooked to an I.V. The only sound in the room is the whir and beeping of the hospital equipment. His skin, always a shade lighter than mine, looks pale and waxy from the lost blood. His shoulder is covered in white gauze. With the sheet pulled down a little, I can see his whole left side. Now I see the ink. I knew about the dollar sign he had on the inside of his wrist, but now I see tats crawling up most of his arm—stars and lettering and numbers that I can't quite decipher. But I know one thing—they're the markings of a crew.

I think back to that officer outside the door. Maybe he's here to investigate who shot Wes. But maybe he's here to arrest Wes whenever he wakes up. It wouldn't be the first time that's happened around here. Wes grunts in his sleep and I lean in, thinking maybe he's about to say something. His eyelids flutter in a dream, but he stays asleep.

I think back to a summer day before our sixth grade year. We were at the park, shooting around, when some older kids rode up. They were in high school, all sneer and swagger. Straight off they told us the court was theirs. That was the summer Wes and I really started to separate in size—like he was rooted to the ground while I inched toward the sky a little more every day. So I told those guys if they wanted to run, I'd run with them. But Wes just bowed out. He slinked to the sideline and sat. And that was the last time he ever played ball with me. It's not like he had all this untapped potential on the court, but now I think back to that day—I hung in there with the older kids, getting some rips and buckets here and there, while Wes lay sprawled in the grass, defeated—and it seems like maybe that was the moment we really started in different directions.

Or maybe it was our freshman year when his dad stood him up and didn't visit on Christmas. Or maybe it was sophomore year when he got his head all screwed up over a girl. Or maybe all of that's oversimplifying things. It's like the more I try to find a real reason why he's lying in bed with a gunshot wound and I'm getting scholarship offers, the less any of it makes sense. Are our fates just different because I'm 6'4" and Wes is 5'6"? Is that all there is? Chance?

I know the deal. I'm supposed to lean over Wes and talk to him. Whisper all kinds of encouraging words that sink in even as he sleeps. But I don't. It's not because I'm anxious or anything, but because I just don't believe in that kind of stuff anymore. Sure, some guys make a turnaround. They get scared straight or find religion or move away and hit reset. But the truth is Wes is on his path, and the vast majority of guys don't get off of it until they're locked up or dead. I don't want that to be the case, but I'm not young enough to pretend anymore.

One of the nurses said that Wes' mom was there earlier, but I've been here for more than an hour and she's been a ghost. I know what that means—she took one look at her son and couldn't handle it. She's off now, lost in a stream of booze. If not something harder than that. And his dad? Maybe he doesn't even know yet. Maybe he'll never know. I imagine him somewhere in the west now, sleeping alone in a dingy apartment. Ignorant of what he's guilty of. So maybe that's the real chance—the lottery we enter to determine whether or not we get good parents.

The door whooshes open slightly. When I turn, all that's visible at

Kevin Waltman

first is a sliver of light coming into the room. Then a hand curls around the door and pushes it open slowly, as if whoever is on the other side is afraid to wake Wes up. When the door's open enough, a head peeks in. Lia. It's clear she's been crying. It's not like she ever knew Wes that well, so I know those tears are for my benefit. She hesitates there, like someone who just stepped into church while the preacher's in mid-sermon, not sure if they should come on in or just slink away so as not to intrude. "Come on in," I whisper. "He's just resting."

Quiet as a cat, Lia slinks in. She's got her arms folded tight around her chest, warming herself against the sterile cold of the hospital. She walks to Wes' bedside and then stops and stares. She shudders once. I pick up the second chair and set it down for her. She doesn't sit right away, like she's afraid to move. I run my hand gently across her back. "It's okay," I say.

Then we sit next to each other in silence. A couple times Lia turns to me, her eyes still glassy. I don't know if she wants to say something or if she expects me to fill up the silence. But each time she turns her gaze back to Wes, because, really, what is there to say? Finally, she simply reaches out with her right hand and puts it on my knee. There's nothing sexy about it, just a quiet touch to let me know she's here for me. I take her hand in mine and we just sit there in silence. Lia and I have had a lot of things go wrong between us, but for now—as the clock creeps toward midnight—we hold steady and keep a quiet vigil for Wes. I guess we're stand-ins for the couple who should be there instead of us.

PART III

20.

A basketball game now seems obscene. But you've got to take what the schedule says. And it's been there since it came out—Muncie Central on the first Saturday in January. The people of Muncie don't care that someone shot Wes. All they care about is hoops. They're decked out in their purple and white, buzzing as the teams warm up. The cheerleaders kick in the air. The concession stands push out bags of popcorn. The band blasts the fight song. And back in Indianapolis, Wes is at home, healing up and refusing to speak—not to the cops, not even to me.

I stand at mid-court, dribbling a rock back and forth between my legs. Around me, my teammates get loose. Gibson's good on his word from the other day. He sees Xavier hoist up a twenty-footer and he gets right in his grill. Over the thrum of the crowd, I can hear him yell "Game shots!" Then he turns to Reynolds, trying to get him amped a little. I can't hear any of that conversation, but I know the drill—he's letting Reynolds know that we need him ready to roll the second he subs in. Then he's off to check on Fuller, who's sporting one of those old plastic masks to protect his broken nose. Even through the plastic, you

Kevin Waltman

can see how nasty the bruise is. With Fuller, Gibson's calm. He even reaches up and adjusts one of the straps on Fuller's mask. Then he must crack some kind of joke, because they both laugh a little.

"You okay, D?" It's Kid, coming out to mid-court to check on me.

"Yeah, I'm straight," I say. It's about the most we've spoken to each other since we had our big dustup. Other than to help break the news about Wes, Kid's barely set foot in our door. I know he still sleeps there because I see the blankets on the couch every morning. But I only see him at practice. I know we've got to get settled with each other, but now—front and center on Muncie Central's court, two minutes left in warm-ups—just isn't the time.

"You even take a chance to get loose?" he asks, motioning toward my teammates who are all working up a little lather.

"I'm good," I say. Then I think about that knee. It's felt better lately, but the last thing I need is to aggravate that old injury. I flip the ball I've been dribbling to Kid. I bend down for some hammy stretches, paying close attention to the injury. It feels "normal," I guess, warm and loose below the wrap I still wear. But my whole body feels tired. Part of me feels like walking off that court and heading home. The schedule demands to be played, but maybe someone else should be playing it at this point.

Murphy walks over, making his rounds. "Let's get after it tonight," he chirps. Then, as I'm all the way down in a stretch, he gives me a hearty pound on the back.

It's almost callous—how can a coach be that ignorant of what's going on with his player? But maybe that's the point—it's Murphy's way of telling me to lace 'em up tight and forget about everything else. Whatever. At this point, the whole thing feels like a crazy joke. I laugh once and continue stretching.

It takes me less than a minute of live action to forget all the other noise—not because of what Murphy said, but because I don't want to get my ass embarrassed. Muncie's 13-1. Got their best squad since the days when Kid was suiting up against them, and they bring it at us pretty quick. Their main man is Jeff Stanski. And he *knows* it. They control the tip, and he sprints to the left wing. Catches at about twenty-three feet and—zap—rips off a trey that's so pure the net doesn't move. Then, as Gibson brings the ball up, Stanski checks me—he's naturally their point guard, but they must want to put best on best on the defensive end.

I've got two inches plus some bulk on the guy. Every instinct tells me to forget running the set—just race for the block and post this kid up. But I know better. Our squad's barely holding together right now. One wrong move could shake us apart. So I widen to the wing and wait for Gibson to bring it up. Then I do the right thing—rub off a back-screen from Jones and then look to cross-screen for Fuller. Same old set.

Muncie's done their homework. They beat us to every spot, get out in front of every cut. Plus, we're moving in slow-motion, like our legs are still heavy from the holidays. Finally, I get a touch just off the elbow. Again, the instincts—I see a little crease and know I could power dribble and then rise up over Stanski. But on the wing Gibson claps twice quickly. "Ball!" he snaps. He's doesn't have that old sneer to his voice, but he's pretty adamant. I know that I've got to give it up. Besides, might as well save up some moves for crunch time.

Kevin Waltman

So I rifle it out to Gibson and we plow through more offense—ending with a tough leaner from Jones that clangs off the back iron. *Could have gotten a better shot than that any time*, I think. What I say, though, is "Keep at it, Jonesy. They gonna fall." That last part's a lie, but it's one I feel compelled to tell.

It gets late early in Muncie. *Late early*—that phrase Kid would always use when you could feel a game hanging in the balance even though there were more than five minutes left on the clock. And here we are, down 46-39 with 5:30 left. Our ball. It's only seven points, but Muncie Central's been so efficient and crisp it feels like a dozen. Stanski's got 19 of theirs, and I know in crunch time they're going to get him touches every trip. I've got 13, though I know if I forced it I could have twice that. Gibson knows it too. As he brings it up, he whistles at me. I stop where I am, and he dribbles toward me. "You get a look, take it," he says. "No more waiting around."

"Got it," I say.

Then we both jog into the front-court. First move is still the back-screen. Then I sprint across the lane to set a screen for Reynolds—he's basically split minutes with Fuller, who's clearly uncomfortable playing behind that mask. Reynolds comes flying off my screen. I see it in his eyes—he thinks *he's* supposed to be the one to step up and bury the big shots. He's got a little space off the screen too. Gibson hits him in stride as Reynolds flashes to the free throw line. He's so eager to fire that he doesn't even set his feet. I spin back toward the lane, sealing Stanski behind me. I race toward the right block, knowing Reynolds is going to miss in the direction he was leaning. I snatch the ball between their bigs, but once I grab it they basically give me the put-back—the last thing they want to do is foul me.

All it takes sometimes is seeing the rock find bottom to get the blood flowing. Murphy's quick to react from the sideline. "Full! Full! Full!" he screams, urging us to pick them up in a press.

Gibson darts into the passing lane, cutting off the entry to Stanski. I plaster to my man. That leaves Muncie Central's three man as the next option. He's trotted past midcourt, and now has to sprint back to the ball. Reynolds—shaken out of his sluggishness—sprints with him. He arrives with the ball and tips it away. Gibson's the quickest to it. He scoops the ball up near the right wing. Any other year, I'd be rolling straight to the rim, looking to receive an alley-oop. But now I just jab step that way to get my man leaning. Instead, I flare back to the wing. Gibson spots me immediately and rifles the rock cross-court. I catch with plenty of time to set my feet. Show off that stroke I've had all the time in the world to work on. That thing falls and all of a sudden we're in a two-point game.

Muncie Central calls time. Their players jog to the bench. A few of them shake their heads, bothered by our sudden burst. Stanski squints up at the scoreboard once. He shrugs real quick, unfazed. Meanwhile, our bench is all up and into it. Fuller strides out to meet us, thumping his chest with his fist. Even through his mask I can see the fire in his eyes. Kid's about fifteen feet onto the court. He fires off two chest bumps for Jones and Xavier. In his heart, Kid wants to throw on a uni and throw down on the deck.

Murphy springs into coach-mode for real. Finally guys are juiced enough that he doesn't have to go through his rah-rah routine. He just uncaps his marker. "You know they're looking to Stanski," he starts. Then he diagrams what he thinks they'll run—a fake double for Stanski, where he peels back to the wing on a back-screen. My man would be the one setting the back-screen. Murphy jabs his marker at me. "Don't give it away early," he says. "But you can anticipate and jump that pass to the wing."

We break, feeling good—like we're destined to win, even if we're still trailing. We have our teeth in this thing now and we're not letting go. Sure enough, Muncie Central runs the exact play Murphy drew up. Ball's out top and Stanski goes flying to the lane toward a double screen. My man crosses to the spot Stanski vacated. Then, two steps from the screen, Stanski reverses for that back-screen from my man. I cheat just an inch, waiting for my chance. And when Stanski comes ripping off that screen, hands outstretched for the rock, I peel off with him. I turn my head, see ball. It's in mid-air, waiting to be plucked. I reach for it, get a hand on it—but it just skims off my fingers, rolls harmlessly out of bounds. Everyone on our bench *ooohs* at the missed opportunity. They immediately snap back to attention, clapping and encouraging. But everyone saw that—a pick of that pass and I had a free run to tie it. Instead, we're going to have to dig in on D and grind it out.

The Muncie players seem to relax a bit. They know they dodged a bullet. They just run their normal sets. No hurries and no worries for them. The clock just runs and runs, then after about a full minute, they get a quick look to one of the bigs. Jones fouls to prevent the easy deuce, but give their guy credit—he steps right up and sinks his freebies. Back to four.

Gibson brings it up for us again. All the Muncie guys are puffed back up with confidence. They chatter away on defense, suddenly as fresh as they were in the opening minutes. That means we have to work too. It would be great to get a quick score, but we know we can't take bad shots now. Even trigger-happy Reynolds passes on a glimpse from range. We work to the post. Back out. Reversal. Another reversal. Finally a reset to Gibson out top. Talk about getting late early—suddenly we're under three minutes. We need a bucket *now*.

I catch on the wing, but there's no room to work. Jones comes out to set a ball-screen, but I wave him down to the block. I dribble back so my feet are behind the three-point stripe. Then I just give a twitch—my man lunges at it, scared of that stroke from three. That's enough to let me get by. The bigs challenge, I drop to Jones, and he gets hammered for an obvious foul.

Only problem is he splits his two instead of getting both. Down three.

We can't get any closer than that for the next two minutes. I get a deuce in the lane. Gibson drops a little runner. Xavier even muscles in a bucket. But Muncie Central keeps getting bailed out with whistles on the other end.

Finally, Gibson brings it up with only forty seconds left. We're down five again. For some that's desperation time. For me, it's winning time. I don't even use a screen. I just flare to the wing, clap for the ball. Gibson delivers it, but my man gets up into me. I drop my shoulder and give him a little rocker step like I might drive. He doesn't really bite, but he has to give me some room so he doesn't foul. All I need. I rise up with him in my grill but drain a deep one anyway. Two-point game.

Kevin Waltman

Then it's Gibson's turn to make a play. He stays with Stanski on the press, mirroring every cut. Muncie Central's got timeouts left, but their man panics. With the five-count coming, he forces the orange toward Stanski—and Gibson's all over it. He deflects the pass, then races after it before it bounces out of bounds. He lunges and flips the ball up over his shoulder to save it. The ball carries all the way out toward mid-court. Xavier hustles and outleaps everyone to grab it.

We've got our chance. Xavier looks lost for a second, not used to having the rock that far from the rim. But Reynolds is on top of it. He sprints to the ball and bails out Xavier. Instead of forcing, Reynolds waits for Gibson to untangle himself from where he landed in the second row of bleachers. Meanwhile, I station myself on the block, waiting. As soon as Gibson touches it, he attacks. He gets by Stanski, but the D pinches down as he finds the paint. This is an easy read. I just pop out to the corner and get my feet set. Gibson finds me, whipping a no-look laser for a little flavor. Even before I let it rip, I hear the Muncie crowd groan. They *know* this trey's finding bottom.

I do not disappoint.

Timeout Muncie Central. Our lead. Twenty seconds to go. The whole gym is a murmur of disgusted fans seeing a victory snatched away from them. Well, the whole gym except for our bench. It's one big explosion. I get mobbed—a frenzy of guys shaking my shoulders and hugging me and bumping chests.

Murphy gets us calmed down enough to talk us through the final set. But when we break, it's obvious right away there's no "play" to defend. Muncie Central just flattens out and gets the rock to Stanski up top. I thought they'd try to get a quick one—give them a chance for a put-back or a foul if they missed—but Stanski's got nothing like that in mind. He dribbles leisurely, glancing at the clock now and then. Their crowd starts screaming for him to *go*. But he waits. And waits. And waits. Ten seconds left. Eight. Six. Five.

Stanski attacks. Gibson's got the quicks to stay with him. He cuts Stanski off at the right elbow. Defends a cross-over to the left. Two seconds to go. All Stanski has left is a crazy-hard turnaround from seventeen feet—with Gibson's hand right in his face.

It doesn't matter. Stanski drains it at the buzzer.

The crowd storms the court. Someone hoists Stanski up in the middle of the mob and he pumps his fist in the air, triumphant.

Us? We hang our heads and slink to the locker room. A loss, even when everything went right. Big shots fell for us. Gibson and I worked together. Even Reynolds and Xavier made hustle plays. But it's another L around our necks. And this one feels heavier than all the others put together.

By all that's right in the world, I should be with Lia. Who was there last year when I had my surgery? Who was there the other night when I visited Wes in the hospital? Lia.

But when Jasmine texted me, I mashed it right back for her to come over. I didn't even think about it. Well, I did think a little—I knew if she came to my place we couldn't get up to anything we'd regret.

Grace merely whimpers in her sleep now and then, rather than her full-out cry. So after Mom and Dad whisper through some small talk with Jasmine—shooting disapproving glances at me the whole time—they excuse themselves to try for some shut-eye. Jasmine coos

Kevin Waltman

to them about how adorable Grace is. Even through their heavy-lidded gazes, Mom and Dad light up at that. But Dad throws me another warning look. It's not that he dislikes Jasmine. But he doesn't want me doing something crazy to screw it up with Lia.

Luckily for Dad—and maybe for me—Jayson has no intentions of giving us privacy. As soon as Mom and Dad ease their door shut he turns up the volume on the T.V. It's garbage—some slasher flick he's seen before—and any other time I'd be pretty annoyed with him. For once though, I'm not trying to get busy even though Jasmine's perched next to me on the couch.

She turns to me, leans in a little. "How you doing, Derrick?" she asks sympathetically.

Like an idiot, I start talking hoops. "Ah, I'm good," I say. "That's how basketball is. You can play your heart out for thirty-two minutes, play well enough to win, and then get iced at the buzzer. Besides, we got time to—"

I stop when I finally register Jasmine's reaction. She's shaking her head at me, a slow and pitying move like a teacher gives when some student pops off an ignorant answer in the classroom. "I'm not asking about that," she says. "I mean about Wes."

Even Jayson sits up now. He knows this is sacred stuff. He mutes his movie.

I measure my words carefully. If I just let it go—let it all spill out about Wes—then I'm worried I'll end up crying like a fool in front of Jasmine. "What happened to Wes," I start, "is on Wes. I know he had a bad run of it, but he had chances. He had people there for him. I was there for him."

I'm not sure how true that last sentence is, so I pause. Jasmine leaps in to fill up the silence. "I'm not talking about whose fault it is," she says. "Whose fault? How about the guy who shot him? Or the guy who sold him the gun? Or the people in charge who let things get so wrong we need guns to feel safe where we live? Don't get me started on that, Derrick." She takes a deep breath to slow herself. When she gets worked up, she can rival even my mom in a lecture about how dirty we've been done in Indianapolis. "What I want to talk about," she begins again, "is how you feel about it. I'm here for you, Derrick."

I've known Jasmine long enough to know I'm not getting away without some kind of answer. The girl's a pit bull sometimes. Jayson leans forward too. "I'm fine," I say. "For real. It sucks, but I've got to keep my own head straight."

"Oh come on, D," Jayson chimes in. "You know I'm not all, like, let's share our feelings and shit. But don't lie to the girl."

I glare at Jayson. He knows teaming up on me is a cold move. He knows that I'd like to cross that carpet and shove the remote down his throat. And he also knows I'm not going to so much as touch him with Jasmine around. "Fine," I seethe. "It's not like Wes and I have been tight lately. Not since last year, but you know that story." Jasmine nods. She heard about it all—Wes getting busted with weed in my car, then almost getting me capped when I had to stand up for him after he ripped off a dealer. "But we go way back, you know? And now he just sits up there"—I motion up the block toward his house—"smoking up and wasting his life. And I get it. That's what half the guys our age do. It's just that he won't even talk about it. Not even to me. Forget cops or counselors or any of that garbage. But if he could just, like,

Kevin Waltman

acknowledge it to me, then maybe we could cope somehow. I can't fix his world for him, but we could still be friends, you know? But this silence! It's like he's already dead."

And on that last word, it happens. My voice cracks. I don't fall out into a full-on cry or anything, but Jasmine and Jayson have what they want. They see now how raw it is with Wes.

"Derrick," Jasmine whispers. She reaches over and puts her hand on my knee. Used to be that touch would electrify me. Now it just offends. I spring off the couch, leaping as fast as I would for a rebound.

"Don't!" I snap. It's loud, but when I listen out, I don't hear Grace stirring. "I don't want your pity. I don't want any of this."

Jasmine backs into her corner of the couch. She looks hurt by my outburst. "It wasn't pity, Derrick," she says. "You always think the worst of people."

I glance over at Jayson to see if he's got anything to add now. He just turns back to his movie. It's still muted, but he acts like it's riveting stuff.

"Then what?" I ask. I keep my voice level this time. "Why are you even here, Jasmine? Why aren't you off at school?"

Now it's Jasmine's turn to look evasive. She gazes toward the door like she'd suddenly rather be out in the blistering wind than here with me. "Because schools sucks," she says. "I hate it. I'm barely passing any classes and I think about quitting each day. You happy?"

"No," I say. "Not happy. I—" But I don't know how to go on from there. To hear Jasmine talk about college that way is crushing. She already admitted it was a struggle, but she was the *one*—smartest kid to come out of Marion East in forever. But I can't put that weight on her.

I feel it sometimes too—like it would be a lot easier if I were just some under-the-radar player who might get a chance at a mid-major.

Jasmine takes up the slack in the conversation again. "It's okay," she says. "I'm the one that started this whole thing. Asking tough questions and making people talk." She forces a little laugh. Then she gazes down at her hands, lost in thought for a few seconds. She looks back up at me then. "But you asked why I'm here. That one's easy, Derrick. You're my friend. This is what friends do."

Part of me still wants to fight. It's like I'm worked up into the heat of battle and then someone blows a whistle and calls the game off. I don't know what to do with all this energy.

Jayson senses it. He smirks at me and rolls his eyes. "She's got you again," he says. "Don't even try saying something back. You ain't never gonna win with her."

I give him my meanest stare, but he doesn't flinch. He knows he's right. I know it too. I throw my hands up in the air, exasperated. "You two about to kill me," I say. Then I ease back down onto the couch and we all share a tired laugh. Jayson punches that remote again, and the volume comes back up. Not too loud though, since he doesn't want to wake Grace with the screams of pretty white teenagers inflicting violence on each other.

Later, when Jayson's finally given us some privacy, Jasmine lets her hand creep over toward mine. We lace fingers. A couple years ago, I would've leaned in for more. Try to get busy right there on the couch. But it's different now.

"What you gonna do next?" I ask her.

She blinks a few times, her eyes a little wet. "Move back home, probably. Maybe try classes at IUPUI." She says this like it's an admission of guilt.

"Come on, now. You're gonna make it." I give her fingers a little squeeze for emphasis. "You know that, right?"

"Thanks," she says, but she looks away.

I unlace my fingers from hers. I put my hand on her shoulder, then wait for her to turn back to me. "I mean it. You're too good not to make it." She's still not buying it. So I try to change the mood. "Besides, you don't want to be going to school down in Kentucky anyway. And Louisville? Come *on*. How can you go to a school that was running freakin' prostitutes for their basketball team? You're better than that place."

She smiles at last. "Thanks, Derrick."

We sit in silence for a few seconds. It occurs to me that this might be one last opportunity to make it with Jasmine. But at this point, I don't even want that. I mean, I *do*, but I want it like this more—us just being cool with each other, having each other's backs.

"You're gonna make it too, D," she says.

"Yeah, well."

Then she gets me one more time. "Who knows, maybe after some credits at IUPUI, I'll transfer again. Land where you go."

I have to just smile to myself. That was our goodbye, I know. She stands to go. I have no idea if I'll ever see her again. But even as she walks to that door, she's got me thinking about some imaginary night in the future. Some place where we'll be different, on surer footing, and there won't be any cause for her to leave me again.

21.

Kid's such a rarity at home, I'm surprised to see him walking out the front door. He's got Grace in her car seat, ready to take her somewhere. In the other hand, he holds a tiny squeaky bear that Gracie loves. He gives it a little squeeze every few seconds to keep her entertained. I don't even ask. Just give him a nod and a *'Sup*.

"Hey, D," he says. He glances down at Grace, who fusses in her car seat. He squeaks her bear a couple times, then bounces the whole contraption up and down, shushing her. She quiets, easy as that. The man does have his ways. "Just taking Grace out for a little drive," he says. "Puts her to sleep."

"Okay," I say. Then we stand there, awkward with each other.

"See you at the gym later," he says, referring to our game with Guerin tonight. It's been a full week since that washout in Muncie, but from here on out there's a steady rhythm of games. Starting next week, it's games every Friday and Saturday until Sectionals on the first weekend of March. If we're going to make it happen, it's got to start *soon*.

Kevin Waltman

"Catch you there," I say. Then I step aside, making room for him as he shuffles past me with the car seat. He doesn't even look at me again. Just heads for the car. When he hits the bottom step, I can look down on him even more than usual. I see the bald spot on the back of his head. I see his shoulder strain with the weight of the car seat. Something about it makes me hang my head. "Hey, Kid," I call.

He stops and turns. He doesn't say a word, just waits for me to speak while he keeps bouncing Grace in her seat.

"I've got Monday and Tuesday off to take my Alabama visit," I say.

"Yeah. I know. I'm the assistant coach, remember?"

"Well, why don't you come with me?" I say. I remember a promise I made to myself long ago, that I'd get Kid on these campus visits. After all, back in the day these should have been the trips he was making. "You know more about what I'm looking for than anyone else."

He responds briskly. Not mean, but businesslike. "I've got to stay and coach," he says. "Besides, that's a parent's job."

"Kid," I say, pleading.

"What, D?" he snaps. Now he is angry. "I don't want charity."

"Kid," I say again. But he's gone. He pops the car seat a little roughly into its base in the back seat of Dad's car. Then he hops into the front seat, jangling Dad's keys in his hand. Turns the ignition. Takes off. He pushes it pretty hard to the end of the block, but I see him ease onto the next street—with Grace in the back, he's going to drive as careful as if the car were strapped with explosives. "You're not a disaster, Kid," I say, finishing the thought I started before he split. But what good does it do to say it to myself? What good is anything I do?

We get run. By Guerin. Now, don't get me wrong. Guerin's got a decent enough squad. Got some shooters. A little size. But a bunch of white boys from Hamilton County aren't supposed to ride down to the city and rip off a twenty-point win.

In the locker room afterward, I don't even want to see anybody. I keep my eyes on the floor. I see the carpet, stained and worn thin. I see my duffel bag by my locker. I see the wet cement of the shower room. That's it. I know, around me, guys are talking—trying to pick each other up, bitching about blown calls, even whispering about what they'll get up to later. But I know that if I open my mouth, all that will come out is a scream. I dropped in 20 and grabbed 12, even dished out 5 assists. For what? To see Xavier go 1-9 from the field? To see Reynolds pop off the bench and cough up 6 turnovers? To see Jones look as lost as a freshman on the defensive end? Forget it. All of it.

I douse my head, rinse off the sweat. Then I grab a towel and head back to my locker. I glance up enough to see Murphy walking to the center of the room. As guys filter back from the showers, he clears his throat. He motions for them to sit.

"Tough one," he says at last. "But listen, guys. You got out there and competed. Winning is the most important thing in sports, I'm not gonna lie. But losing's the second best. Because when you lose, it means you got out there and gave it your all. Losing is nothing to be ashamed of as long as you competed. You just have to keep working, guys. I believe in you."

I want to spit. He *believes* in us? Lord, what team is he even

Kevin Waltman

watching? I don't believe in us. When I cut my eyes to Kid, I can tell he's thinking the same thing. There's real anger in his eyes. It's one thing to get a beatdown. Another still to get it from suburb kids. But to just *take* it? To give some optimistic bullshit to the team afterward? That's a sin to me. And to Kid.

I wait a few more seconds, make sure Murphy's done. Then when he claps his hands to signal he's finished, I stuff my gear in my bag, zip it up. I throw on my street clothes in about two seconds, and I'm history. I don't leave for Alabama until tomorrow morning, but I'd just as soon hit the road right now. As far as this locker room's concerned, I'm as gone as gone can get.

22.

It's so early it hurts, but I know the old man's up. I've barely slept, feels like. We did the Bama trip Sunday, saw them beat Florida Monday night, had some more meetings Tuesday morning before mashing it back up I-65. We didn't get in that late, but I couldn't sleep. Too much noise in my head, too many nerves jangling.

So, the old man. Before school starts on a Wednesday, I ring the doorbell on his little cottage house and wait. It's the cleanest place on the block, but even here there are signs of decay. The driveway has cracks spiderwebbing across it. All the paint around the front windows is starting to flake off. Even the screen door sags heavily when you open it. I wait a minute, then bang on the door a few times.

"Hold your damn water!" a voice rasps from behind the door. There it is. My coach. He finally opens the door, blinks a few times in the thin winter light, then registers who it is. "Derrick, you ever think that when a man retires one of the reasons would be so he doesn't have to drag his bones out of bed at dawn anymore?" Then he smiles—an expression that's always made it look like Coach Bolden's face will crack in two—and invites me in.

Kevin Waltman

The place has that same spare and scrubbed feel his office used to have. There's an old couch in one corner and two uncomfortable chairs along the opposite wall. A T.V. that looks straight out of 1977 sits against another wall. Past it, a dark hallway leads to the rest of the house. Bolden doesn't look quite as put together as he used to though. He's wearing some old blue sweats with a small hole at one knee, plus a Marion East t-shirt that looks so faded it might be from the year he was hired. Beneath it, he appears bony and frail. He's got some gray stubble on his chin too, and his eyes look tired. I used to think of him as the "old man," but now I really see his age. Then, when I take a deep breath, I smell it: that old-person scent that hovers around a place.

"Well," he rasps. "You got something on your mind, I bet."

I start by apologizing for waking him up. He just laughs it off and tells me he's giving me hell—he's been up since 4:00 am. So at least he's still a step ahead of me mentally even if he looks like he's angling for the grave. "I just got back from Tuscaloosa last night," I say. "Visiting Alabama."

"Yeah? You gonna go be a good Southern boy? Roll Tide and all that?" There's some sarcasm in his voice, but I can't tell if it's specifically because of Alabama, or because he just wants to knock me down a peg like always.

"Nah," I say. "They were nice enough. Cool town and school. But, man, we get more people at high school games than they got for an SEC game. I don't think some of the people down there even *know* they have a basketball team."

Bolden laughs at that. He rubs that stubbly chin. "You said it there," he says. "So where you gonna go?" I explain that it's down to Clemson and Indiana really. I still could take visits to Marquette and Michigan, but I feel myself cooling on them. Then Bolden leans forward, and I see that old orneriness blaze up in his eyes. "That's what you came for? Talk schools? Boy, you got a family for that." He claps his hands in front of him, the way he used to in practice when he wanted guys to snap to attention. "Now go on and talk about what you want to talk about," he demands.

I take a deep breath. Every time I get around him, I'm a freshman again, head swimming. But then I remember all the things he and I have been through. And I remember that in the end—every time—Bolden had my back. I can ask the man what I want to ask him. "Why'd you up and quit on us?" I say.

That question drains all the fire from his face. He purses his lips and looks to the window, where the morning light peeks through the blinds. "I didn't quit on you," he says. "You always think you know the whole story with people." It's a crack at me, I guess, but his voice is softer than I've ever heard it. He shakes his head and looks at the floor. Then he motions, palm up, toward that dark hallway. His voice is barely above a whisper now. "My wife got sick, Derrick. People forget that players and coaches have lives away from the court, and most of the time that includes a woman who's holding the whole damn operation together all by herself. You realize I never even changed a diaper on our three kids? I was just off playing with the boys while she got them cleaned up, got them walking, got them to school, on to college. They're all grown now. Oldest has a family of her own. And I visit them and hold my grandbaby and I know all of that—the woman my daughter's become, the men my sons are becoming—is because of my wife. *Mary*,"

Kevin Waltman

he says, raising his voice on that as if her name is a golden truth I should always remember. "So last summer when the doctor told her she had cancer, it wasn't some *choice* I was making. The team didn't even factor in. It was time I stepped up and helped someone under this roof."

"Coach, I'm sorry," I say. "Is she—" But I trail off, lacking the courage to finish the question.

He raises her eyebrows. "Is she okay? Ha!" His laugh cracks the quiet like a gunshot. "She's good. Gonna outlive me. She's too damn competitive to die first. And she's sick of me hanging around the house worrying over her."

"Well, then come back to the Marion East gym."

He shakes his head again. There's a little smile, and I can tell he's flattered by the idea. But he's not having it. "I always swore when I retired, that was it. No comebacks for coaches. We can't have one foot on the platform and one foot on the train like all these athletes who don't know when to hang it up. I'm done." Then he raises an eyebrow at me, stares with that old hawkeye. "Besides, you ever think Coach Murphy might have something to say about that? It's his team now, you know."

I roll my eyes. Can't help it. I know from years of experience that kind of attitude gets under Coach's skin—but if he's not my coach, he can't make me run stairs anymore. "You know I like Murphy," I say. It's the truth still. He's a good guy. "But he's not *being* a coach. He's still just trying to pump guys up. That's cool, I guess, but it doesn't work if you're not around to drop the hammer."

From down the hallway, I hear someone stirring. I figure we ought to keep it down. Instead, Coach just stands and crosses to the kitchen. Opens a cupboard, pulls out a bag of coffee, and starts the machine going. When he's done, he leans on the kitchen counter, which opens out to the living room. "Drop the hammer?" he asks. "Was that all I was good for?" I start to explain, but he shakes his head. Just messing with me again. "Look, Derrick, you ever think that Murphy has his own style? I never expected that I'd hand the whistle over to him and he'd try to coach just like me. Bunch a different ways to run the show. Now that I'm done with it, I'm not even sure my way was the best."

I get it. He doesn't want to bad-mouth his old assistant. It's not like I actually expected Bolden to do anything. I know he's not stepping back in mid-season. But I thought maybe I could at least coax some of that old fire from him again. Maybe he could help me get my head right. "He's losing the team," I tell him. "We had a fight in practice the other week. Haven't won since."

Coach cocks his head at me. Behind him, the coffee machine starts to sputter and cough. "Now let me see. I think I recall a team that got in a fight in practice and still turned it around for the stretch run." He rubs his chin, pretends like he's trying to think back. Then he levels his eyes at me. Here it comes. The fire. "Oh, yeah. It was your team when you were a freshman. And it was you getting in the damn fight." He strides back out of the kitchen now, walks directly to my chair. He towers over me. "As far as the Marion East team this year, it's not really my problem anymore. But if it were" —he pauses, leans down—"I'd hope I had a senior leader who could come talk to the coach to get things straightened out."

There's my answer. The same answer I always got from Bolden— it's all my fault. The thing is, I kind of expected it would turn out this way. Hell, maybe I hoped it would. Maybe I needed someone to light a fire under me again.

He stands up straight again and takes a step back. His wife calls his name from down the hallway, asking about breakfast. Bolden points at the door. "Now hoof it, boy," he says. "I need to start on the food."

I do as I'm told. Marching orders.

But before I hit the door, he tells me to wait up. "Derrick," he says, "get it right. You don't, you'll never forgive yourself."

All I want is that last bell. For most kids, that means time to cut loose. Hit the streets. Hang with friends. Find trouble. For me, it's going to mean a chat with Coach Murphy. Long overdue.

But before last period, I get something else that's overdue. A glimpse of Wes. I'm shocked to see him, especially at school. At this point, he shows up only a few times a month. I wonder why he bothers at all. There he goes though, strutting down senior wing like he's some bad-ass. Thing is, in some circles of this city, that bullet wound—and the fact he kept his mouth shut about it—earns him mad respect.

"Wes," I shout. He keeps on. "Come on, Wes," I holler again. This time he recognizes my voice and stops. I jog down the hall to catch up.

Wes waits for me to get all the way there, refusing to budge to meet me halfway. "'Sup, D," he mumbles when I get close. I can tell by his eyes he must have smoked up at some point during the day. Or maybe that's just the way he *always* looks now.

Whatever. I press on. "Nothing's up," I say. "Just haven't seen you in a long time. We got to, like, catch up."

Wes snorts out a laugh. "If you say so." He turns his head and gazes down the hall, like he's in some hurry to get to a class he's failing.

"Wes," I plead. "It's me. I'm not trying to put anything on you. I just…" I trail off. What am I supposed to say? I've been in this spot countless times with Wes in the last couple years. I realize it at last—the way it finally hits a team that's down double digits with a minute left. It's never going to turn around. There's this distance between us, and no matter what I do it's just going to keep getting wider.

Wes hangs his head for a second. For all that strut and tough act, he looks so small right now he's like a middle schooler who wandered into Marion East by mistake. When he looks back up at me, he seems on the verge of tears. He knows it too—this is it. Maybe it snuck up on both of us. "I know you're not trying to mess with me," he says. His voice is soft, almost a whisper. "But let's be real, D. It's not like we can *catch up*. There are too many thing that have happened."

"That's what I mean, Wes," I say. I almost reach out to put my hand on his shoulder, but his body seems so tense I feel like a touch would shoot out sparks. "You got to at least talk to somebody about what happened."

At that, he sneers. "I ain't got to do a thing, D."

Around us, kids hustle to their classrooms. Teachers stand at their doors, ready to crack on kids who are even a millisecond late. The hallways thin out. The last bell rings. Wes and I are officially late for class, not that it matters at this point. "Why you even here, Wes?" I ask. "You've given up on everything else. Why even set foot in school?"

"I still got a chance to graduate if I can kill it this semester," he says.

Kevin Waltman

It's infuriating. Sad too. Wes can be cynical about the guy who used to be his best friend one second, then in the next breath say something so naïve he sounds as foolish as someone still believing in Santa. *Graduate?* He's missed so much time he's got a better chance of walking on the moon. There's no good to come from telling him that. So I nod, let it slide. "Then I guess I ought to let you get to class," I say.

Wes nods, but he doesn't leave. Neither do I. It's like we're both waiting for something better to come of the conversation, hoping that something will save our friendship. Nothing does. Instead, we just hear the clack of Principal Markey's heels coming down the hall. Time to split.

We start in opposite directions. Then Wes calls back to me. "D?" I turn to face him. He's got a smirk on his face, but it's not anger—just resignation. That look that so many kids get around here when they see that big dead end rushing up on them. "I know you've been trying with me. I just want you to know that no matter what happens, I appreciate that."

"It's all good," I say. "But, Wes, you gonna be all right?"

He laughs once—it's a sharp sound, like a door slamming shut. "Probably not, D. But I'll try."

·

Gibson sits beside me. By rights, it ought to be Fuller and Jones—they're seniors—but at this point it's pretty clear which guys are piloting our plane. Murphy sits across from us, smiling. With a few months to make it his own, he's spruced up what used to be Bolden's office. His desk has things scattered across it—an iPod and earbuds, a stopwatch, a whistle. A ball autographed by Magic Johnson perches on the corner. He's got a couple posters of old school ballers from back in his day—

Dominique depositing a dunk on the Celtics, Barkley back in his Sixers days. Then there's a guy in an old Mavs uniform I don't recognize. Neither does Gibson, and he points and asks, "Who dat?"

Murphy cranes his neck to see, then smirks. "*Dat*," he says, imitating Gibson's fake street-speak, "is Rolando Blackman."

"Rolando who?" Gibson asks.

"Blackman!" Murphy shouts. "The guy only dropped twenty a game for more than a decade. If there were any justice in the world, he'd be in the Hall of Fame!"

"I dunno, man," Gibson says. He's sporting a little grin now, egging Murphy on. "Looks like they ought to keep him out just on account of that nasty mustache."

Murphy almost has to gasp for air he's so worked up. "You make four All-Star games and you can look any damn way you want!" Then he kind of mutters to himself. "Crackin' on a baller because he had a mustache. Kids don't know nothin'."

I smile. Watching Murphy go off like this reminds me of a bus ride sophomore year, when he about fell out because Coach Bolden started talking up Larry Bird. Good times. I'd like to get back to that kind of vibe. Which, I remind myself, is why we're here. "Coach," I say, "Gibson and I wanted to talk to you about the team."

Murphy smiles, right back to his cheery demeanor. "Well, I figured you two were here for something other than a lesson on old school NBA."

Then he waits for us to put it on him. Suddenly, Gibson doesn't have a thing to say. It's one thing to bellyache about a coach behind his back. Another entirely to step up and say it to his face. Thing is, I feel it too. In a way, Murphy's optimism just makes it harder. It's like he's so upbeat, he thinks the next word's going to be another ray of sunshine. I almost hate to break the news to him that the season's going sour, even though it shouldn't be *news* at all. But it's my senior year. I'm not letting it crater just to spare Murphy's feelings. Time to rip off the Band-Aid.

"Coach, we don't have much time left in this season," I say. "And I don't want to waste any of it."

"I hear you," he says.

I shake my head. "I don't think you do," I say. "I mean, with all due respect, you jumped us harder about Rolando freakin' Blackman than you did about getting run by a team like Guerin."

Murphy offers me a real patient smile. He takes a breath and fiddles with the stuff on his desk, acting like all of a sudden he really needs to reorganize. "I know you're used to how Coach Bolden ran things," he says. "But I can't be him."

"I know that, but—" Murphy raises a hand to cut me off.

"Derrick, wait a second. I know you can take that kind of yelling, but some of the young guys can't. And I couldn't come out guns blazing on a guy like Jones. I have to let him know I'm on his side first. Do you see where I'm coming from?"

I'm about to answer, but Gibson beats me to it. "I feel you, Coach. But I'm new here and I figured if I half-assed things I'd get called on it. You don't have to act like a maniac, but you've got to yell sometimes. When you don't, it's like you don't care if we win or lose. This ain't intramurals, y'know I mean?"

I want to chime in too, but I realize that Gibson's said precisely what I've been feeling all season long.

Murphy's smile is gone. Very deliberately, he picks up that iPod and winds the earbud cords around it. But this time it's like he's doing that instead of strangling us. "I am well aware that this is not intramurals," he says. Then there's silence. He just stares at us. He might not have that old evil eye that Bolden did, but it's pretty clear we've struck a nerve. It feels like an eternity passes before he speaks again. "You got anything else to say?"

We both shake our heads.

Murphy points to the door. "Then I'll see you at practice tonight."

Murpy bides his time. He lets us get through warm-ups, then some walk-throughs against Pike's defensive sets. We run some inside-out drills, letting our bigs work on where to look when Pike doubles the post. Murphy lets us go through some help-and-recover drills even though they're kind of disastrous—Gibson keeps breaking down the defense so bad he either scores or nobody can get back to the shooters.

But when we start running fives, Murphy strikes. First trip down I take a quick one—not a bad look at all, a little pull-up from fifteen. It catches back iron and spins off, then Murpy's whistle pierces the air. He thumps his heel on the floor and yells. "What the hell, Derrick? One touch? We get one pass out of that possession and you jack one up?"

I bite my tongue. This—Murphy lacing into me after one missed shot—isn't what I had in mind when we met with him this morning. But fine. If this is what it takes to pump some life back into our team, I'll take it. "I hear you, Coach," I say.

"Okay," Murphy says, satisfied. "It's not a terrible shot, but you

Kevin Waltman

can get that whenever you want it. Make the defense work a little." Murphy's voice has come back down to a respectable decibel-level, and it seems like everything's going to smooth right back out. But there's a mumbling from near the rim, then a laugh—Xavier, talking nonsense to Jones. Murphy's on Xavier in a flash. "What's the big joke?" he asks, his voice still even.

Xavier smirks. He doesn't seem to realize he's dealing with a different Murphy tonight. "Just thought it was about time someone called out the great All-Stater for being a flick."

Murphy flat out *cracks*. "What the *fuck* do you know about it, Xavier?!" he screams. He closes the ground between them in three swift strides, getting right up in our freshman big man's grill. Xavier's got a couple inches on him, but all of a sudden you can remember that Murphy must have been a bit of a beast back in the day. "You know why Derrick's got a chance to be All-State?"

Xavier doesn't answer. He looks away, smirk still on his face, like this is all some big game. He even looks at my Uncle Kid like he expects some sympathy, but Kid just returns a stony stare. The rest of the gym is quiet as the grave.

"I asked you a question!" Murphy shouts.

Xavier rotates his head back toward Murphy now, looking a little indignant. "I guess because Derrick's *so talented*," he says, his voice dripping with sarcasm.

Murphy's eyes bug, but he starts out in an even tone. "Talent? Aw, that's part of it. But everyone in this gym is talented." He scans the whole team now, trying to make a larger point. "Derrick's not getting Big Ten offers just on talent. He's getting those things because when he was a freshman"—and here he turns back to Xavier, his voice rising in volume with each word—"he stayed after practice every day to work on his game instead of spending the whole season *being a lazy dumbass!*"

All that attitude in Xavier's face just drains out. Just like that, he goes to looking like any other scared freshman. He deserves this long overdue lecture, but all of a sudden I feel bad for him. It's never easy getting called out. And Murphy's not done.

"I've spent months trying to pump you up," he says. "Calling you *X-Man*, giving you your props every time you so much as make a gimme. I do that because you could be a real load for us. But instead you want to fuck around! You want to just *play* like we're in some church league. Well, this is big boy basketball, Xavier. And if you don't step up and work at it, you're gonna get left in the dust. All that line I ran after last game? *The second best thing is losing because it meant you were out there competing?* Well, that's only true if you've actually busted your ass. Otherwise, losing just means you got your damn teeth kicked in again."

As Murphy's hollered at him, Xavier's head has slowly lowered, so now his chin's almost on his chest. I realize, too late, that maybe Murphy's going too far—like he's been storing all this up since November and he just can't stop himself. Kid must realize it too, because he steps toward Xavier, offering a consoling hand on his shoulder. No dice. Our big freshman spins away. He walks off the court, heading for the locker room.

Now Murphy, his chest still heaving and his eyes still blazing, looks my way. He doesn't have to say a word for me to know what he means—I'm the one who wanted this, so I better step up. I know from experience not to wait. When I was a sophomore, I let Reynolds huff

Kevin Waltman

off in practice, and we almost lost him for good. And as much as I've bristled at Xavier's attitude, I know deep down we can't afford to lose him—he's the most gifted big man we've got.

I hustle over to meet Xavier just before he hits the locker room door. He doesn't want any part of what I'm bringing. "Out the way, D," he mutters. He reaches past me for the door.

I get up in his chest. Not rough—I don't want to start static again—but enough to knock him off his course. "Come on, Xavier. You don't want to do this."

"Hell I don't, D," he says. "I don't need that shit." He points angrily back toward the court, toward Murphy. But at least he's not headed for the locker room anymore. He's standing there, waiting for me to respond.

"Yeah, you do need it, man," I say. Xavier rolls his eyes and starts for the locker room again. I grab him by the elbow and he stops. "Listen, Xavier. You leave now you're walking out on your future. I know you don't want to hear it. But it's the truth. You walk out the doors to this gym and the world outside will kick your ass."

Xavier stares at me, considering it. Deep down he knows it's true. Anyone who goes to Marion East knows it's the truth—these are the easy years, even if they're a lot harder than we'd like them to be. I lower my voice now, try that same patient tone my parents use when the dust has finally settled after an argument. "Look, man. Between those lines on the court? You get second chances. All you got to do is walk back over there and jump in. Ain't a soul gonna think less of you. That's what teammates are for. We screw up and then we man up. But you walk the other way—?" I let my voice just trail off. He gets it.

Hesitantly, he takes a step back toward the court. I run ahead of him, give him a "Let's go now" like we're hustling back on D during a game. When I look back, Xavier's got his head down, legs churning. Atta boy.

Murphy's at least got the sense to let everyone shoot free throws. Let those raw nerves settle a bit. I trot over to the goal Gibson's shooting at, rebound for him while he works on his form. He smiles at me. "Well, we got our fireworks," he says.

I raise my eyebrows. "Damn," I say. "I thought maybe he'd get mad and have us run sprints or something. I didn't think we'd get that kind of show."

Gibson and I laugh a little, but we keep it quiet. We don't want to set off Murphy again. Kid must have been eavesdropping because now he strolls over.

"For real?" he asks. "You two *asked* Murphy to jack people up?"

Gibson and I glance at each other, then nod to answer Kid.

Kid shakes his head. "Aww, you guys don't even know," he says. "I played with Murphy for one year back in the day. Man was an *animal*. Fight you soon as look at you. This whole mellow thing he's got going? He had to work on that for years if he was ever gonna coach. You can't throw down at mid-court when you're supposed to be in charge of teenagers." Kid laughs to himself, then adds, "Now you two knuckleheads went and let the tiger out the cage."

Kid starts off again, but I follow him. I catch him at the hash mark, a safe distance from any of the buckets. Nobody can hear us, so it probably just seems like we're talking strategy for the Pike game Friday.

"Look, Kid," I say.

Kevin Waltman

That's all it takes. He smiles at me, pulls me in for a quick hug and pound. "Don't even go through it, D," he says. "We're family, man. Always will be."

"But that thing I said?"

He holds his hand up, stopping me again. "It hurt, but only because it was the truth. But, D, it's not like you told me something I didn't know. And it's not like I'm gonna hold my mistakes against you." Then he leans it toward me. "Listen, Derrick. We're good. We don't need to go through some big apology scene. You my boy, got it?"

We bump fists, and I feel a weight come off my shoulders. Being on the wrong side of Kid was a killer. He was always the guy—taking me to the park, working with me on my game, talking me down from bad losses. It's good to be back on the same page with him. Then I glance around the rest of the gym. I might be back in stride with Kid, but I don't know which direction the rest of these guys are going to head.

23.

For once, there's quiet at home. Kid's got Gracie again, so everyone's chilling. And I need it—Murphy hasn't let up all week. The man is a tornado now.

When I step in the room, Jayson raises his eyebrows from his play just for a second. He just nods at me, then goes back to it. I start prepping my bag for tonight—kicks and sweats and headphones. Then I lean back on my bed, trying to picture how it will go. This is a big one—Pike. They grabbed the Sectional championship last year when I was hurt. Then they went on and cruised through Regionals, only to get cut up by that Evansville Harrison machine at State.

But titles don't matter right now. What matters is they've got two studs—two more guys who were slotted above me by the *Star* way back when. Devin Drew and Scout Thurmond. Drew's their point. For real. Not a great shooter, but good enough. And he can match any guard in the state—except maybe Kernantz—quicks for quicks. Then Thurmond—a young guy, but big and rangy. At 6'6", he's got the height to bang it out down low. Sometimes he does just that—

snatching 9 boards a game doesn't happen by luck—but he loves to work on the perimeter. Loves to use that height to rise over people with his smooth J.

I feel like it ought to be me checking Drew. But I know Murphy's sticking with Gibson at the point now. I'll get a few looks against Thurmond, but he slots more at the three spot, meaning Fuller's the one with his hands full there. All I can do, I remind myself, is take care of my job—which means flat *owning* the match-up at the two. That doesn't mean I've got to drop 40. But I've got to shut my man down and cause enough nightmares on our end to open things up for everyone else.

Jayson finally lowers that script from his face and peers over at me. "What you doing?" he asks.

"Thinking about the game," I say.

"Well, try not to think about how you guys stunk up the gym last time out." I sit up and glare at Jayson. But I wouldn't have it any other way. The one thing I can always count on with Jayson is that he'll stir it up if he's got a chance. "For real," he says. "I don't want to waste my time watching games where a team half-asses it."

"Like you know anything about it!" I shout. He's got me worked up again.

I'm sure Jayson would keep on, heckling me about everything from my schools to my choice of music in my headphones. We get interrupted though by an explosion of noise in the living room. At first I think something's wrong, but then I hear a high-pitched squeal from my mom—girlish excitement I haven't heard from her in forever. Jayson and I both drop everything and head out.

When we reach the end of the hall, we see Uncle Kid still standing by the door. He's got Grace, in her car seat, in his hand. He gently bounces her up and down while Grace sleeps peacefully. Which means that whatever the excitement's about, it isn't focused on Kid and Grace. Then I hear Dad's voice. "It's just so good to see you, April."

April? Now *that* I didn't expect. I'd be readier to believe Fuller flushes one in Thurmond's grill tonight instead of the fact that April—Kid's ex—would show up at our house today. The family's only seen her once before—last year when Kid brought her by to show her off. And now, just like then, the whole house brightens. Mom immediately apologizes for the mess and starts darting around tidying up. Dad straightens up in an almost military posture, smiles like he just scratched off a winning lottery ticket.

But none of them top Jayson. He practically elbows me out of the way to walk up to April. He holds out his hand, says, "Can I take your coat?" April laughs, but she sheds her coat and folds it neatly into Jayson's arms like she's bestowing a gift.

"All right," Kid says, "can we just sit down and act normal?" He sets Grace's car seat down, unbuckles her and hands her to Mom. Then he hands Mom the squeaky bear too, which has now become like a safety valve for anyone holding Gracie. Grace starts to stir, but instead of crying she gives a big coo, on best behavior around April.

I'm excited to see her too. But I'm wary. Any time Kid walks in the door with good news, there's something bad trailing close behind it. That's bad to say, but it's what we've come to expect. Finally everyone sits down—except for Mom, who stands and bounces Grace—in the living room. I ease in between Kid and Jayson on the couch. Dad pulls up a kitchen chair, and he lets April have his recliner. Then we all just look at each other.

"Sooooo," April says. She glances nervously at Kid.

"Drinks!" he shouts. "You want something to drink?"

Kid stands in a hurry, but Dad, close to the kitchen, waves him off. He calls over his shoulder to tell April what we've got. But all the fuss just makes her look more uncomfortable. After repeatedly telling my dad she's fine, she accepts a glass of ice water.

Finally Mom just cuts to the chase. She shifts Grace to one arm and leans in toward April. "So you really want to give this guy another chance?" she asks, pointing to Kid. We all laugh, relieved that the question that's been on everyone's mind has finally been asked.

April raises her eyebrows and looks at Kid again. She measures him, like she's only now been introduced to the idea that there's something not totally perfect about the guy. "Well," she says, "we kept bumping into each other at a lunch spot near where I work. At first I thought Grace was his, and I realized how jealous I was. Made me think maybe there was something still there. So we talked a few times. And maybe we can call this some kind of probationary period."

Now Jayson finds his old attitude again. "Ah, Kid, knows all about probation, right?"

"*Jayson!*" Mom and Dad seethe in unison. Dad walks across the living room to hand April her water and apologizes to Kid.

Kid just smiles. "It's okay, big brother. I got this one." He slaps both hands down on his knees and rubs them back and forth a few times like he's trying to warm himself up. "It's not like my history's a secret. And there aren't gonna be any secrets anymore anyway. No lies."

He looks at April again, his face as earnest as I've ever seen it. "I messed it all up trying to be someone I'm not. I'm finished with that."

April nods. She's obviously run through this all with him already. "I told him I don't need anything fancy. I've got my own money." I remember now that she's a nurse at Methodist, which around here puts her in a pretty high tax bracket. "So I have no problem dating a guy who's a bartender." Then she throws one more meaningful look at Kid. "I do have a problem dating a guy I can't trust."

Kid doesn't even blink at the dig. Instead, he just cocks his head. "Hey now. I'm not just a bartender. I'm a basketball coach too."

"And a really damn good one," I chime in. Mom and Dad raise their eyebrows at me. Any other time I'd get cracked on for that *damn*—as long as I'm under their roof, they'd remind me—but they let it slide, not wanting to harsh the mood.

"He's also a grade-A babysitter," Dad adds. Then, suddenly embarrassed, he backtracks. "I'm not saying that matters to you. I mean, it *matters*, of course. I just mean I'm not trying to say that's what you're interested in, April. I mean, maybe you are, but—" Finally, he just stops. He looks at Mom. "Bail me out here?"

Mom shakes her head. She just gives April a look, like, *Men! What can you do?* They share a little laugh, but then Mom shifts her attention back to Kid. "Speaking of babysitting," she says, "I get it now. Here I thought you were taking Grace out of the kindness of your heart. But, Kid, you were taking my baby to help pick up women. You were, weren't you?"

I can't tell if Mom's genuinely angry or not, but a hush falls over the room while we wait on Kid's reply. Used to be, I could count on

Kevin Waltman

him to evade the question, but he just got finished professing how all honest and true he is now.

Kid clears his throat. "I was absolutely not using Grace to pick up women," he declares. Then he looks at April. "I was using Grace to pick up April."

Laughter all around. With that, Kid wins the day. And I can turn my attention again to who will win tonight.

Pike's got some swagger. Any team trotting out a 18-1 record would. But they just saunter between the lines, jawing and juking, like they own this place. And Thurmond's the worst. He stops to yap a couple times with fans in the front row. I can't tell what he's saying, but it's not like he's wishing them a happy new year. He wasn't even eligible last year. Grades. But he's pretty full of himself now.

The more I watch him, the angrier I get. Gibson feels it too. He takes a break from warming up and stands next to me by our hashmark. "We got to shut that mug up and send him home with an L."

"I feel that," I say.

Then Thurmond trots out toward half-court. He spots us eyeing him. Sneers. Mouths something at us. While I can't make it all out, the one thing that's pretty obvious is an f-bomb.

"Aw, hell no, he didn't just do that," Gibson says.

"He most definitely did," I say. Then I watch as Devin Drew, Pike's senior point guard, races out to corral Thurmond before any real static can start. Thurmond's no big fan of that either. He swats Drew's hand away, then stares us down a few seconds more before returning to warm-ups. Thing is, he's big and bad enough to act that way. 6'6" and cut up. Got that menacing look too—the kind you don't want to see on your block late at night. He'll ink high major someday if he can keep his wits enough to make it that far.

We get through the rest of warm-ups without incident. Then starting line-ups. Even then, Thurmond gets people riled. He struts out to mid-court, head bobbing. He claps his hands rhythmically, then stomps the last few steps. When our crowd boos, he just motions for them to get louder. They do just want he wants, and he eats it up, grinning and laughing. Not even a tick off the clock yet, and it's war.

When the orange goes up, Thurmond doesn't waste any time making his mark. Pike controls and Thurmond races right down to the block. Drew finds him quick. He spins—gets that chicken wing out to seal Fuller, but there's no call. He flushes one with some flourish, giving a big yell—"Aaaaaaaaahhhhhh!" Then, trotting back on D, he lets it rip again—"Aaaaaaahhhhh!" Then more clapping, more foot stomping.

I've been around the block a few times. I've seen these acts. What this guy really wants is for us to take the bait. Get emotional. Try to show out on him. But that's not what we need to do. Best way to handle some fool like Thurmond is to stay cool. Gibson knows it too, because he's in no rush to bring it up. And when he crosses mid-court he just motions to the rest of us—a little pat in the air with his hand, like, *We cool. No hurry.*

Gibson bounces to me on the wing. I look to Jones low, but there's nothing. Back out top to Fuller. A reversal to Gibson. He drives middle on Drew, but can't get a look. It's enough to draw some help though, and I take advantage. I float to the baseline and Gibson finds me. A quick J from fifteen finds bottom and we're all tied up.

Kevin Waltman

That seems to settle everyone a little. I see Fuller take a deep breath and hustle back to check Thurmond. Even through his protective mask, I can read that expression on Fuller. He's ready to dig in. But Thurmond rides him down to the post and—when the refs aren't paying attention—gives Fuller a big shove with his elbow. The crowd catches what the refs miss. They point and scream for a foul, but there's no whistle coming. It's exactly what Thurmond wants—more turmoil. He claps his hands emphatically and bobs his head. But when Fuller comes back to check him again, Thurmond's all business—he gets those feet set and posts up like a pro. I can tell right then Thurmond will be a handful all night—both between the lines and between our ears.

We're in the locker room for halftime. It's been tight throughout, but Pike finished on a little spurt to take a 30-26 lead into the break. All anyone can talk about is Thurmond.

"Can't believe they haven't caught any of that garbage," Reynolds gripes. He checked in mid-way through the first and caught a stray Thurmond-elbow about twenty seconds in.

"It's like he fouls so much they can't call everything or he'd be gone in five minutes," Gibson says. "But, man, that kid is out of control."

"Already got welts from those 'bows," Xavier says.

"It's bush league stuff too," Jones says. "I mean, yeah, all those elbows. But he keeps stepping on my feet when I'm going up for a rebound. Driving me crazy."

Everyone looks to Fuller, expecting him to chime in. Instead, he just sits at his locker, shoulders slumped. He's taken off his mask and it dangles from his hand as he stares into space. The look is part fatigue and part frustration, both of them simmering toward anger.

"You okay, Fuller?" I ask.

He shakes his head slowly. "I'd be okay," he says, "if I could get a stop on that kid to shut him the hell up." He lifts that mask up like he's going to fling it across the room. But he stops short, just grabbing it with both hands and shaking it like the whole ordeal is its fault. This is about as emotional as I've ever seen Fuller. It makes me burn against Thurmond. He hasn't done anything to me but offer a crack about me being nothing but a spot-up shooter, but at this point I hate him on Fuller's behalf.

"Hey!" Murphy yells, his voice knifing through the locker room. He's got that fire in his eyes that hasn't gone out since the moment Gibson and I left his office. "You're all hurt because some sophomore thug is swinging elbows and talking shit. But you're so busy worrying about him, you're losing the game that matters. We've stopped helping on Drew's drives. We're losing shooters on the perimeter. We're getting worked on the boards." He stops, his chest heaving from the effort. He glances over at Kid, checking to see if he's got anything to add.

Kid steps forward. "We've all been there, boys. But nobody's going to shut Thurmond up for you. Only way to get revenge is on the scoreboard."

After that, Murphy diagrams a few sets for us. He shows us how they've beaten us a few times, then gives us a new offensive entry to start the second half. Then he gives us a few minutes just to catch our breath before we head back out to the court.

As soon as we exit the locker room, Thurmond's at it again. He

Kevin Waltman

glares from Pike's end of the floor. Then he saunters out toward mid-court to get my attention. I know I should just ignore him, but I can't help myself. "What?" I snap.

He smiles. All cocky. "Man, my boy Drew told me you had some quicks to you. I ain't seen none of that. You just any other shooter. Ain't no D-Bow here no more."

I feel my blood rise. I know he wants me to lose my cool, so I just take the hit and remember what Kid said—only way to hurt him is to beat him.

Soon enough, we're back to live action. We have the ball first. We use that entry Murphy drew up. It's a slick little ball screen for Gibson out top while Jones and Fuller double for me. All the action is going toward my side, but it empties out the lane for Xavier to slip that ball screen. It works like a charm and Gibson bounces it to Xavier right in rhythm. Only Thurmond isn't about to let us start the half with a dunk. He peels off of Fuller late and flat *hammers* Xavier at the rim.

Xavier goes down hard, landing on his shoulder. The refs jump in immediately, but it doesn't stop everyone from stepping up to Thurmond. But all it amounts to is some chest-puffing and jawing. The refs separate the players. They check to see if Xavier's all right. And then they call a regular foul on Thurmond. No flagrant, no nothing. Just his second whistle, same as a hand-check out top.

Our crowd goes nuts. They're screaming for him to be tossed, hurling obscenities at the refs. I glance at my family and see Jayson stomping his feet on the stands. He walks down the aisle a couple rows and I think he's about to storm the floor—but he's just trying to get a few feet closer to the refs so they can hear him.

Then I look at Thurmond. That smile again.

All we can do is play through it. Xavier splits the pair to make it a three-point game. And then the noise *really* starts. Murphy's not the only coach to draw up a special at half—Pike comes down and throws a new set at us. Sure enough, it ends with Thurmond popping free to the rim. Fuller hustles to challenge, but all he does is get a face full of Thurmond as he throws down a nasty dunk. He hangs on the rim for a second—just a hair short of what the refs would whistle for a tech—then draws his knees up into Fuller's face. Fuller falls back and his mask goes flying down to the baseline.

This time it's Murphy who loses his cool. He's almost to mid-court, stomping his feet and gesturing at the refs to call something on Thurmond. He gets a whistle all right—a big fat technical for leaving the coach's box.

The crowd starts throwing things—plastic water bottles, wadded up popcorn bags, whatever they can get their hands on. It's an ugly scene. A tornado swirling around Thurmond who's finally accomplished his goals. When the dust finally settles, Drew walks to the line to sink the technical free throws. Then, on the in-bounds, he shakes Gibson and drains a fifteen-footer. It's a six-point possession, and suddenly we're down 36-27, all out of sorts.

The boos rain down as Gibson walks the ball up. I know they're not directed at us, but I can't take it—this kind of scene in the Marion East gym. Four years I've busted it here, and it seems like everything is falling apart around me. Then there's Thurmond—nodding and clapping, nodding and clapping.

Gibson enters to me on the wing, and I don't even think. I

Kevin Waltman

just catch and—*boom, gone*. Drew flashes at me, but I dart toward the baseline. Then it's a power dribble toward the rim, with Thurmond racing over to challenge. I explode toward the rim, Thurmond rising with me.

I keep rising, head near the rim. I cock back the rock. Then I put that thing right in Thurmond's grill. A moment later, I land. I hear the whistle for the and-one. And I hear the crowd erupt—it's a wild, guttural scream from all corners of the gym. Pure release for seeing someone finally give Thurmond his.

Thurmond tries shrugging it off, walking along the baseline and shaking his head. I follow him. I don't have to say a word. Just a long staredown to let him know who's boss. A ref comes over to pull me away, and I let him. No sense in getting T'd up now. And only then do I realize it—I was so in the flow that I wasn't even conscious of what I was doing. That rip past my man? That rise up and over Thurmond? All those old quicks, all that old burst. It's back. *I'm* back.

The roar of the crowd keeps rolling down in waves. It subsides just for a few seconds while I drain the freebie, then swells again. We're still down six, but our people *feel* it.

After Drew brings it up, they get it to Thurmond on the short corner—a step beyond his range. He's got a wild look in his eyes, frantic to show out after getting punked on the other end. He lowers his head, puts it on the deck baseline. Fuller just flicks at the rock, taps it off Thurmond's knee and out of bounds. Our crowd loves it. And I see Fuller chirp just a little at Thurmond. Unable to take his own medicine, Thurmond wheels toward Fuller and gives him a quick shove. Finally, the refs catch him. It's an automatic T. And a quick trip to the pine for

Thurmond. Just a few seconds ago, it was the home crowd losing its cool, but now—heading to the bench—it's Thurmond boiling over. When his coach gets in his ear, he pulls away from him. Shouts over his shoulder as he hulks away. A few teammates get up to calm him down, but he just keeps jawing. And our crowd loves the whole show, riding him mercilessly.

Our comeback is just as merciless. I drain the technical freebies. Then, when we enter it and I catch on the wing, all I have to do is lean—just a slight shudder toward the baseline—and my man jumps like he's been electrocuted. Amazing what a rip and throwdown will do to the D. It gives me all the space I need to launch a trey. Money. Trims the lead to one.

Pike calls a timeout, but there's nothing that can stop our run. They come out and turn it over again, then Gibson draws and dishes to Xavier for a deuce. Then it's a Fuller leaner from twelve. A Jones turnaround from the block. Gibson with a pick and run-out for another deuce. Even Reynolds pops off the bench and promptly drops a three from the corner.

Drew does his best to keep his boys in it, but he's a one-man show. Thurmond comes back off the bench and misses three straight shots. And we're lights out. By the end of the third quarter we've left them in the dust.

Kevin Waltman

24.

After that Pike game, we just keep mashing. We ride up to Logansport
and win by a cool dozen. Sweep Northridge and Howe in a weekend
tournament. Ring in February by hammering Speedway by 35.

It's not just the Ws or even the margins of victory. It's the way
we're winning. We started slow against Howe and were behind by a
deuce at the end of the first. Aside from that, we haven't trailed for a
second. It's like that ball goes up and the boys in Marion East colors
ain't even *playin'*. Just jumping on people from the first tick until triple
zeroes.

My personal stats are popping too. I'm dropping 25 a game, but
I'm taking fewer shots to do it. That rediscovered burst is getting me
to the line, getting me easy looks at the rim. And it's made life easier
for everyone. Suddenly, it's not just Gibson who can rip it past people.
We've got two killer guards out top. With both of us turning ankles, the
looks from other spots come so easy my *dad* could step out there and
ring up ten a game.

The state is on notice. Our recaps in the *Star* are getting a little more attention every time out. But it's not that rag that matters. It's the word around the city. A month ago people were wondering what was wrong with Marion East. Now they're talking about us like we're the high school version of the Golden State Warriors. They call us the D Day Invasion, or the Double D Show, or they just say what the owner of Ty's Tower told me last time I poked my head in there—"D-Bow and D-Train! Best backcourt in this state since Jay Edwards and Lyndon Jones." I had to ask him who those kids were, and he just smiled. "Before your time, son. Before your time. Let's just say you and Gibson keep it up, they'll be comparing people to you thirty years from now."

That's not the only notice that's going on. Since I'm still uncommitted, the recruiting game has gone crazy. Every day I power my phone back up as I walk home from school and scroll through the texts. Today, there are thirty of them. All those schools who cooled on me when I went down are pretty breathless now. I walk toward Patton and check the list—Ohio State, Oklahoma, Iowa.

Delete. Delete. Delete.

Then, when I get home, I head to my room and take the time to text back to Clemson and Indiana. I can feel them getting nervous. They thought they had the inside track, but they're not fools—they know other schools want to scoop me up from them.

I've got a few minutes of privacy to rest on my bed and gather my thoughts. Then there's a knock at the door. Kid.

"You don't get enough of me at practice you gotta hang with me here too?" I say.

Kid knows I'm messing, but he gets that old hang-dog look of his. "Sorry, D," he says. "I don't mean to be all up in your business."

I just wave him in and tell him it's no problem. When he steps into the room though, he looks even more uncomfortable. There's nowhere to sit, but I can tell it's not just that. "Spill it, man," I say.

Kid takes a deep breath. "I just wanted you to know that the offers keep coming."

"What now?" I ask, but I sit up on my bed a little. There's something about the way he says it that makes me think he's taken something. He's made a turnaround, but you never know when that old shady Kid will rear his head.

He laughs, almost to himself. "You been tearin' it up pretty good, D. It's like the moment you started trusting that knee again, every athletic department in the country found a little more juice in their bank accounts. I mean, you're getting Mr. Basketball hype now."

I swell with the compliment. Mr. Basketball from an Indianapolis Public School? I know Trey Lyles won it out of Arsenal Tech a few years ago, but before that you have to go *waaaay* back. But before I start daydreaming too much about that, I come back to Kid. He never really answered the question. "So," I say, "what is it now?"

"A car. A long stack of green to go with it."

"You take it?" I ask. It's pretty blunt, but I'm tired of dancing around the question.

Kid shakes his head. "Nah, D. Come *on*. We been down that road already."

"Who offered?"

"Does it matter?"

I don't have to answer that one. He knows it doesn't make a bit of difference. But, like always, part of me itches to know. And, like always, part of me wants to jump at it. If they're throwing a ride and cash to my uncle, what else could I milk them for? What if, just once, I took the easy way? Got mine while I can, like Moose told me? But I let it go. I've learned that the easy path doesn't stay easy for long. Hell, it would get hard fast the moment my folks found out.

That itch lingers for a while, and so does Kid. He's still standing near my doorway, shifting from one foot to the other. Finally he looks at me again. "That's not why I came in," he says.

Now I'm worried something's *really* off. I figured his shiftiness was just about being tempted by a hand-out. I spring off my bed and stand in front of him. He's leaning a little, so I actually look down at him a tad. "Spill it, man."

He straightens at my tone, showing off that he's still got a half-inch on me no matter how grown I get. "Aw, man, you always suspect me," he says. "I just came in to say I'm packing up and moving out."

Kid coming in to admit he's in trouble. Fessing up that he took some dirty money from a booster. Even something stupid like using up the last of the coffee before Mom and Dad had theirs. Those are the things I've come to expect from Kid when he has something to admit. Certainly not that he's stepping up and moving back to a place of his own. And, suddenly, I feel his absence in advance. It's not like he's even been around that much, but there's always the pillows and blankets—sometimes folded neatly, other times wadded in heaps on the floor—by the couch to remind us he's staying here. That knowledge that Kid is still here has turned out to be comfortable—like throwing on a ratty old sweatshirt on a cold Sunday morning. I know now that I'll miss the guy. But I also know I can't let him see that. No self-respecting man is going

Kevin Waltman

to tell another grown man he'll *miss* him. Instead, I scrunch up my face and shake my head. "Well, it's about time, man. Give me some elbow room around this place for once."

Kid laughs. "I figured you'd say that."

I lay it on even thicker. "What are you, fifty now? Finally stepping out on your own?"

"Easy," Kid says, acting all hurt. Then he puffs his chest out. "I'm a long way from fifty. And even when I get there I'll still run your scrawny ass."

Then we both laugh, knowing that his days of running me are long gone. "For real," I say, "where you gonna be?"

He tells me it's a small place just off of Central. Cheap. Probably pretty sketch. But it's something he can afford honestly. "And," he adds, "if things go according to plan, I'll be spending most of my time at April's anyway." He raises his eyebrows at me a few times for effect.

Then there's a holler from down the hall. Dinner's on. We open my door and head toward the bustle of the house. Dad and Jayson bickering about something silly while they set the table. Gracie whimpering in Mom's arms. The background chatter of the T.V. Jayson forgot to turn off. As we approach, Kid slaps me once on the back. "Hey, D," he says, "I'ma miss you too."

It's a Sunday morning. We're fresh off thumping Bowman Academy and then putting away Zionsville on the road late. A fine weekend. Which means by all rights I should be able to skip church and sleep in for once, rest my muscles. Maybe knock out some homework before vegging out in front of the feature Big Ten game.

Dad's got other plans. I wake to him shaking my shoulder. It feels impossibly early, but when I peep at the clock it's pushing 7:00. Still, the rest of the house is sleeping—even Gracie—so Dad puts a finger to his lips to remind me to be quiet. Then he whispers to me to get dressed and come with him. I slip out of bed and throw on some old clothes piled on the floor. When I hit the living room, looking pretty scraggly, Dad pops up off the couch, ready to roll. He's shaved and showered, wearing clothes fit for service. But I know we're not heading to church this early. Through my sleep fog, I begin to wonder what in the world is up with him. Just as we're about to leave—door open just an inch and the February air bristling in—the first cry from Gracie floats down the hall. I look at Dad. He waits for a second. Doesn't hear another cry. "Come on," he says, and he's out the door so fast he could have ripped it past me on the deck.

I'm too tired to ask Dad any questions yet, so I just lean back and let him drive. He heads over to Keystone, then north. I figure I know where he's headed—The Donut Shop, his time-worn favorite. But he stops a few blocks short of that, then hangs a left into a shopping plaza. Finally, I have to ask. "What's up, Dad?"

He smiles at me. "Nothing's *up*, Derrick," he says. "Just, with Gracie and basketball and recruiting trips and everything, it's been a long time since you and I have been able to just sit down and talk."

Oh, man. It must be bad. You know when someone wants to *sit down and talk*—especially if that someone is a girlfriend or a parent—there's a storm about to hit. Dad parks, then points to a façade of the strip mall, where the word "DELI" appears in red, capital letters. "There we are," he says.

I trudge to the place, hunching my shoulders against the cold February morning. When I get inside, I relax a little. It's a classic Dad spot. A greasy dive. Already, the place is nearly packed, everyone from disheveled college kids to old men grumbling about politics. There are people decked for church grabbing a bite before service, a few young couples staring longingly at each other over steaming cups of coffee. Young, old, black, white, brown—it's a mix of Indy at the tables. The place is loud with conversation and the clatter of pots and pans in the kitchen. The walls are plastered in pennants from Indiana teams, and behind us where we wait in line is a larger-than-life black and white of Frank Sinatra and JFK.

I can tell without even looking that you'll be able to get a full belly in this place for about five or six bucks—the number one quality a restaurant can have in my dad's book. After a few minutes we're at a table near the window, waiting on pancakes and sausage and hash browns. Even though I'm more relaxed now, I still wonder what's going on. Dad's clearly got something on his mind. He's content to make small talk until the food arrives—what do I think about Kid moving out, how do I think the Pacers will fare in the playoffs. Then, when they slap those heaping plates in front of us, he pauses with his fork in the air. "Things are going pretty well for you, aren't they, Derrick?" he asks.

"Yeah, I guess so," I say. I don't want to say anything too definitive. This has to be building to some kind of lesson.

Dad slurps some coffee down, then encourages me. "You guess so? Come on. You guys are on a roll. You've got every college in the country begging you to come. I think that warrants more than an *I guess so.*"

"Okay, sure," I say, still tentative. "But I don't want to get too full of myself. We still have Sectionals. Hopefully Regionals and State after that. These wins now don't mean a thing."

Dad smiles, nods. He keeps nodding as he chews on some pancake, as if I've just offered him some deep and penetrating truth. When he's done, he looks me in the eye. "You've got a good head on your shoulders, Derrick. That's not exactly common for guys in your position. You realize that, don't you?"

"I guess," I say again. Here it comes, I think. This is where it turns into some rundown of how I've screwed up. Maybe I've neglected chores at home? Haven't fussed over Gracie enough? I don't know what, but it's coming.

Dad must sense my expectations because he shakes his head. He puts his fork down on his plate. "Relax, Derrick," he says. "You're making me feel guilty here. I know your mom and I are tough, but I swear this isn't some chance for me to come down on you."

"What is it then?" I say at last, a little exasperated. It comes out a bit loud, but with the noise of the place swirling around us, nobody seems to notice.

Dad slumps down and shakes his head. Now he actually *is* a little mad since I've raised my voice at him. He rattles the next words off at me quick. "I wanted to take you to a nice breakfast to tell you how proud I am of you for being a stand-up guy in a game where it's a lot easier to do just the opposite. I wanted to tell you that I hope this season ends up with a championship, because if any player in the world deserves it, it's you." Then he pauses, sighs. "But it seems like you'd actually *prefer* it for me to be a little angry with you, so you can be happy now."

244 Kevin Waltman

After that, we both eat in silence for a while. But suddenly I've lost my appetite. I take a few bites, then just push my plate away. "Thanks, Dad," I say. "I'm sorry I ruined the whole thing."

He offers a little ironic laugh. "Don't sweat it," he says. "The truth is I'm worse at giving compliments than you are at taking them. It's a Bowen curse, so get used to messing up nice moments for the rest of your life."

He reaches over and pats me on the back once. Then he points to my plate, urging me to eat—God forbid I don't finish every bite of a breakfast that didn't even cost him a Jackson. But I do as I'm told. And the two Bowen men do something we *are* good at—shut up and crush some good eats.

25.

Ben Davis, our floor. Senior night. Last game before the playoffs.

Pre-game, they parade the seniors out. It's me and Jones and Fuller, accompanied by family. As a baller, you're not supposed to get emotional. I *hate* it when I see guys crying on the bench when they lose in the tournament. I mean, man up a little. But as we're drowned in cheers, I take a quick glimpse at my classmates. Next to him, Fuller's mom and dad are just flat-out crying—tears streaming down their faces. She leans over and kisses her boy on his cheek, and I see Fuller's eyes get a little glassy. Jones only has his mom there with him, and I can tell from one glance she's a tough one—tall and wiry, got that hard edge to her that Jones wishes he had. But when he bends down and gives her a bear hug, I see her melt a little. She doesn't cry like Fuller's parents, but she looks down at the floor for a second, takes a deep breath to steady herself.

Then I feel it—my mom reaches over and curls her fingers around my hand. It's just us. With Kid on the bench, it would have left Jayson in charge of Gracie and he begged off of that duty. So Dad's in the stands, holding her. There's something that gets to me about Mom holding my

Kevin Waltman

hand, and out of nowhere I start welling up. I do just like Jones' mom—look down quick like there's something real interesting on my kicks. I swipe my free hand across my face to erase any tell-tale signs. Take a breath to gather myself. Then I turn and look down at my mom. She's decked out for this one. She's got on a red dress and heels, even went to the hairdresser this afternoon to do it up right. I remember what Dad said the other morning about Bowen men always ruining nice moments. So for once I forget about trying to act all swole on the court. I lean down and hug Mom tight—who cares if I look a little sappy? You only get one senior night.

Into my chest, she shudders once with emotion. Then I hear her, even through the crowd noise. "You got grown fast, boy," she says. "Way too fast."

And then that's it. We escort our moms back to the stands, and re-join our teammates on the bench. "Glad that's over with," Gibson says to me. "Like a damn chick flick out there. Let's get back to ball." He's kidding, but only a little. I think about how much he bristled against his folks on my brief visit. I make a little mental note—if my college schedule lets me, I'll have to get back to the Marion East gym for next year's senior night just so I can watch the mighty D-Train get all teary-eyed between his parents.

But he's right about one thing. It's back to ball. Murphy's got a few seconds for last-ditch instructions, then we're at center court for tip. I still feel a little raw from that moment with my mom, and I remember that these things can go two different ways. Sometimes a team gets all amped up for something like senior night and they just steamroll the team on the other bench. Other times, the emotions get too much and they lose their edge.

That ball goes up and Jones springs after it, getting about three extra inches on his normal vertical. He taps it to Gibson who races ahead. A quick dish to Fuller on the wing. Shot fake and go. The defense collapses, losing sight of everyone else. I crash toward the rim for a possible rebound, but at the last moment Fuller eyes me. Instead of a shot, he lofts up a perfect lob—right at rim level.

I pluck that thing from the air and even have time to cock it back with my right hand before hammering it home.

Just so everyone knows—*that's* how this senior night emotion is going to play out.

Ben Davis is no joke, but we treated them like one. We got it all rolling. I loosened up the D with some bombs from range, then we got Jones and Xavier making noise in the post. Reynolds popped off the bench to give me a spell and didn't miss a beat—drained a trey and then got a teardrop runner to find home for a hoop-and-harm.

By mid-third all that mattered was getting the seniors some love. I'd already had a highlight reel, so Gibson made a concerted effort to get the other seniors theirs. He made sure to tell me so at a dead ball—didn't want me thinking he was up to his old game of freezing me out. He just wanted to be sure that Jones and Fuller got some senior night buckets too. And they sure enough did. Gibson started carving up that D with drives and dropping dimes—Fuller from fifteen, Jones for a dunk, Fuller on a slash to the rim, Jones on a pick-and-roll. Then came the icing. Gibson turned his man inside out and knifed into the lane, then backed it out even though he had a look—setting up Fuller for an easy back-door and throwdown at the third quarter buzzer. Crowd went *insane*.

Kevin Waltman

Murphy sent the starters back out there for the beginning of the fourth, even though we were up 23 at that point. But it was just for effect. First dead ball, he subbed Reynolds in for Fuller. Standing O as Fuller trotted to the bench for the last time on his home court. Next dead ball Jones got the love. Then he waited an extra minute for me. A couple chances to sub me out passed, and I realized he was giving me time to drop one last deuce in front of the home crowd. I hunted a dunk, but by then the Ben Davis D pinched into the paint as soon as I so much as leaned toward the lane. So instead, I got a nice look at a pull-up from sixteen. Two points just the same. And I held that follow through for a few seconds, savoring it. I wanted it etched in my mind—the rock finding bottom, the lull in the sound of the crowd before they reacted to the shot, the big men all jostling for position with their necks craned to follow the ball. Even Gibson. He had one arm raised in premature celebration, that old cocky smirk on his face—a look that used to make me tremble with anger when it was directed at me but now it felt just right.

Next buzzer, I was done. And the crowd thundered out their approval. I took my time walking off, pumping a fist for them. But by then I wasn't caught up in the senior night emotion anymore. I was already hungry for Sectionals at Pike.

Now, it's Lia time. We're at her place, alone. But instead of getting busy from the drop, we just hang on her couch and chill for a while. Things have been so crazy we don't even feel like we get a chance anymore. Growing up, I always thought ballers got all the girls. And it's true, I guess—if last year I had been just another junior shuffling through Marion East instead of some blue chip recruit, no way would Lia Stone have looked my way. But if ball gets you female attention, the games and practices and recruiting visits and bus rides and team meetings mean you get a lot less time to spend with a girl once you get her.

I look at Lia sitting on her couch. The lamp beside her casts a harsh light and it makes her look older, a little tired. She gives a weak smile and reaches for an old blue blanket behind her. She curls her knees up and smoothes the blanket across her. The pose pushes her back away from me a little, her knees and feet like a barrier I can't cross. Suddenly I wonder what Lia would say about basketball and *boyfriends*. Chances are she'd say ballers aren't all they're cracked up to be.

"Lia, I'm sorry it's been such a mess with me," I say. "This season's gonna be done soon, and then—"

"Then you'll be packing your bags for some other place," she cracks. It takes the wind out of my apology. She senses it, reaches over and pats my arm—but it's a brittle motion, no real warmth behind it. "I didn't mean it that way," she adds. "You know I've got to give you a hard time about it."

We've had the T.V. on, but we're not really watching it. Just some low level noise in the background. The news, which now switches to sports. Instinctively, I start to watch the highlights from the action around the state—but I catch myself. I reach for the remote, wedged between the cushions and click off the set. "It doesn't have to be like that," I say. "I could pretty easily end up in Bloomington next year. You could be with me as much as you want."

Lia smiles and shakes her head. "You say that, but—" She lets it trail off. A couple times she starts to talk but catches herself. The sound comes out like a gasp instead. Finally, she stands. Lets the blanket just

Kevin Waltman

slide off her legs to the floor. She's above me now, a chance to look down at me. I gaze up at her and shudder a little at how hot she is, even now. I just can't help myself with her. She senses it and moves closer. Tempting me. I could reach up, grab her hips, pull her into me. She leans down, putting her hands on either side of my head, her lips close while she whispers.

"There are other schools within driving distance, you know," she says. She leans in that last inch and gives my ear a little bite.

I can't stop my hand from running up and down her leg now. My heart is pounding so loud I can feel it in my temples. "Uh huh," I groan. "I'm listening."

Then she says it. A Kentucky school. It doesn't matter which one really. *Not* interested. I give a quick laugh. Then I lean into her, kiss her neck. "You crazy, girl," I say. "You know not a thing in this world could make me go there."

Just like that she stiffens and backs away. "Not a thing in the world. Including me," she says. She folds her arms across her chest. "I knew it. I told them you wouldn't go for it."

Now it's my turn to tense up. I pop off the couch, my pulse racing with leftover lust and a sudden anger. Lia flinches beneath me and I remember how big I am next to her, realize the scowl I must have on my face. I soften my stance and take a step back, but I still ask. "Told *who?*"

"Those coaches. Or not coaches, I guess. A booster or whatever." She hangs her head, unable to look at me.

"They were trying to use *you* to get me there?" I ask.

She looks up again, eyebrows pinched down. Outside a car rolls past slow. Its lights wash across the windows, and the bass thump rattles the walls. But it's not that noise that threatens to shake the place apart. "You don't have to act like the idea's *that* ridiculous," Lia says. Pure ice.

"I didn't mean *that*," I say. "It's just, what? Were they offering you something?"

She nods. She unclasps those arms from her chest and slumps her shoulders. She walks to the chair—her dad's chair—and sinks into it, defeated. "They said they could get me in there. Make it work with admissions or some bullshit like that. Or if not they'd get me set up with some stupid job in the athletic department." She shakes her head, angry at her own actions. Then she rolls her eyes. "God knows what they would have given you."

There's not much to say then. I keep waiting for her to get up, shake it off. In some ways, nothing has changed between us. We're right where we were before she brought the whole thing up. If anything, I just make myself a vow to take it to that school when I get a chance, revenge for playing dirty with Lia. Stupidly, I say, "We're okay, Lia. It doesn't change anything."

She glares at me from the chair. "It changes *everything*."

"Because I won't go where you want me to?"

She shakes her head slightly, but keeps that glare on me. It's like she blames me for what the school did. "No. Because every time I look at you I'm going to remember what this makes me feel like."

I take a quick inventory. I want to remember this place. That threadbare couch and the old blue blankets. The lamp on the nightstand that wobbles. That old T.V. that must be from before Lia was born. Her Dad's chair, its cracked brown leather. And I try to forget the

Kevin Waltman

person sitting in it, at least like she is now. I close my eyes and think about how she looked when she flirted with me at that party junior year. Or the way she laughed when we were out having fun. And, sure, the way she peered at me as she led me out of this room toward hers. Because I know without asking this is the last time I'll be over here, and I don't want the image of her now—tucked into a ball on the chair, too ashamed to even look at me—to be the one that sticks.

Like I said, there are no promises Senior Night will go the way people hope.

26.

We lost enough early in the season to get a tough Sectional draw. After a grinder against Lawrence North, we feed straight into Pike, who's rested after a blowout of Roncalli. And at home. And still smarting from the whipping we gave them a few weeks ago.

During warm-ups, it's clear our boy Scout Thurmond has learned his lesson. He doesn't so much as *think* about talking smack. Doesn't even glance at our end of the court. When that ball goes up though, we've got a whole different problem than some sophomore punk getting loud—Devin Drew means business. He's a senior, intent on showing why he's one of the best points in the state and why he's good enough to sign with Illinois. That dream I've got of cutting down the nets as my exit move? Yeah. Drew's got the same dream.

He chases down the opening tap and races ahead. Throws a crossover at Gibson and then loses him on a spin. Pull up from seventeen is wet. Next time it's pure speed—right past Gibson and to the rack before any big can get over to challenge. Then he just gets nasty. He sees an outlet and races into the frontcourt like he wants a pull-up from range. When Gibson comes to check him, he gives a false

Kevin Waltman

step and ducks past. Gibson's good enough to check even that—but he's not good enough to recover on Drew's ridiculous step-back. It creates enough space for a look at a three—and of course it falls. That gives Pike an early 7-2 edge. Murphy pops off that bench like he sat on a tack. Calls time.

What needs to be said has nothing to do with Xs and Os. So before we hit the bench, I get next to Gibson. "You got this," I say.

"I know," he seethes.

He's angry—at getting turned inside-out by Drew. But nobody likes to get a lecture a mid-court so I let him get to the huddle before I get in his ear again. "For real," I tell him. "You *got* this." I point toward the other bench. "Drew's good. And he's feeling it. Home crowd. Knows they bounced us from Sectionals last year. He's *real* comfortable."

Gibson nods. He takes a big swig of water and slams the bottle down at his feet. "You telling me things I already know, D."

"Well, make him *uncomfortable,*" I say. "Remind Drew that you got some quicks too. Show him that when the D-Train's coming he best step off the tracks."

Gibson can't help but smile at that.

Murphy draws something up in the huddle. He probably thinks it's a great play. But when we hit the deck, we start to run his set and then I get a touch on the wing and stop. I wave Gibson over to me and we run a little hand-off. Then I just empty out the side. Let Gibson solo up Drew for a change. He gives a couple rhythm bounces, then— *poof*—he's gone like it's a magic trick. Drew recovers late, but all he can do is hack at Gibson before he gets a shot off. Foul. First on Drew.

We set up for the inbounds. From the bench, Murphy signals for us to run our #3 entry—a way to get Xavier free on the blocks. But again when I get a touch, I set up Gibson. Oh, I give a look Xavier's way, but ain't no way in the world I'm giving him the pill. We get it to Gibson, clear out again. This time, he starts right like before. When Drew jumps it, Gibson whips the rock behind his back and knifes into the lane. Drew just lets him go. Doesn't want that second whistle this early. It's an easy path to the rim for Gibson to silence the crowd.

Then Gibson jumps Drew full court. Now, no way is Gibson going to pick it from him, but the look on Drew's face is enough—he's annoyed that he's not getting a free inch of hardwood. Angry that some white point guard he'd never heard of before the season has the brass to challenge him on his home court. He's just as uncomfortable as we could ever hope for.

Thurmond is tame. The one time he gets a little puffed up after a rebound bucket, I jog down the court next to him. "You mouth off, I'm-a put one in your grill again," I say. And it's like if he can't talk trash he can't do anything else either—can't make a shot, can't keep track of Fuller on the other end, can't be anything more than a mediocre forward getting worked over when it counts.

And Drew gets reckless. By early second half, he's pretty sure that he's going to have to play savior. So he turns into a flick. He gets some to fall, but it basically freezes out his teammates. And he doesn't get *enough* to fall to keep them in the game.

We just keep coming at them. Fuller keeps losing Thurmond for mid-range Js. Gibson keeps turning Drew's ankles. Our bigs get busy on the blocks. And I get mine. No big show-out like last time. Just this steady drumbeat—a leaner from the foul line, a spot-and-shoot from eighteen, a put-back of a Jones miss. Bucket. Bucket. Bucket.

By early fourth, we've stretched out a 59-40 lead. The Pike crowd stays, hoping for a miracle that will never come. But they're quiet. All you can hear is our crowd living it up. Getting louder with each Pike miss, every shot we bottom out. The last few minutes feel like a long coronation. Marion East as Sectional champs. As it should be.

We let it loose at the buzzer. Xavier runs to Murphy and hugs him, lifting our coach a foot off the ground. Kid hops up on the bench and waves a towel around, pointing to our crowd. He's acting like he's been out there on the boards, but I say let the man do his thing. And the rest of us woof and holler. We keep it to each other, except Fuller. He hunts up Thurmond as he's sulking away. "Yap now, big boy! Yap now!" Thurmond tenses once like he's going to stop and throw down. Drew doubles back to grab Thurmond and stop any drama. Then Fuller turns around to celebrate with the rest of us. Hugs. High fives. Some dancing. Then we line up and take turns on the ladder to snip down the nets. All the stuff you get to do as champions.

But by the time we hit the locker room, we're settled down. Guys are still laughing and hollering, but nobody's acting like we just won the NBA crown. Murphy says a few words to tell us he's proud, but he senses it too. "Look, guys," he says at last. "A month ago I didn't know if we'd get this far. But now that we're here—" He breaks off his sentence and looks around. Everyone stops in the middle of peeling off socks and jerseys or joking around with the guy next to them. They give Murphy their undivided attention. Then he starts again. "Now that we're here, I don't see a single damn reason to stop at a Sectional championship." He stomps his foot on the locker room floor. "I'm talking about a Regional championship! I'm talking about more than that. I'm talking about Marion East as the Indiana state champs!"

And that draws the biggest celebration from his players all night.

Someone must have given Hamilton Academy the same speech. It's only fitting they're the ones standing between us and State. My first two years, they were the alpha dog in Indiana—stocked full of high major talent, with back-to-back undefeated seasons until we clipped them my sophomore year. And they're the school who wanted me to transfer so bad when I was a freshman. It's like every time I see them, I'm seeing some alternate version of my basketball life—and I can't let the alternate version turn out better than the real one.

But of course it's them—the Hamilton Academy Giants. We both cruised through the opener in Regionals and now we're warming up across from each other in Hinkle Fieldhouse—the most storied court of all Indiana courts. They've got a nice balanced team—shooters at every spot, some size on the blocks. It's Kalif Trueblood who's the standout. Like Thurmond from Pike, he's a 6'6" sophomore. But where Thurmond was all muscle, Trueblood's pure silk. He's got leaps, but finishes with finger rolls more often than jams. Has a crazy array of leaners and pull-ups and turnarounds. And his range? If he's in the same zip code as the bucket, you better challenge.

As soon as the tip goes up, it's clear we're in for more of a dog fight than we had against Pike. Sure, Pike jumped on us early, but it was just the Devin Drew show. We slowed him down and that was that. Hamilton Academy is more than Trueblood. Their first touch, they zip it around at a fast clip—a schooled and patient team. Every guy who touches offers fakes, looks to the post, then finds the open man. When Trueblood catches and beats Fuller baseline, our whole team sinks down to help. He just rifles a cross-court pass to an open shooter on the baseline. Bang. 3-0.

But the biggest difference between them and Pike is on the defensive end. Pike you could catch napping. Not these guys. It's like they share a brain. They're always in ball-you-man alignment. Always help on drivers, but never over-commit like we did. Their bigs aren't special, but they've got the footwork to keep from getting sealed by Jones and Xavier. And they put Trueblood on me. I could take him, but it's not like I can just turn that rangy kid inside out like I do other guys. We work and work, but can't get a look. Finally, Gibson tries a runner from fifteen—a shot he can make, but a real tough take. It scrapes, Hamilton corrals, and they patiently set up again.

As the first half wears on, we get more and more frustrated. Even when we get open looks, we're so worn down from the effort to get loose that they come off flat. And with each miss you can feel our crowd deflate. They started the game at a fever pitch, but now they're just sitting there. If anything, we can some disgruntled hollers of bad advice—*Get out and run,* they yell, or *Shoot the three,* never mind that you've got to get clean stops to run, and you've got to get open looks before you fire off treys.

We head to the locker room discouraged. It's only a seven-point gap—25-18—but it feels like a lot more. We're just not used to being held to 18 points in a half. As soon as that locker room door swings open, guys start griping. They can't help it. There's no finger-pointing, but just about everyone wants to point out to Gibson and me that they're getting open.

"Just get me some touches," Xavier complains. "I can take my man."

"They're losing sight of me all the time," Fuller says. "Just watch for me on the wing."

Gibson starts to point out that neither one of those statements is entirely true. He looks at me for some support, and I jump in. "Look, I've been here against these guys before," I say. "We've got to stay patient."

Now it's Jones. He roars in disapproval. "Patient?! Shit. We get any more patient, we'll be stuck on eighteen points until next season!"

At the front of the locker room, Murphy offers two loud claps. "Keep it together!" he yells. "Let's not go back to who we were in January. We're frustrated, but we're gonna fix this." Then he nods toward Uncle Kid.

Kid steps forward. The man with the plan. But as he starts to speak he sounds a little nervous. "Now, they've got Trueblood on Derrick," he says. "That means we can't, you know, just flatten out and expect Derrick to save us, right?" He glances around the locker room like he wants an answer. But people just stare. Kid coughs once, then starts to slump his shoulders in that old shifty Kid pose. He needs some support.

"Then what do we do?" I ask. It comes out unintentionally sarcastic, the opposite of how I wanted to sound. Kid stares at me, hurt. "I mean it, Coach," I say. "Tell us what to do. We trust you."

Kevin Waltman

That's all Kid needs. He smiles. He claps his hands in front of him and starts striding around the locker room while he talks. Looking guys in the eye. "Now, listen! We *know* we're a better offensive team than what we showed. We have the best damn backcourt in the state. We've got big nastys in the post. We've got shooters on the wings. The problem's not the players. It's the offense." He jabs his finger back toward the court. "They're too disciplined for what we've been running. They've watched some film on us, boys. So the new offense is simple." He huffs a big breath, a touch winded from pacing around. Then he straightens up, nods his head as he speaks. "Screen for Derrick," he says.

After all that build-up, we were expecting more. Guys hang on, waiting for some added explanation. When it doesn't come, they all lean back in their chairs, disappointed. The grand plan amounts to everyone working to get me open. Jones voices what everyone else is thinking. "For real? Season's on the line, and your whole plan is try to get Derrick open."

Murphy steps back in, standing up for his assistant. "*For real,*" he says. "Thing is, you pups forget Kid and I been around a little. This will work." He leans forward and repeats it for emphasis. "This *will* work."

We get to test it out right away. Our ball first, and Gibson brings it into the frontcourt. I widen to the wing, Trueblood plastered to me. Then the screens start coming. A back screen from Jones. A down screen from Xavier. Another back screen from Fuller.

And Trueblood glides past each one. Forget me getting buckets. This offense doesn't even get me open. Even if Trueblood trails for a step, Hamilton reads it and hedges to stop me. They're not going to get fooled by an offense that just funnels the rock to one guy.

But right then, I hear a sharp shout from out top. "Ball! Ball *now!*" It's Gibson, demanding the pill from Xavier. From the look in his eye though, it's not because he's just going to solo, try and go all D-Train. No. The kid sees something. Xavier bounces it his way, and then everyone stands for a second. Gibson yells at us. "Go!" he shouts. "Screen for D!"

Well, if Hamilton Academy had any confusion about our plan, it's cleared up now. Our point guard just announced it to the whole damn gym. But guys do as they're told. It's Fuller first. He comes for a cross screen. I try to set Trueblood up—jabbing baseline before rubbing past Fuller toward the foul line. But it barely gets me a step. And Fuller's man helps out just to discourage any look my way. And *zip*. Gibson puts a *laser* into Fuller's mitts. He catches at fifteen and pauses, surprised at how open he is. He's still got time to re-set and launch. It rattles around and rolls home.

Instinctively, everyone looks toward our coaches. There Murphy and Kid sit. They just nod at us. Kid nods a little more emphatically, like, *See, I know what the hell I'm doing.*

Oh, that next trip down the floor *everyone's* eager to "Screen for D." Because we're no fools. The plan's not to get me open. It's to get Hamilton jumping and helping so the screener gets open looks. Baby, those looks are *abundant*. Jones slips to the paint for a dunk. Xavier faces from ten. Fuller frees himself again. Reynolds checks in and promptly buries an open trey. Then, when Hamilton Academy is really turned in circles, Gibson just knifes through everyone for a sweet scoop shot in the paint.

Of course, it's not like Hamilton Academy forgets how to shoot on their end. They keep sniping away from range. And Trueblood starts turning Fuller inside out. But it's driving them crazy that they can't stop us. And the kicker is that we're using their own best instincts—help defense—against them. Kid's a genius.

By end of the third we've doubled our first-half production. We're still down 40-36, but they're feeling the pressure. As we break the huddle for the fourth, I glance down at their bench. Their coaches are worked up. All decked out in coat and tie, they're demonstrating how they want their players to defend. They flash their hands in one direction, then shuffle fast the other way, their hard soles clacking on the hardwood. Even from my vantage point, I know the lesson—they're reminding their players they've got to recover to the guys they're guarding after they help on me. I shake my head. You can't have it both ways. If they're worried about recovering, that means any help shading my way is just show.

We get our first possession down five after they split a pair at the line. Gibson lasers one to Fuller just like he did to get our run started, but this time Fuller catches with a hand right in his face.

Gibson and I share a quick look. We both know it—all those easy buckets are gone. Time for us to show that we really are the best back-court in the state. The first test is to see what Trueblood's really got on D. I've been flaring to the perimeter on every screen, trying to draw the defense further from the bucket. But next chance I get, I curl tight around a screen from Xavier. Gibson puts it on me in rhythm and I keep rolling right to the rim. I feel Trueblood close behind me, so I shield him away with my body and float one up left-handed. It drops, but a left-handed scoop in traffic isn't exactly something we want to turn into a steady diet.

On the other end, Hamilton Academy stays patient. They work through Trueblood. He backs Fuller down until Jones has to help. Then Trueblood shuffles one to the open man—but not before Xavier jumps the passing lane. Our ball, down three. We don't have numbers, so it's a half-court set again. This time Gibson finds me again off a screen. I try driving baseline, but Trueblood cuts it off—time for the other half of this back-court to shine. I dribble back top and run a little hand-off with Gibson. He rubs shoulders as he catches it, making his man trail—and no matter how much Hamilton preaches help defense, Trueblood doesn't want to leave me. That gives Gibson a head of steam at the rim. He takes advantage, beating a big to the rim. Gibson can't get the finish, but he gets the whistle. Steps to the line and sinks two to cut it to one.

Our crowd rises as we trot back on defense. They've been vocal this whole comeback, but now they taste it. Stop here and we've got a chance for the lead. Trueblood shuts them up fast. He catches on the right wing. Jab steps. One dribble right. Then between his legs to get back behind the stripe for a three over Fuller. A sick, sick, sick move. Back to four.

And that's how it goes for most of the fourth. Gibson and I trade off hoops on our end, then Trueblood answers for Hamilton. With a few minutes left, Hamilton has basically abandoned that whole team-first philosophy—they get the rock and just flatten out for Trueblood, who keeps singeing the nets.

With a minute and change left, it's 53-50. Dead ball, Hamilton Academy possession. Murphy calls time. Most of the year we've spent time-outs zoning out on what Murphy tells us, but there's no shortage of attention now. We're locked in. This is do or die, season on the line. He lets us catch our breath, then leans in. "Look, we can get the buckets we need to win," he says. "We need stops. D-Bow, you switch onto Trueblood." I nod. Even Fuller nods. The guy's got all the heart in the world, but he knows he just can't check Trueblood. Murphy claps his hands, demanding our attention back. "Here's the thing, D. When I say you got him, I mean *you*. We can't help off their shooters. You got to check that kid straight up. You got it?"

"Straight," I say.

Then we break.

It's not like it's some puzzle for Hamilton to figure out. They bounce it in to Trueblood, and there I am. He sizes me up. I see a little grin on his face. He *wants* this match-up. Just like I would have wanted to square up against an All-State senior when I was a sophomore. He waves his teammates down to the baseline. He wants to solo me up just like he's been doing with Fuller. His coach calls from the sideline that there's no hurry, to work the clock, but Trueblood isn't having it. He dribbles toward me and I get into him at a few feet outside the stripe—no way do I want him getting a look at a three, no matter how deep. He gives a little bump with his hip. Nothing big. Just wants to see how much strength I have. Then he gets down to business. Steps back. Shudders right, then crosses left. Hard. I jump to cut him off, but he lowers his shoulder to edge past. All his long frame is crouched down now, and I know what's coming. He takes one more dribble to get to about fifteen feet then explodes for a pull-up. His frame extends and he gets serious lift.

So do I. And I meet him right up top on his shot. When I get a piece of the rock, I hear the crowd gasp. They didn't think I had that kind of jump left in me.

Fuller scoops up the loose ball—because Fuller gets every loose ball everywhere. He doesn't waste time. He throws a long pass ahead to me. Trueblood's trailing me, and their point is back. I could rip it to the rim. But I didn't work on my jumper for four years to let this opportunity pass. I set my feet and let fly. Wet. Tie game with just under a minute left.

Our crowd roars. Murphy and Kid are both stomping their feet and pumping their fists. The whole bench is screaming for us to get one last stop.

Hamilton Academy pushes into the frontcourt and then slows up. Their coach leaps to his feet, index finger in the air—one shot. They go ahead and get it to Trueblood out top, but he just dribbles near mid-court. Milking clock. I go out to challenge, but every time I get that five-count close, he gets enough space to reset. Twenty seconds to go. Ten. Six. Everyone in the gym gets on their feet. Winning time. One way or another.

Trueblood attacks. A lightning-fast rip to his right. But I match him quicks for quicks. He picks up his dribble at twenty feet out. My hand right in his grill. And at last he shows he's a sophomore. Instead of calling for time, he panics. His eyes go wide and he floats a cross-courter for their point guard. Gibson reads that thing so easy the Hamilton crowd groans while the pass is still in the air.

Then it's just D-Train time. He plucks it clean. Glances at the clock. Two ticks left. For mortals, that's just enough time for a dribble and a desperation heave. But for Gibson, that's an eternity. He races all the way to the rim. Floats that baby up just a hair before the buzzer. And it falls—true—as the horn sounds.

Our crowd goes berserk. They storm the Hinkle floor, spilling out the stands in streams. The place is a sea of rocking red and green. In the madness, I find Gibson. "They gotta know to get off the tracks!" I shout at him. He just hugs me in return. Then there's a mass of arms around us—Jones, Fuller, Reynolds, Xavier. Then it's Kid and Murphy piling in too. All the bench guys. But this time we don't even wait for the locker room to get the message out.

"Enjoy it, boys," Murphy yells. "But remember! We ain't finished! You hear me? We're not done until we're the last team standing!"

We all hoot and holler at that. So do some fans who overhear.

Evansville Harrison better lace 'em up.

27.

The days creep. It's like each one lasts a week. Every day at school is a pep rally, the school more worked up than if a Jay-Z show broke out in our auditorium. And each day I come home and I can't even bear to think about idling through dinner, through homework, through channel surfing. Even my parents—who have always tried to keep everyone reined in on hoops mania—can't take the wait. Every night, they try to steer the conversation to something else—politics, weather, how Kid's doing at his new place, anything. But after a few minutes it always fails and we're back to the only topic anyone's kicking around this week. Can we corral Kernantz? Can we keep Scotty Sims in check? Can we actually do what nobody's done in a year and a half—beat Evansville Harrison?

Those answers are yes, I know. In fact, what people forget is that the last team to crack that Evansville Harrison code was us—last year right before I got hurt. Granted, they've taken it up a notch or ten since then. And they tore us up pretty good earlier this season. But we've got ourselves cranked up too.

Whatever. The talking is pointless. My family knows it too. So tonight, like every night this week, we exhaust the topic, and then I sigh with impatience. "We'll find out in a couple nights," I say.

Jayson nods. "You'll get 'em," he says. Then he starts clearing dishes and humming out a song. All nervous energy. "You *gotta* get 'em," he says, but it's like he's trying to convince himself.

After he's helped wash dishes, Dad changes into his work clothes and takes off for a night shift. Mom gets Gracie settled to sleep in her swing. Then she calls a friend on the phone. Jayson and I chill in front of the tube, volume low so we don't disturb Grace. There's not a thing on worth watching, but we're way too antsy to go back to our rooms and crack books for school. Mom emerges from her room to announce that she's going down the street. "Ms. Taylor needs some eggs." She holds up a carton of eggs as if it's proof of testimony. She pulls on her coat and starts for the door.

Jayson grunts at her, barely paying attention. Then, just as she puts her key in the door, he almost leaps off the couch. "Mom!" he whisper-shouts. "What about Gracie?" He points frantically toward the swing in the kitchen, as if Mom had forgotten about her daughter's existence.

Mom fixes a cold stare on Jayson. "She's asleep, Jayson. And if I can't count on you two to take care of a sleeping baby for two minutes so I can leave the house—for once in longer than I care to remember—without her in my arms, then we have got some problems." She pauses for effect. "Do we have some problems, Jayson?"

"No, Mom," he says. He turns back to the T.V.

Then Mom turns to me. "If she wakes up, just get her squeaky bear out," she says. "She likes that. And if that doesn't work—Lord save me for saying this—just try to do what Kid would do with her."

I tell her we got this, and then she's out the door. As soon as it's shut behind her, I feel that same dread Jayson does. *What if Gracie wakes up?* I did say we got this, but now it seems a little like the way a nervous freshman talks about clutch free throws right before he bricks a pair. I glance over at Gracie in her swing. She seems so peaceful. How can I be this scared of a three-month old?

I whisper to Jayson that I'm going to get a Coke from the kitchen, and I ask if he wants one. He just shakes his head *no*, refusing even to whisper for fear of waking the baby. I edge past Grace, my eyes on her as I walk. Burglars have nothing on me for how gingerly I'm stepping. If she so much as breathes quickly, I stop. Wait for her to return to normal.

And then I take one big step right onto that squeaky bear, left like a trap on the kitchen floor. Under my weight it gives off a long, high whistle like a tea kettle. Before I even have time to form my lips into a *shhh*, Grace is awake. And howling.

Jayson races into the kitchen, panic on his face. "What the holy shit, D?" he says. "What are you doing?"

I start to explain that I didn't mean to wake her up, but her cries get so loud that they knife right through our argument. *Waaaa. Wa-aa-aa-aaaaaaah!* "Okay," I shout. "We can do this. Get her out of the swing and we'll rock her!"

Jayson crouches down to unbuckle her. He's shushing and telling her everything's all right and trying to fumble through a song Kid sings to her all at the same time. But he's rattled by the cries. He can't get her

Kevin Waltman

undone. After a few seconds of trying, he looks up at me. "How do you get her out of this thing?!"

I bend down. With Grace screaming at us, we maul the thing. We're careful not to hurt her, but we're like two dogs just pawing around. Finally, through sheer luck, one of us hits the right button and the buckle comes undone. Jayson scoops her up and starts to rock her. He supports her head and bounces her gently, just like Mom has demonstrated a million times. But by now we've hit full-bore Grace-fit. She's shaking with her cries, face red, eyes squinched up in pain.

"What do we do, D?" Jayson asks.

I gaze around helplessly. Her cries come so fast that it rattles me. I feel an icy panic spread through my body.

"D?" Jayson keeps saying, getting angry at me for not responding.

Finally, I remember the culprit that started all this. That bear. I scoop it up and present it to her. I smile, all calm now. "Here you go, Gracie," I say. Then I squeak it a few times for her.

The squeaks startle her out of her cries. She looks at it. Then she shudders in Jayson's arms and starts crying again. Even louder now.

"Good one, D," Jayson snipes. "That helped."

"I don't need you getting mad at me," I say. I keep my voice level so I don't scare Gracie even more, but I feel my own temper rising too. Somehow, I want all this to be Jayson's fault. I know that's crazy, but it's how I feel right then. "Bounce her a little more gently."

That really angers Jayson. A darkness flashes across his face. He just stops. He's gentle with Gracie, but he holds her out to me. "You try," he says flatly.

I take her. She's screaming and shaking, but I hold her as gently as if I were picking up an active bomb. Jayson turns away from me and huffs back to the couch. His shoulders rise a few times with deep breaths, but then he comes back. "I'm sorry," he says. He has to raise his voice now just to be heard over Gracie. "We can't get mad at each other. That just makes it worse for her."

I nod emphatically. Meanwhile, I start rocking Gracie by doing deep knee bends. She's still howling pretty good, but it seems to help. Then I remember what Kid always does, so I give her quick pats on her bottom while I bounce her. That helps a little too, but we're a long ways from getting her settled. "Where do they keep the pacifiers?" I ask Jayson.

He nods in recognition, then walks to a drawer in the kitchen. He rummages around, plucks out an orange pacifier that came home with her from the hospital. He starts washing it. I'm about to get angry with him again for wasting time, but I know he's just trying to be safe with his little sister. He finishes. I stop my bouncing so Jayson can offer it to her. She doesn't take it at first, but Jayson coos to her a little and keeps gently pushing it into her mouth until she latches on. That stops the crying, but she still whimpers and shakes even as she sucks on the pacifier. We're not home yet.

I look at Jayson and raise my eyebrows. *Any ideas?*

Jayson starts to say something, then stops himself.

"What are you thinking?"

He shakes his head. "Nah. Mom'll be home soon."

"Jayson," I say, "we can't just count on her to save us. I don't want her walking back in on some disaster. We need to step up for her."

He sighs. "Okay," he says. "This is when they usually change her diaper."

Kevin Waltman

We go about it silently and solemnly. We're like white people driving through a bad part of town late at night—sure that any word or sudden motion will bring disaster. Jayson spreads a towel on the couch, then puts the new diaper on top of it. I start to put Gracie down, but as soon as I do she spits out the pacifier and starts crying. I snatch it from mid-air, put it back in her mouth and resume bouncing. I look at Jayson. He nods, knowing the deal—we're going to have to change her while I hold her. I slow my bounces to long, methodical motions, so Jayson can keep time with me. I hold her with her head back against my belly and her legs toward Jayson. With all of us bobbing rhythmically, Jayson unsnaps her clothes, then undoes the diaper. He holds his breath and pulls it off. We both exhale with relief to see it's just wet. "Thank God," Jayson whispers. Then he sets back to work. He wraps the new diaper around her, but gets it on backward. It takes him a few seconds to figure it out, but finally he gets it on right. Then he snaps her clothes back up. Job done.

By now, Gracie's pretty calm. I cradle her in my arms again and go back to the knee bends—slow and not so deep now. She looks up at me with those startling, wide eyes and locks onto mine. I run a thumb across her tiny cheek. Jayson hovers over her too, and her eyes shift over to his face. He smiles at her then, softly, starts to sing the song that Kid always sings to her to get her to sleep. It's a stupid oldie. Some Sam Cooke song that Jayson always makes fun of—but now, it turns out, he knows every word. He keeps singing. I keep bouncing. And, at last, Gracie's eyelids flutter and she's asleep, peaceful as can be.

"Think we can get her back in the swing?" Jayson whispers.

"Let's give it a shot."

I nestle her into the seat. She starts to stir, but I pat her from underneath the seat, just like I've seen Kid do a hundred times. Jayson snaps the buckles back together like an old pro, and we turn it on. Then, for a few seconds, we just watch her swing. We're attentive to any possible motion, any disturbance. But when it becomes clear we've actually done it, we look at each other. Big smiles. I silently pump my fist in the air as if I've just sunk a game-winner. Jayson heads back toward the couch, stepping well clear of that squeaky bear that's ended up on the floor again. I follow him. Once we're away from Gracie, he turns to me. He's still whispering, but he says, "I am the *man*, D! And *you* the man too!"

I'm about to respond in kind, but a different voice floats our way. "Oh, you two are big men all right," it says. We look, and there's Mom standing by the door, coat slung over her arm.

Jayson's face falls into disbelief. "For real?" he asks. "How long you been there?"

Mom stifles a laugh. "Long enough to see you get religious over a diaper."

Now Jayson's all indignant. "You could have *helped* us," he says. "You just stood there and watched us struggle?"

Mom hangs her coat up. She steps into the room and plops down on the couch. She smiles at Jayson again. "You're right. I did. But if I stepped in and bailed you out, you wouldn't feel so proud now, would you?" She waits for Jayson to respond, but for once he's got nothing to say. She pats the cushion next to her and Jayson sits beside her. She gives his arm a squeeze. "You and Derrick were my babies first," she says. "And I'll always be there if you *really* need me. But, hey, what you

Kevin Waltman

two just did? That tells me you're grown up way more than anything else ever could." She looks at me now. "You keep wondering why your Dad and I always make you do things the right way even when it's harder? It's so you can be the kind of man you can feel good about being. Nothing more than that. And I saw you two. You feel pretty good about yourselves right now, don't you?"

Again, we don't have anything to say to that. Because, again, Mom's right.

Mom was right that taking care of a baby takes more of a man than winning a basketball game. But that's not what I feel in my heart as we sit in the locker room of Bankers Life Fieldhouse. Crowd filling the seats in the arena. Clock out there ticking toward game time. My teammates buzzing about me. Suiting up. Getting taped. Talking trash.

What it feels like is this. Everything—my whole life—has led to this moment. And I know I'll have more games somewhere else someday, but it feels like this is the *only* game. Like Evansville Harrison is the *only* opponent I'll ever face. Like my entire career will be judged by the next two hours. If the past few years have taught me anything, it's that there are more important things than hoops. I've seen my uncle lose his car and apartment because of nonsense. I've seen my dad laid up from a car wreck. I've seen my career almost go up in flames because of an injury. I've seen my coach—the hardest driving guy I've ever known—walk away from it because his wife got sick. I've seen my best friend almost get himself killed. And I've seen my baby sister get born. I know, in my head, that all those things are more important than life between the lines. But I run out of that tunnel into the bright lights. Hear that band blast our fight song. See the swirl of colors in the stands. And in my gut it feels like this game matters more than anything else in the world.

Everyone's pulse is running a little fast. For once, instead of trying to amp guys up, I take a couple seconds at mid-court just to gather myself. I don't want to burn up all my energy in warm-ups. I glance toward the other end. There's Kernantz, Sims, the Evansville Harrison juggernaut. I know this about hoops, too—there are no promises. No destiny. Maybe people wearing Marion East gear think the universe *owes* us this game or something. But the people in Evansville Harrison gear think just the opposite. In reality, the universe doesn't care. All you've got is thirty-eight minutes to make history bend your way.

I hunt up Fuller and Jones. We stand off by the hashmark in a little triangle. Murphy gave us the emotional pre-game speech about laying it all out there. We've been through so many battles together, there's not a whole lot left to say. "Whatever happens now, it's been a ride," I tell them.

Jones sneers at me. "Don't go getting all soft," he says. "None of this *Whatever happens now* crap. We gonna run these fools."

Fuller nods emphatically. He gives Jones a fist bump, then offers his fist to me. I show him some love, but I can feel these guys are a little over-hyped. I try again to ease them down a notch. "I know we gonna run them," I say, "but we play like we've always played. It's just one more basketball game. That's all. Let's be the senior leaders and stay cool, alright?"

That meets with approval from Jones. "Aight," he says. "I feel that."

But then he leaves our little huddle and promptly snatches up a ball and fires a twenty-footer. It falls and he hollers for everyone to hear. "Rain! All night long! Let's get this!"

Murphy comes out on the court, making his rounds. He gets to me and wraps an arm around my shoulders. "Last one, D-Bow!" he shouts.

I give a little laugh. "You just sayin' that because you'll be glad to have me out of your hair."

Murphy shakes his head. "No way, baby. I know it took us a while to click, but I've never wished away the best guard in the state."

I look him in the eye and serious up for a second. "You're a good coach, Murphy," I tell him. But then I scan the floor with him. I can feel the energy rippling off our guys. Too much. It's not just Jones trying shots from outside his range. It's almost everyone. So I turn back to Murphy. "You might have to be a great one tonight."

Pretty soon there's no more time for talking. The clock hits zeroes. The place hushes for the anthem. Then erupts as they announce starting line-ups. I told myself last night that I'd soak it all in, remember every last detail, but it's like time races ahead at double speed. Everything's a blur until I hear my name—last time as a member of Marion East. I explode off the bench and race to mid-court. A quick handshake with Kernantz. The crowd in a frenzy around us. The T.V. lights shining down. The recruiters packing the place to peep the talent. The cheerleaders kicking their legs high. Then a mob of my teammates, jumping up and down in unison. I'm in the middle hollering "Game time!" like I always do, nobody can hear a thing at this point. We break, and then the place settles down while the starters walk to mid-court.

Then the ball goes up. It is *so on*.

Evansville Harrison controls the tip. Immediately Kernantz starts probing our D. Gibson's a little readier for that burst, so he cuts off drives. Gibson gives it up to the off-guard and I jump in his grill, trying to turn him. He just backs it out, looking for a man to pop open. He fires to the right wing, then it's a quick entry to Scotty Sims, their best big. He faces against Jones, gives a jab-step baseline, then tries a fade. Too strong. It skims off and Xavier snares it.

Outlet to Gibson, who pushes. Nothing there with Kernantz back, so Gibson backs it out. He hits me trailing, but I've got nothing, so we set the offense. Back to Gibson. To Fuller on the wing. Then Jones baseline. I see it right away—Jones is still over-amped. He puts it on the deck, a no-no for a big. Then he steps back. Back again until his feet are behind the three-point stripe. He launches.

And hits. Our crowd loses their minds. It's Jones' first three-point attempt of his career. He buries it to open up the scoring in the state championship. He trots back down on D, arms raised in celebration. I love the early lead, but that's about the last way we want to attack Evansville Harrison.

Kernantz pushes it right back at us. This time he gets Gibson turned. Kernantz snaps it back between his legs and knifes right down the lane. A quick deuce to trim our lead to one.

I grab the ball to inbound it to Gibson, and I wait a beat before I do. I give him a nice, slow bounce pass so there's no way he can try to rip it back. "Let's get things calmed down," I shout at him. He just nods, knowing. If it comes to it, we can break out the D-Train and D-Bow show, but right now our job is to slow things down a little.

Kevin Waltman

Gibson walks it into the front-court and we start our offense. Problem is, as soon as Jones gets a touch, he's got that look in his eye again. Gibson practically screams at him—"Back out! Back out, big man!"—but Jones is having none of it. At least he doesn't launch another trey, but he tries to take Sims on the bounce. Kernantz reads it easily. He drops into the paint and plucks the pill away from Jones. Then he's off to the races.

Gibson and I both get back, but it takes the two of us to cut Kernantz off from the rim—leaving a shooter wide open at range. Kernantz finds him in rhythm and just like that it's 5-3 Evansville Harrison.

Our next trip, Jones actually passes the ball back out of the post. But now that he's not flicking it up there, the rest of us have a tough time hunting up a look. I know I could get mine, but there's no sense in forcing this early. Jones already proved that. Finally, Gibson tries a tough runner against Kernantz. It misses. Then Xavier has a follow-up roll off the rim.

Evansville Harrison ball again, and they come ripping it at us. They get Sims a touch again, but Jones defends him expertly. No look. He throws it back out to Kernantz, who goes to work on Gibson again. He tries driving into the lane, but Gibson stones it. Kernantz backs up, and even Gibson has to give him some space because of that Kernantz burst. It's all he needs. He clips off a little step-back from eighteen that finds bottom.

All that love we were getting from the crowd after Jones' three is gone. The only noise in the place is coming from the Evansville Harrison section. Just a couple minutes in and they taste their third straight title.

They keep it rolling too. I finally get a bucket to stop the bleeding, but they get another trey and one more filthy Kernantz step-back sandwiched around a Murphy time-out. Kernantz spends the rest of the first quarter setting other guys up. He finally gets Sims going on a lob—though Jones has done a great job on him otherwise—then dials up a few of their shooters for more threes. Then, with the clock emptying out on the first quarter, he freezes Gibson again. He fakes a drive that Gibson has to respect—then drains another step-back to make it 23-9 at the horn. Gibson's got enough quicks to stay with Kernantz, but he doesn't have the length to challenge that step-back move.

Guys slump back to the bench slowly. There are some anxious glances at the scoreboard. Some shaking heads. Some muttered obscenities. Kid reads the body language and comes onto the boards about ten feet. "Get in here!" he yells. "It's just one quarter. Don't you dare hang your heads. We gotta dig, boys! Now come on."

That gets some chins back up, but when we sit for the break, we know that we're going to need more than some optimistic talk. We need a different plan. Murphy and Kid step outside the huddle to chat for a few seconds. Then they share a look and a shrug. Whatever they've hatched, it seems more like a last-ditch plan than something they have a ton of confidence in.

Still, Murphy crouches down in front of us and breaks out the clipboard. "On defense," he starts, "we're going triangle-and-two." We know the basic principles, but he breaks it down for us. One guy checks Kernantz. Another checks Sims. And the other three create a triangle zone to defend everything else, always looking to help on Kernantz and

Kevin Waltman

Sims rather than guarding anyone else man-to-man. He explains that Jones and Xavier will rotate on Sims to prevent foul trouble. And then there's the kicker. "Derrick, you've got Kernantz." He glances at Gibson. He doesn't want hurt egos to get in the way now, so he explains that my size will give Kernantz a little more trouble—and that Gibson can use his quicks to jump passing lanes out of his spot on top of the triangle.

"Now, on offense," he says. He pauses, scratches his head. Then he starts walking us through our sets again. I can tell it worries some guys that there's nothing new to offer here. Finally, Reynolds leans in from behind Murphy. He's only seen a couple minutes of action, but rather than sulking he's trying to contribute however he can.

"Coach Murph?" he says.

Murphy whips around. "What, Reynolds?"

"I know we got here by sharing the looks, but I don't think they can check D-Bow if we clear out for him."

Murphy hesitates. He doesn't really want to rest our state title hopes on a suggestion from our back-up swing man. But then he gauges the looks on everyone else. No protests there. "Okay," he says. "We'll keep running sets to get everyone touches. But if we don't get a good look after a few reversals, we're flattening out for D." Then he looks at me. "You ready to shoulder the load."

"I got this," I say.

We all put our hands in the center of the huddle. "Ain't nothin' easy for Marion East," Murphy says. He grins. "It's how we do it."

Then he slaps the top hand in the stack. "Team!" we all shout.

We stride back onto the floor. No more slumped shoulders. We know we've got to get to work. Our ball first, so we run a set looking for an entry to Xavier. We get it to him, but he's pushed off the blocks a few feet. I can tell he wants the look—he hasn't had a shot all game—but he's grown since early in the season. He kicks it back out to Gibson, who whips it to me out top. Then they spread the floor to let me work. I don't waste any time. I rip it left, then whip out a spin move at the elbow. I pull up in the paint and fire a 12-footer before help can come. There's more than a deuce riding on this shot—and when it falls, I feel our whole team rise in spirits a little. Maybe we can get this done.

For the rest of the half, I'm *on*. I get to the rim a couple times. Drop a trey. Another pull-up J. Some freebies at the line. And I get my teammates involved too. Every time I beat my man, help has to come. I just revert back to my old point guard mode, distributing for open looks. So by the end of the half I'm popping the stat sheet—18 points and six assists.

The other end is trickier. The first time Kernantz gets it and sees me across from him, he attacks. And I've been softened up by playing two-guard for so long. I'm just not used to this kind of speed. He whips me a couple times before I adjust. I have to give him space so I don't get blown away. As soon as I do, he sizes me up for that J he was dropping on Gibson—but when he rises for it, I extend to challenge. I get just a fingertip on the orange to tip it off course. And just like that, Kernantz realizes things are going to be a little more of a grind the rest of the way.

Meanwhile, Jones takes every move Scotty Sims can throw at him and flat kills it. Sims is going to a high major next year, but right now he can't buy one against my fellow senior. He does draw a couple fouls

Kevin Waltman

on Jones, and then two more on Xavier. So we finish the half small, with our two best bigs riding pine.

The other guys slowly start to figure out their responsibilities in the triangle. There are some hiccups. We overcommit when Kernantz gets past me. Two guys jump to the same player, leaving another one open at the rim. But we settle in. By the end of the half, the Evansville Harrison supporting cast is still getting some looks—but they're tough. A step beyond their range. A hand in their face. And they start tucking the ball back in, looking for Sims or Kernantz to bail them out.

Then, right at the end of the half, we get the kind of defensive play Murphy had hoped for. One of their wing players picks up his dribble. I clamp down on Kernantz so there's no outlet there. So he floats one back out top. And Gibson, at the top of our triangle zone, pounces on it. He snares it for an easy run-out to end the half.

There's just one problem. It only slices the lead to 43-34. For all our success, we've only chipped five points off the deficit. But as I trot to the locker room, Fuller hustles to get beside me. "That's all we gotta do," he says. "Gain five points a quarter. Down to four at the next break. Then a one-point lead at the buzzer."

It's a grind. Not because I'm worn down or unable to shoulder the load. But because Evansville Harrison opens the third by switching Kernantz onto me. No more easy rips at the rim. I have to back him down some. Muscle him into the lane for tougher looks.

They're more patient on the offensive end too. They remember they've got the lead. And no shot clock. And a killer point guard. But mostly they make a concerted effort to get Sims going. He finally gets one to fall on a tough spin move around Jones. Then he loses him on a cross-screen for a thunderous dunk. And then the whistles come. Jones picks up his third on a silly reach. His fourth on a brutal call that probably should have been a charge on Sims. So in the opening minutes of the fourth quarter, our best big man heads to the bench. Coach sends Reynolds in to replace him—meaning we're going small again. Xavier's our only big and he'll have to check Sims.

When Kernantz sees that, he knows what to do—feed the big boy and watch him eat. They pound that rock right to Sims and Xavier's got no chance. My boy Xavier will be a load someday, but right now he's a freshman in over his head. And there's no other big men to help him out. A turnaround. A shot fake and power to the rim. An alley-oop. A bad beat on the offensive glass.

We had done just what Fuller had hoped for—trim that big lead down to four by the end of the third. But just like that it's stretched back to 62-52 with five minutes left. That's a tough mountain to climb against anyone, let alone Evansville Harrison. Coach Murphy calls time.

Mostly it's to let us catch our breath, but then he crouches down in front of us. Sweat is beaded up on his face, his eyes full of fire. There's no more strategy. Just passion. He holds up his right hand, fingers spread. "Five! Five minutes, boys. You've got to play the best basketball of your life for five minutes." He levels a finger at Xavier. "Jones is coming back in with three minutes to go. That means I need just a couple stops out of you. I know you can do it."

Xavier nods. Then one of our bench-warmers chimes in from the back of the huddle. He's trying to be encouraging, but he says

Kevin Waltman

that other guys have to step up. "Derrick can't make all the buckets himself," he says. It's just chatter, the kind of things guys say just to get nervous energy out.

But Kid wants none of it. "The fuck he *can't!*" Kid yells. He reaches over and squeezes the freshman's shoulder, letting him know it's nothing personal. Then he hammers home his point. "The best guard in the state is on *our* bench. Let's keep getting him the rock." There are nods all around. Nobody's got time for bruised egos now.

Our ball. Gibson inbounds it to me. I take a deep breath. Then it's attack time. Kernantz comes almost to mid-court to check me. But instead of sizing him up, I just kick it into full speed. I drive right, Kernantz riding my left hip. I power into the lane, draw the bigs to me. I rise over them all for a look.

Back iron. Off. Fuller comes crashing in like a madman to snare the board. His mask is knocked lopsided by a stray elbow and he dribbles clear out to the hashmark before he pauses to adjust it. Then he kicks it to Gibson on the wing. A dribble exchange with me. I attack again, but this time Kernantz anticipates my move. Back to Gibson. Reset one more time. This time he knifes into the lane and tries his floater. Front rim. Again Fuller comes barreling in. He can't snare it this time, but he keeps it alive and Xavier tracks it down.

They trap him in the corner. He pivots and lobs it way out top to me. A dangerous pass. Kernantz sprints to pluck it away, but I get there at the same time. I outleap him for it, and his momentum carries him out of bounds. I attack immediately. Now Evansville Harrison's in disarray, scrambling to defend. Everyone swarms to defend my drive. When I look opposite baseline, I see an open man. Reynolds. The forgotten man. He can sulk. He can mope. But he can also shoot the hell out of the rock.

I put the leather on him and he buries the trey. Our crowd and bench explode, hearts full of one last hope. 62-55.

Kernantz brings it up. As soon as he crosses mid-court he makes a circle motion with his index finger. *Work clock.* I've been able to keep him in check because of my size, but there's nobody in the world that can catch him when he's playing keep-away. Every time I get into him to start a five-count, he slips past. He darts. Zigs. Zags. The clock expiring with every dribble. After what seems like an eternity, I force him to the left sideline. Gibson knows what to do. He sprints over from his spot and we trap Kernantz. Solo, he could take either of us. But not both of us. He picks up his dribble. Gives it up. As soon as he does, he sprints back out top and calls for the ball, but now it's a different story. He can flash open, but his teammates are scared of my length. They don't want to float a weak one into a passing lane and have me pick it.

But they do know they've got the monster down low. So they bounce it to Sims on the block. Kernantz is still screaming, practically begging for the ball. But a special ops team couldn't pry that rock from Sims now. He wants to seal this game right here. He backs down Xavier. Muscles him near the rim. Then he rises up for a jam—an exclamation point.

Xavier has a surprise for him. He gives every last bit of energy he's got and meets Sims right at the rim, capping him clean. The orange drops down, clips off Sims' shoe and trickles out of bounds. Our ball.

There are no gimmes against this D, especially with Kernantz

Kevin Waltman

up into me. So we still have to take more time than I want. But at last Gibson whips past his man. Kernantz flashes a hand, not even really helping—but that's all the space I need. Gibson puts a dime right on me. A seventeen-footer from the wing.

Ring it up. 62-57.

Timeout Evansville Harrison.

Jones checks in for us. Reynolds heads to the bench. But instead of sulking, his chest is puffed out. He knows he did his part. Now he can't even bear to sit. He stands and urges us to get another stop. "Dig, boys," he screams. "We got this."

But the message to Evansville Harrison in the huddle is evident right away. No shots. They just give the rock to Kernantz and spread out. Our crowd boos, hating that they're just trying to run the clock out on us. But everyone watching knows this is the smart move. We'll either have to steal it from Kernantz—not likely—or make him give it up and put someone on the line.

We chase Kernantz. And chase him. And chase him. Then, when we do get him to give it up, we're not sure who to foul. In the time it takes us to look down at the bench—and see Murphy and Kid shouting desperately to foul anyone but Kernantz—they get the ball back to him. And the chase is on again. Finally, Gibson and I corral him. Force him to give it up. And Fuller fouls the first guy to get a touch. The clock has bled all the way down to 1:30.

The guy we send to the stripe is a shooter. He's been spotting up all game. But he's also a sophomore. As he strides to the line he smiles to his teammates. Nods. But then that leather hits his hands and he tightens up. He rolls his shoulders, trying to stay loose. Our crowd makes as much noise as they can, trying to rattle him. Nobody ever knows if that kind of thing works, but it can't hurt. And when he lets it fly, he pulls the string. Short.

Jones rebounds and we're off. Outlet to Gibson. Push ahead. He tries taking it all the way to the rim but gets cut off. Back to me on the wing. I know there's no time to work for an easy one now. I just have to make it happen. Kernantz is glued to me. A shot fake from range doesn't shake him. So I throw everything I've got at the kid. Power dribble left toward the middle. Snap back between the legs. Cross back left again. Then spin hard toward the right baseline. He's still right on my hip as I rise—a real tough fade from seventeen. But it's a clean look at the rim. And I am not going to be denied now.

Shot's wet. 62-59. Just over a minute to go.

Then the chase is on again. It feels frantic, like the horn's going to go off with Kernantz still dancing away from me and Gibson. But the clock in my head tells me that we still have time. We just don't want to resort to fouling Kernantz. I don't think the kid's missed a free throw since Christmas break.

Again, we make him give it up. And, again, he gets it to the same kid. This time Xavier gives up the foul, putting him right back at the line. Our crowd's even louder now. And the pressure is even higher. Kernantz grabs his teammate by the elbow and shouts some encouragement in his ear, but I can see it on the kid's face. He's *tight* now. Sure enough, he overcompensates for his last miss. He goes back rim this time. Rebound Jones.

Push again. I catch on the opposite wing behind the stripe. A three to tie it? I offer a fake, and this time Kernantz has to jump at it. I

Kevin Waltman

don't hesitate. I power it left and attack the rim. Sims starts to crash at me, but he doesn't want to foul. Good thing for him, because I *elevate*. Thunder home a dunk. The rim rattles and the arena shakes.

62-61. Thirty seconds left.

Kid jumps up and down, waving for everyone to pick up full court. Murphy's on his hands and knees, pounding the floor with his fists. "One more stop!" he screams.

I try to deny the inbounds to Kernantz, but he's too quick. He catches and the chase is on one more time. Gibson has basically given up any defensive responsibilities other than helping me track down Kernantz. Still, he pushes past us into the front-court. I glance toward our bench, waiting for the signal to foul Kernantz. At this point, even if he drained both, we'd have a chance to tie it with a three. Murphy glances at the clock, then shakes his head. Not yet.

Kernantz drives middle, then back to the opposite wing. Darts a step toward the baseline, then reverses back out top. Opposite wing. Back out top. Tick tick tick. I give one last look to the bench. Finally, Murphy signals for us to give up the foul on Kernantz. Gibson and I both race after him, and I get ready to hack him. But we actually have Kernantz pushed into the corner. Gibson recognizes it first and instead of fouling, he just defends. Kernantz doesn't dare pick up his dribble, but Gibson gets a peek at the orange and stabs at it—just a touch, but it ricochets up off of Kernantz's chest and right back to Gibson. He grabs it and calls for time.

We head back to the bench and I glance at the clock. Six seconds to go. There's no real strategy left from Murphy. Just an entry to me and then clear out. He reminds me to find an open shooter if I don't have a look, but everyone knows it's on me now.

We break the huddle, and I stride onto the deck for the last time in my high school career. I take one last look into the stands. I see my family, their faces flush with passion and hope. Mom's got her hands clasped in front of her mouth like she's praying. Jayson's jumping up and down nervously. Dad's holding one hand to each temple like he's in pain. Back home, a babysitter is trying to hush Gracie and watch this on the T.V. at the same time.

I know there are a lot more people in the crowd with their hopes hanging on this too. Coach Bolden's out there, dying with each shot. Moose is up there, maybe next to Nick, both of them urging us to the glory they just missed in their playing days. On the sidelines, Murphy and Kid are clinging to belief in me—wanting me to deliver them a trophy, and more importantly a story they can tell for the rest of their lives. Jasmine's up there somewhere. And Lia. Both of them on pins and needles no matter how much they deny caring about hoops. Wes is up there, cheering and carrying a scar from a gunshot. The guy who gave him that scar is probably up there too.

People can yap all they want about *no I in team*, or put up slogans about how the strength is in the hive. But most of the time sports is about getting yourself what you want. The next bucket. A scholarship. A ring. It's about *you*. But right now I feel all those dashed dreams from the people of Marion East. I feel all those near misses—the wouldas and couldas and shouldas—in our crowd. I feel all the people who never quite made it. Who have to get up tomorrow win or lose and hustle some dead-end job or, worse, a dead-end life. They need this. It won't change anything really. Won't get Wes' life back in order or give Moose or Nick or any other player a second chance at hoops glory. It won't

Kevin Waltman

make the leap to college any easier for Jasmine. And it won't undo all the bad things that keep happening to people in those stands. But it'll make it all feel worth it, if just for one night.

What comes next is up to me. But it for sure is *about* everyone who's ever set foot on my blocks too.

The ref trills his whistle. Time to go. One last possession. Evansville Harrison's coaches aren't dumb. They know the pill's headed my way. So I get a jerseyful of Kernantz plus one of his teammates. They bracket me on the inbounds. I know the back-up plan would be to get it to Gibson instead, but I sprint hard toward mid-court, then plant and cut back for the ball. Fuller puts it on me, but I'm double-teamed immediately.

I attack the side away from Kernantz. Push it with my left into the frontcourt. As I cross half-court, I give a hesitation like I might spin back right. Just enough to freeze them for a second—and enough for me to power left again and get my shoulder past. Past the hashmark, near the three-point stripe. I know I've got a couple ticks left, so I look to get into the lane—but Kernantz takes an angle and catches me, hedging me back toward the left wing. It's into traffic too. Fuller's spotted on that baseline, so there's less room to work. And the other defender from the double-team has caught up to me too. The clock in my head knows it's time to get a shot off. I can hear the anxiety in the crowd, their noise rising in volume and pitch. Everyone—teammates, fans, coaches—screaming *Shoot!*

I'm twenty-six feet from the bucket. Double-teamed. Zeros coming. But I've played this kind of drama out in my head a million times since I was a kid on the blacktop. I was born for this.

I just give a hitch in my dribble and square my feet like I'm going to rise. Both defenders jump, ready to challenge. And—zip—I split right between them. There's your quicks. I only have time to pick up the dribble at about eighteen. A little off-balance. But it's a look.

And it's so true.

Euphoria. Bedlam. Pandemonium. These are the words I bet the announcers kick around. But the celebration is too crazy to put into words. What I remember afterwards, when I'm glowing in the locker room, all of us basking in the biggest win of our lives, are a few images. Fuller doing the world's most awkward dance at mid-court. Xavier hoisting Reynolds onto his shoulders. Jones leaping up on the scorer's table and ripping his jersey off to wave it above his head. Murphy snipping an extra piece of net and presenting it to Coach Bolden in the stands. And a series of the unlikeliest hugs—Kid and my mom. Kid and Bolden. And me and Gibson.

The whole time, all anyone keeps saying is *We did it. We did it. We did it.*

OVERTIME

In Evansville they're holding a press conference. Sims is announcing that he'll go to Louisville with Kernantz next year.

ESPN broadcasts live to show an LA big man choose from a series of college hats spread out in front of him. He fakes like he's grabbing the UCLA hat and then puts on the Arizona lid instead.

It's the circus that is Signing Day.

We could do that here too. But that's not how we roll at Marion East. The only time camera crews come here is for bad news. And, well, for when we won the state title. But instead of a press conference, I just take a letter to the main office and ask to use the fax machine. Kid and Coach Murphy are there, presiding. So are my parents. But nobody except me knows where that fax is headed.

The machine beeps and churns as the letter reaches its destination.

"Well?" Dad asks. Everyone wants to know. Did that go to Bloomington? Clemson? Ann Arbor? Did some school make a late charge to snag me away?

I savor the moment, the last seconds before I share my secret. "Awww," I say at last, "I been balling in Indiana since the day I was born. I'm not going to stop now."

ACKNOWLEDGMENTS

I want to thank Bobby, Lee, and John Byrd, and all the people at Cinco Puntos Press for giving me a chance to write this series. Writing is too often a pursuit that occurs in solitude, broken up only by rejections, so when Bobby Byrd told me they wanted this work—all of it—I was immediately grateful, and remain deeply so. Thank you.

Along the way, I received a lot of help, professional and otherwise. The people who have offered this are too many to mention, but Brant Rumble, Jim Giesen, John Kitch, Ben Osborne, and Rick Ray all warrant special mention. Thank you all.

Thank you, too, to Carole Waltman, Sue Kidd and Jack Kidd, otherwise known as Gram and Mah and Dack. You've offered me endless support, both in terms of time and energy, and more importantly you are incredible grandparents that make life richer and happier for Calla and Holling.

My father, Royce Waltman, was a basketball coach, and a damn good one. He introduced me to the game when I was tiny and cultivated a love for it in me. So, obviously, his voice has whispered to me constantly as I've written this series. Sometimes I feel these are as much his words as mine. Of course, as I've written these books I've come to understand that they are not so much about basketball as about fathers and sons and growing to become a man. When I think back, I realize that some of those basketball lessons I could have learned elsewhere. Becoming a man, though, couldn't have been learned better from anyone other than Royce Waltman. Thank you, Dad. I miss you every day.

Writing can be a selfish pursuit. There are countless times I've clung to private hours so I could work, when I could have been helping elsewhere instead. I've been afforded those hours by my wonderful wife, Jessica Kidd. But you have given me so much more than time, Jessica. You give me support daily, and when I'm feeling overwhelmed or distraught you always help bring me back around. More importantly still, you've shown me that the world is as beautiful and rich as one is willing to make it. Our life is rich and beautiful and joyful because you've made it so, Jessica. Thank you.

And finally, my kids. Calla Kidd Waltman and Holling Fordham Waltman. I have been asked on more than one occasion how I'm able to get writing done while raising two small children. Well, the first answer is a credit to so many of the people listed above, who give me help time and again. The real answer though is this: every day, you reinvent the world for me and in doing so you make it clearer. When the world is clearer, my role in it is clearer. And thus easier. Everything I do is *easier* because of you two. Everything I do is *worth doing* because of you. I love you both more than the sun and the moon and the stars in the sky, more than the mountains and the valleys and the whole of creation. I love you more than words can ever say, and I love you forever and ever.

D-BOW'S HIGH SCHOOL HOOPS SERIES

NEXT
D-BOW'S HIGH SCHOOL HOOPS SERIES BOOK ONE

"Waltman's series opener features plenty of basketball action fueled by hoops slang that will set basketball-mad readers right onto the court...avoids slam-dunk answers, leaving readers poised for the next book. Like Derrick, this series is off to a promising high school career." —*Kirkus Reviews*

SLUMP
D-BOW'S HIGH SCHOOL HOOPS SERIES BOOK TWO

"As in the series debut, Waltman wrings drama from believable day-to-day trials and triumphs...he spikes the plot with extended play-by-plays called in Derrick's voice, putting readers on court in the middle of the action. Things are far from settled with arch-rival Hamilton, or with Jasmine, for that matter, and teens who have now reached series halftime will certainly be back for third period."
—*The Bulletin of the Center for Children's Books*

PULL
D-BOW'S HIGH SCHOOL HOOPS SERIES BOOK THREE
"As a childrens/YA bookseller, I LOVED THIS BOOK. The language, the characters, the basketball—they are all spot on perfect...I am so excited about this series."
—*Cynthia Compton*, 4 Kids Books, Zionville, Indiana